She'd be safer here ~~vacant house until~~ he got back.

But, just in case, he pulled his pistol out from under his shirt at the small of his back and wrapped her hand around it. "Keep this with you. Only put your finger on the trigger if you intend to fire."

He headed out the back door they'd come in, brushing aside the small curtain on a side window to look out first and check for neighbors who might see him leaving.

"Jake?" she called, stopping him.

"Yeah?"

She hesitated, her expression puzzled and her gaze fixed on the ring on her left hand. "Never mind. It will keep."

"What is it, Paige? Tell me."

She sighed. "Well, I was just wondering… Am I married…or not?"

Dear Reader,

I'm having so much fun writing THE BANCROFT BRIDES series! In *The Bride's Bodyguard,* Paige Bancroft is ready to walk down the aisle when a disaster beyond anything she could imagine throws her life into chaos. Orderly, organized Paige doesn't do chaos. Thank goodness she has ultra-hot, former Navy SEAL Jake McCall at her side, helping her dodge bullets! Paige is in for a wild ride and about to discover that love can bloom in the most difficult situations and with the person you'd least expect.

As I write this letter, I'm in the final stages of wrapping up book three (Zoey's book), and I admit, leaving these three sisters is going to be tough! Having grown up as the middle of three sisters, I pulled bits and pieces of my own experience into creating Paige, Holly and Zoey. Their love for each other, their widely different personalities, the occasional sibling rivalry…even the camping in a pop-up trailer come from memories of my youth.

I hope you enjoy Paige's story, and stay tuned for Zoey's book, coming in mid–2011.

Happy reading,

Beth Cornelison

BETH CORNELISON

The Bride's Bodyguard

ROMANTIC

SUSPENSE

SILHOUETTE BOOKS

Recycling programs
for this product may
not exist in your area.

ISBN-13: 978-0-373-27700-1

THE BRIDE'S BODYGUARD

Books by Beth Cornelison

Silhouette Romantic Suspense

*The Bancroft Brides

BETH CORNELISON

started writing stories as a child when she penned a tale about the adventures of her cat, Ajax. A Georgia native, she received her bachelor's degree in public relations from the University of Georgia. After working in public relations for a little more than a year, she moved with her husband to Louisiana, where she decided to pursue her love of writing fiction.

Since that first time, Beth has written many more stories of adventure and romantic suspense and has won numerous honors for her work, including a coveted Golden Heart award in romantic suspense from Romance Writers of America. She is active on the board of directors for the North Louisiana Storytellers and Authors of Romance (NOLA STARS) and loves reading, traveling, Peanuts' Snoopy and spending downtime with her family.

She writes from her home in Louisiana, where she lives with her husband, one son and two cats who think they are people. Beth loves to hear from her readers. You can write to her at PO Box 5418, Bossier City, LA 71171 or visit her Web site at www.bethcornelison.com.

To my sisters—Martha and Lenna. I love you guys!

And in memory of Nate. I miss you.

Chapter 1

"Do you, Paige Michelle Bancroft, take Brent to be your lawfully wedded husband, for better or for worse, in sickness and—"

A strange buzzing filled Paige's ears, drowning out the minister's voice and ramping up the panic constricting her chest. The hand holding her bouquet shook, making the imported orchids tremble. Her mother's antique pearl choker strangled her.

No, no, no, she wanted to scream. *I don't love Brent. I don't want to spend my life with him.*

"—as long as you both shall live?" The minister raised an expectant gaze to her, cuing her to respond.

"I do," she rasped. Her answer seemed to come from the bottom of a deep well, a hollow, disembodied voice with its own will.

Brent squeezed her free hand and gave her a smile, which she dutifully mirrored, despite the legion of butterflies battering her stomach and the doubts shouting in her head.

She cast a quick glance to the front row where her mother

joyfully dabbed her eyes and her father beamed at her triumphantly. Her parents' happiness bolstered her courage.

"I'm so proud of you," Neil Bancroft had whispered to Paige as he escorted her down the aisle moments ago. "Brent is your perfect match."

She'd swallowed the bitter uncertainties that rose in her throat, wanting to reply, "No, he's *your* perfect match. Don't make me do this!" Instead, she'd forced a grin and nodded.

Marrying Brent was her destiny, her obligation. Marrying the man who would soon be the CEO of Bancroft Industries meant control of the family business would stay within the family. More important, she was making her father happy. Her father doted on Brent as if he were the son he never had.

Paige had long ago come to terms with the fact that her marriage was more a business merger than a love match. As the oldest daughter in the family, she knew her father expected her to put family obligations first. When Brent had proposed to her, with her father sitting across the table from them, she'd seen how the prospect of her marriage to his protégé had thrilled her father. Her engagement had earned her unprecedented praise and acceptance from her hard-to-please father.

A tug on her hand called her attention back to her groom, who was slipping an extravagant ring on her finger. "With this ring, I thee wed."

Her heart tap-danced as she turned to hand her bouquet to her sister Holly and receive from her Brent's ring.

Holly gave her a curious look, whispering discreetly, "You okay?"

Another fake smile and a tiny nod. "Of course."

Paige shoved down the twinge of envy for her sister's loving and happy marriage to a handsome doctor. Holly and Matt's Christmas wedding last winter had been a small affair but bursting with heartfelt affection and joy.

Paige drew a deep, steadying breath as she faced her groom with his wedding band in hand and prepared to recite her vows. She could make this marriage work if she kept the right attitude and put aside her childish dreams of a fairy-tale prince to sweep her off her feet. The kind of romantic dreams her youngest sister, Zoey, was chasing.

"I can't pretend I'm happy to see you marrying someone you don't love," Zoey had declared in the same phone call in which she explained her reasons for skipping Paige's wedding. Not having Zoey at her wedding broke Paige's heart, but her temperamental youngest sister had always been stubborn, opinionated and unpredictable. And so Zoey was God-knows-where with her latest loser boyfriend, protesting Paige's practical decision by boycotting the wedding ceremony.

Brent might not be her dream love match, but he had his good qualities. He was thoughtful, intelligent, generous, polite and ambitious. He tried hard to make her happy—and he tried even harder to make her father happy. He was comfortable, like her favorite old pair of slippers.

With a mental kick in the pants, Paige shook off the doubt demons plaguing her and firmed her resolve. Zoey was wrong. Marrying Brent Scofield was the right thing to do. She'd be fine, and she'd learn to love him. She'd make her marriage work.

With shaking hands, she lifted the gold band to Brent's finger. "With this ring, I—"

Slam!

The door at the back of the sanctuary crashed open, and Paige jerked her head toward the source of the distracting noise.

A man in a long trench coat strode down the center aisle toward the altar. "Sorry I'm late. But I didn't want to show up too soon and give the groom a chance to escape."

Brent snatched his hand from Paige's and stiffened as he faced the intruder. "Who are you, and what do you want?"

"Who I am doesn't matter. And you know what we want, Scofield."

Jake McCall surreptitiously reached for the sidearm hidden at his hip under his tuxedo coat and stepped smoothly between the intruder and the groom. He'd been so caught up in deciphering the odd reluctance and anxiety in the bride's expression that he'd allowed his vigilance over the groom's safety to lapse for valuable seconds. He shoved down the self-recriminations that would only serve as further distractions and shifted into battle mode.

Even as Jake drew his SIG Sauer P226 and moved into a more offensive position, Brent shifted out from behind him, addressing the man in the trench coat. "And if I refuse?"

As if on cue, several more men, all armed with rifles, appeared in the balcony and stepped through the side and back doors of the sanctuary.

A murmur of distress whispered through the congregation, and the bridesmaids huddled together behind the altar rail.

Jake's grip on his pistol tightened. Quickly, he began recalculating his best strategy to protect his client and avoid getting anyone else shot in the process. He sent a quick glance around the sanctuary, monitoring the other gunmen, then returned his attention to the ringleader. The man's trench coat, out of place on a rain-free summer day, bothered Jake. Not knowing what might be under that long coat bothered him more.

Trench Coat sent Brent a gloating smirk and jerked a nod toward Jake. "I see you were expecting us." Turning, he narrowed a menacing glare on Jake. "Drop it. Or my men will drop you and anyone else in the line of fire."

Jake hesitated only a moment before setting his pistol on the floor and kicking it toward Trench Coat. Ordinarily, he'd keep his weapon at all costs, but being outnumbered and outgunned with so many civilians at risk changed everything.

"Now…" Trench Coat faced the groom once more. "If you give us what we want, nobody has to get hurt."

"Brent? What is he talking about?" the bride asked, her expression stunned, terrified.

Matt Randall, who'd been introduced to Jake as the bride's brother-in-law, rose from the front pew and eased up behind Trench Coat.

Jake tensed. Clearly, Matt had some form of well-intended, but ill-advised heroics in mind. He tried to make eye contact with Matt to warn him off, but Matt's focus was on the man threatening the wedding party.

Just before Matt reached his target, Trench Coat jerked his head around and whipped open his coat to reveal the explosives he wore on his chest. He pulled his hand from his large coat pocket, his thumb hovering over the switch of a detonator. "I wouldn't try anything if I were you, pal."

The bridesmaids issued a collective gasp.

Brent raised both hands in a conciliatory gesture. "Take it easy. Your business is with me. Leave everyone else out of it. Let everyone else go, and I—I'll cooperate."

Trench Coat cocked his head and twisted his mouth in an eerie smirk. "Good to know. Hand over the bead, and we'll be on our way."

Brent cut a desperate glance to Jake. "I, uh, don't have it."

Trench Coat's face hardened. "You're lying. You knew we were after it, and you wouldn't leave it unprotected. It's here somewhere, and I'm getting tired of asking nicely." He glanced to one of his cohorts. "Scofield needs a little encouragement to cooperate."

The gunman gave a tight nod. Raised his rifle.

And shot the man at the end of the pew closest to him.

Screams rose from the congregation. Terrified people scrambled from their seats to run for the door. More shots were fired toward the escaping crowd as the gunmen moved in to block the door.

"Sit down!" Trench Coat roared.

A terrified hush fell over the church, and Trench Coat turned so everyone could see the bomb strapped to him. "I have enough C4 taped to me to blow this church to hell and back."

A prickle of intuition chased up Jake's spine. He'd worked with C4 during his navy SEAL training. The claylike material Trench Coat wore wasn't C4.

And these men weren't religious or political extremists on suicide duty. They were mercenaries after something Scofield had. Blowing themselves up would serve no purpose. The bomb was likely a fake, a scare tactic to win cooperation from the congregation and deter would-be heroes like Matt.

But the rounds in the goons' rifles were real enough, as they'd demonstrated.

With the hand not holding the fake detonator, Trench Coat pulled a .38 revolver from a coat pocket and leveled the gun at Brent. "The bead, Scofield. Now!"

Jake rocked to the balls of his feet, prepared to launch himself in front of a bullet or knock Trench Coat to the floor in an instant. "Brent, give him what he wants," he hissed through clenched teeth.

How could Scofield play his game of chicken with these terrorists when so many lives were at risk?

Brent sent him a stunned glance. "No!"

Trench Coat's aim shifted twenty degrees. Toward the bride. The .38 clicked as he cocked the hammer.

"No!" Brent threw himself on his bride, knocking her down just as Trench Coat fired.

In one rapid move, Jake dived for his pistol, rolled to his back and dropped Trench Coat with one shot to the head.

Bedlam erupted as the congregation ducked for cover or ran for the door. The other terrorists fired at will, trying to regain control of the frightened crowd.

Jake scrambled forward and seized the .38. The fake detonator lay beside the dead terrorist, forgotten.

Over the gunfire and screams, Jake heard the bride shout, "Brent! Someone help me!"

As he rushed toward the bridal couple, lying together on the floor, Jake spotted the blood spreading at Scofield's tuxedo collar.

He reached his client at the same time as Matt. The other man muscled him out of the way. "I'm a doctor! Let me help him!"

Jake yielded to the doctor but assisted in ripping open

Brent's ascot and tux collar. He balled his own cravat to stanch the flow of blood from the wound at Brent's jugular vein.

The bride huddled beside Brent, crying and clutching her groom's hand. "Hang on, Brent. Stay with us. Matt will help you."

Brent's fading gaze found his bride's, then shifted to Jake's as he rasped, "McCall…"

Guilt kicked Jake hard in the gut. He gritted his teeth in frustration and self-reproach. "I know. You hired me to protect you, and I didn't."

"Listen to me!" Scofield grabbed Jake's wrist with a grip that was surprisingly strong considering how much blood he'd lost.

Jake hesitated when he met the determined fire in his client's eyes.

"New…assignment. Paige has…what they want. Get her… out of here. Hide her." Brent struggled for a breath, the life light in his eyes dimming. "Keep…the bead safe… at all costs. National security…."

Jake frowned, straining to hear over the continued tumult in the sanctuary. "What bead?"

"Homeland compromised. No police "

"What bead?" Jake demanded. "Where is it?"

"In…her…" Scofield paused, gasped, gurgled on the blood in his throat. Brent's gaze darted to something behind Jake. "Go!"

Jake whipped a glance over his shoulder in time to see one of the riflemen approach the altar, then pause to take aim on them.

Hooking an arm around the bride's waist, he hauled her to her feet and shoved her behind the pulpit. He took cover with her, shielding her with his body as the bullets whizzed past, missing them by inches. Peering around the side of the pulpit, Jake fired back at the rifleman. Hit him in the chest. The man slumped to the floor.

Burying his mouth in the bride's hair, he shouted directly

into her ear. "We're going out that side door to the limo. Move fast and keep your head down."

She shook her head, her eyes wide with terror. "But Brent—"

"Just do as I say! We run on three. One, two, three!"

Numb with shock and fear, Paige stumbled as Brent's hulking best man tugged her arm, propelling them toward the sanctuary's side exit. Her foot caught the hem of her Vera Wang gown, and she immediately tumbled to her knees. She bit her tongue as she landed with a jarring thud.

Jake sent her a dark scowl of impatience, as if she'd tripped on purpose, as if running in high heels with yards of satin and lace draped around her legs should have been easy.

Shaking from head to toe, she fumbled to untangle herself, fighting the billows of her skirt out of her way. In a daze of disbelief, she watched Jake knock away the muzzle of the rifle that a thug by the side door had swung toward them. Lobbing a fist to the thug's chin, Jake sent the guy sprawling on the floor, then turned to her. His square jaw was taut, and a lethal intensity blazed in his dark eyes.

Without warning, Jake planted his shoulder in her stomach. Wrapping his arm around her legs, he tossed her over his shoulder in a fireman's hold. The air whooshed from her lungs, and her world turned upside down. Dangling over his shoulder, she scrabbled for something to hold as he charged out the door. Paige fisted his tuxedo coat, but as Jake raced down the steps and across the churchyard, the heavy stomping of his feet bounced her like a rag doll. She groped frantically for a more secure hold, wrapping her arms around the expanse of his wide back.

Jake's shoulder gouged her belly. His fingers dug into her thighs. His feet and the ground filled her line of sight with a dizzying blur of motion. The bright sunshine and thick humidity of the Louisiana summer day beat down on them as he ran toward the front driveway.

A beautiful day for my wedding, she'd thought that morning when she arrived at the church. *The perfect day for my perfect wedding.*

Now bile and adrenaline soured her stomach and threatened to come up as she clung to Jake for dear life. The surreal screams from her friends and family, under assault in the sanctuary she'd been dragged away from, faded as they made their escape.

But the deafening gunfire followed them. A series of blasts thundered through the air. Paige winced as bits of concrete flew up at her when bullets peppered the ground. Bullets aimed at her and at Jake.

"Start the engine! Go, go, go!" Jake shouted to someone. He staggered to a stop, but before she could catch her breath or regain her bearings, he dumped her, unceremoniously, onto the backseat of the bridal limo.

"Let's move!" Jake yelled.

She battled away the curtain of ivory satin that had her tangled in an awkward knot, obscuring her vision. As she scooted across the seat, righting herself and restoring air to her jostled lungs, Jake lunged onto the seat beside her. He swung a handgun out the open car door and fired a couple of earsplitting shots. The limo driver hit the gas, and they rocketed down the church driveway, even before Jake had closed the limo door.

As the limo hurtled down the streets of Lagniappe, weaving through traffic and taking turns at a high speed, Paige was tossed about like a sock in the dryer. Her mind spun as well, reeling from the macabre turn of events. Her wedding had become a bloodbath. Brent had been shot. And her groom's high school friend, a man she'd met only four days ago, had bodily carried her out of harm's way like some tuxedoed superhero.

Dear God, was her sister hurt? Her parents? Her friends? And poor Mr. Diggle had been murdered in cold blood!

She must be dreaming. *If this is some anxiety-induced nightmare, please let me wake up now!*

For the first time, Paige said a prayer of thanks that her

youngest sister hadn't been at the wedding after all. At least Paige knew Zoey was safe.

The limo's back window shattered. Startled by the loud crash and rain of broken glass, Paige screamed.

"Get down!" Jake palmed her head and shoved her to the floor, covering her with his massive body. His weight pressed her back into the plush carpeting and biting shards of the window while his rock-hard chest and wide shoulders ground against the galloping beat of her heart. The heat of his exertion and the faint scent of sandalwood surrounded her. Despite the hell breaking loose around her, the solid wall of his body created a warm cocoon where, for a few moments, she felt marginally protected, fractionally less frightened.

She squeezed her eyes closed, only to see haunting images of Brent's blood, spraying bullets and crushed flowers. Chaos, death and destruction. At her wedding.

She shuddered.

You know what we want, Scofield.

Keep the bead safe at all costs.

Why had Jake brought a gun to the wedding? Had he expected trouble?

Who were those armed men, and what was Brent's link to them?

None of it made sense.

"Hit the highway out of town and don't stop until you're sure you've lost them!" Jake shouted to the driver.

Time kaleidoscoped, and Paige couldn't be sure if she'd huddled beneath Jake's protective cover for one minute or twenty. When the assault of gunfire stopped, he rolled off of her and sat back to take off his tux jacket and rip open the shirt at his throat. Her gaze gravitated to the pulse throbbing on his thick neck. A muscle in his jaw jumped as he gritted his teeth and eased forward to peer over the backseat.

She rubbed the spot at her temple where her head pounded.

"I think we lost them." Jake expelled a deep breath of relief as he pushed up to the seat at the back of the limo. He raked a hand through his short, inky-black hair and lifted a penetrating gaze to her. "Are you all right?"

Paige could only stare back at him, too stunned, too shaken, too confused by the violent attack at her wedding to know what to do or say. This kind of thing was only supposed to happen in the movies, not in real life. Not in her staid, well-planned, organized, boring life.

Jake extended a large hand to her. She studied the crimson smears on his fingers, and her stomach roiled. "You have blood on your hand. Brent's blood," she said stupidly, still too shell-shocked to edit her thoughts for statements of the obvious.

But Jake didn't laugh off or dismiss her banal comment. Instead, his expression darkened, and his jaw tightened. "I did what I thought was best, considering I was outnumbered, outgunned and had the lives of three hundred of your friends and relatives to factor in to my response to those thugs," he said bitterly. He massaged his knee and winced. "I know I screwed up. I know your fiancé is likely dead because of my screwup."

Paige's breath hitched, and a sharp ache sliced through her. *Brent could be dead.*

Jake jerked his gaze to the side window and huffed. His nostrils flared, and pain flooded his face for a moment before he schooled his expression and turned back to her. "I'm sorry."

She blinked, saying nothing for long seconds, realizing he'd taken her comment as condemnation and accusation. His tortured expression, his guilty confession twisted in her chest.

"I—I only meant…you have blood—" She pointed to his hands, then stopped when she saw the blood on her own fingers. She gaped at the red stains, her stomach seesawing as she discovered the smears on her dress, as well—the garish reminder of the violence she'd witnessed, of her futile attempts to help Brent when he'd been shot, of the unknown carnage she'd left at the church. It was *her* wedding. Didn't that make it her responsibility to see to the safety of her guests? How could she flee like a coward and leave everyone else to die?

And what choice in the matter had Jake given her, hauling her away like a duffel bag over his shoulder?

"Are you hurt?" Jake repeated, his tone demanding.

Paige drew a slow breath, forcing air into lungs paralyzed by shock, terror and grief. "I—I don't know." She looked up at Jake, needing answers. "What just happened? How... Why...?"

He leaned forward and put a hand under her elbow, helping her off the limo floor and onto the long seat ninety degrees from where he sat. "Good question. The sooner we get those answers, the better I'll be able to protect you and the bead."

"Protect me?"

Jake gave her a tight nod. "Those are my orders. That's what Brent asked just before we made our big exit."

"Your orders?" She hated sounding like some parrot, re-peating everything Jake said, but her brain was still struggling to comprehend the horror of the past half hour and make sense of the insanity. "Who the hell are you *really?* And why did you think you had to bring a gun to my wedding?"

Jake flexed and balled his hand restlessly. "I really am an old friend of Brent's. But not his best friend—just the one with the most military training. He hired me a couple weeks ago to protect him until after the wedding. My being his best man was my cover. So you wouldn't ask questions."

Paige shook her head, more confused than ever. "Then... why are you here instead of protecting him?"

"Didn't you hear what he said before we made our exit? He told me to hide you and keep the bead safe at all costs." He narrowed a sharp gaze on her and extended his hand. "In fact, you should give me the bead for safekeeping."

Her head throbbed, and she swallowed the urge to scream her frustration with the endless riddles. "What *bead?*"

Jake's jaw tightened, and his dark eyes reflected his own frustration and impatience with the situation. "The one the terrorists who crashed your party were after, of course! The one you're protecting for Brent. Give it to me." He wiggled his fingers, urging her compliance. "Come on, Paige. Brent asked me to guard it. He said something about national security."

Paige barked a humorless laugh. "What does some bead have to do with national security? And what makes you think I have this…this *bead?*"

Squeezing his eyes shut, Jake massaged his right knee again and exhaled an irritated huff.

"Brent said you have what those guys who shot him were after," he said quietly, clearly struggling to keep his tone calm, though tension vibrated from him in palpable waves. "That's why I got you out of the church so fast. According to Brent, you have what the terrorists want, and it is my job to keep this *bead*—whatever it is—safe."

His wording smacked her between the eyes, and she flopped back on the seat, her chest aching, as if from a physical blow. "That's what he said? Keep the bead safe? That's why you hustled me out of there so fast? Why you risked your life to save me?"

Protect the bead. Not her. She was merely a pawn in Brent's dangerous secret agenda.

Jake rolled his eyes and groaned. "Isn't that what I just said? This conversation is getting old, Paige. Just give me the bead, okay?"

Something inside her snapped. Her patience, her composure, her illusions of her safe, orderly world shattered, and she grabbed her head, fisting her hands in her hair, further destroying the salon styling she'd received that morning. "I don't have any bead! I don't know what Brent thinks I have or why he told you I have it!" She hated her shrill tone, her loss of control. But getting shot at, learning the safety of some bead was more important to your fiancé than your safety, having your entire world thrown into chaos did that to a girl.

"I don't know why armed men attacked my wedding! And I don't know why my fiancé thinks he has something to do with national security! None of this makes sense to me!"

Jake's head snapped up, his attention drawn to something out the back window.

"What—"

Before she could finish her question, he grabbed her arm and yanked her back toward the floor. Paige gritted her teeth. She was getting tired of his manhandling.

"Stay down!" he shouted as he lowered the side window and leveled his handgun at some threat outside.

She heard the roar of an engine, too loud and high-pitched to be a car. It sounded more like a motorcycle. Then a hail of bullets hammered the limo, shattering more windows and pocking the far wall of the back compartment.

"I thought you said we'd lost them!"

Jake spared her only a brief glance. "Clearly, they found us again."

He pitched backward as the limo veered suddenly and bumped along the shoulder. His eyes widened, and he bit out a curse. Lunging forward, he climbed over her and shouted, "Hold on to something! Our driver's been hit."

Jake turned on the seat and rocked backward. With a hard kick, he knocked out the Plexiglas window partition between them and the front seat.

Paige scrambled across the floor, groping for a handhold as the vehicle swerved and bumped. She grabbed the pit of a wet-bar cup holder over her head and braced her feet on the long side seat on the opposite side of the compartment. Jake slid headfirst through the opening he'd created, dragging the driver—oh, God, was he dead?—off the steering wheel and into the passenger seat.

Paige bit down hard on her bottom lip, praying for a miracle, praying she and Jake weren't about to be shot or killed in a car crash. Praying she'd wake up from this far-too-realistic nightmare.

Bile rose in her throat, and tears burned her eyes as two truths clarified in her mind.

Brent was involved in something terrible and clandestine.

And her fiancé's dangerous secret might cost her her life.

Chapter 2

Jake fought the limo back under control and steered onto the highway. Checking the mirrors for any more surprise assailants, he took the first exit and headed in the opposite direction from the way the motorcyclist departed.

At his earliest opportunity, Jake pulled the limo off the road and stopped long enough to check the driver for signs of life. He pressed his fingers to the man's carotid artery, despite the glaring hole in his head that screamed proof that the driver was dead.

Paige appeared at the windowless gap between the front and back seats. "Why'd we stop? Is the driver—?"

"Don't look," he barked, harsher than he needed to, but tension had him wound tight. Tact was not at the top of his priorities at the moment. "Get down and stay there. You don't need this image in your head, and I don't know when we may get attacked again."

The rustle of satin and lace told him she'd complied.

"So what do we do now? Where are we going?" The tremble of fear in her voice sucker punched his gut.

"This is a work in progress, darlin'. I'll tell you when I know. First thing we have to do is get rid of this limo. It's conspicuous as hell." He whipped a quick glance over his shoulder to the backseat. Paige's wide green eyes made her look vulnerable, yet he also saw keen intelligence and stubborn determination in her expression that told him she was no frail flower that would wilt at any moment. Good. If this situation was half as dangerous as the past thirty minutes purported, she'd need a little starch in her to survive the coming days.

"First thing *you* need to do is lose the dress."

"*Excuse* me?" she said, her tone rife with offense.

He dismissed her misunderstanding with a twist of his mouth and a short sigh. "You do have other clothes, don't you? Like in a suitcase in the trunk? Packed for your honeymoon?"

"Oh…right."

He heard her embarrassment in her voice, and though he kept his eyes on the road, he imagined her ivory cheeks, flushed red as they had been the night before at the rehearsal dinner when she was the butt of her friends' and family's good-natured ribbing. Her modesty and discomfiture had struck him as unusual for a woman with so much going for her—beauty, brains, wealth, ambition and family and friends who clearly adored her. Most women he knew with so much going for them seemed to feel they were entitled to their privileged lives.

For someone who'd scraped and fought for everything he had, such arrogance was a huge turnoff to Jake.

He cleared his throat. "Not only is the dress conspicuous when we need to blend, it's hardly made for speed if we have to make a break for it on foot again." He searched the side of the road for a place where he could hide the limo.

"Do you think we will…have to flee on foot, I mean?"

He met her gaze in the rearview mirror. "I don't know what we may be up against. But we need to be ready for anything, and we can't call attention to ourselves. They'll be looking for us. So we've got to go to ground until we either figure out what they want," he said thinking aloud, "or know for certain they're not hot on our asses anymore."

"We should just call the police and let them handle it."

"Can't. Scofield said Homeland was compromised. I assume he means Homeland Security, which is exactly who the police will call if they think national security is at stake." He shook his head. "For now, at least, we do this alone."

Jake spotted a vacant gas station and parked the limo behind it, out of sight of the road. Hauling himself out of the front seat, he clenched his teeth in pain as his bum knee, the reason the navy had kicked him out of the SEALs, throbbed a protest. Sprinting for the limo with an extra hundred or so pounds over his shoulder hadn't been kind to his old injury. Refusing to let his pain get in the way of his duty, he tried not to limp as he retrieved a floral-print suitcase from the trunk.

When he yanked open the back door of the limo, she gasped.

"I assume this one's yours."

Paige pressed a hand to her chest and sucked in several deep, restorative breaths that drew attention to the low neckline of her dress and the gentle swell of cleavage the dress had clearly been designed to maximize.

A hot stab of lust jabbed him in the gills, and he gritted his teeth. Now was hardly the time to get distracted by Paige's assets.

"Yeah, that's mine." She reached for the luggage, and he batted her hand away before setting the suitcase flat on the seat.

"Pick something practical that you don't mind getting dirty. Something you can run in, even sleep in if necessary. That includes shoes. No high heels."

"What about you? Your tux doesn't say *blend in* or *ready for action* to me."

"Well, a tux isn't my first choice of attire for this debacle either. But since I'm a good six inches taller and fifty pounds heavier than Scofield, I doubt anything he had packed will fit me, so I'll have to make do for now."

She glanced away and worried her bottom lip with her teeth.

He cocked an eyebrow. "What's that look for?"

"I…need to call someone—my dad or my sister Holly—to see how Brent is. To see what happened after we left, to make sure everyone else is all right, to—" Her words caught on a sob, and her face crumpled. "Oh, God. Mr. Diggle was murdered! At my wedding! I—I can't even stand to think of anyone else being hurt…or *worse*. And B-Brent—"

She dissolved into tears, and Jake's gut pitched. He could handle blood and bullets. But tears left him floundering like a plebe on his first day of training.

Not that he couldn't understand her concern. She had every right to be upset about her family's safety, about her fiancé's condition. He rubbed his suddenly sweaty palms on his tux pants and slid onto the seat beside her. Taking her by the arm, he pulled her onto his lap and gave her back an awkward pat.

There, there, sprang to mind, and he clenched his teeth, refusing to mutter any such asinine mumbo jumbo.

But somehow *shake it off* or *suck it up, soldier* didn't seem appropriate, either. Comforting Damsels In Distress 101 hadn't been part of his SEALs training. And while he was as compassionate as the next guy, expressing his feelings and dealing with other people's softer emotions were as foreign to him as some of the locales where he'd served before a well-placed bullet left him with a career-ending knee injury.

Paige's fingers curled into his tux shirt, and she nestled her head in the curve of his throat, collapsing against him and indulging her crying jag. He plucked a few shards of the broken window from her hair, noticing the tiny cuts the shattered glass had caused on her neck and hands. His hands, too, for that matter.

They were damn lucky broken glass was all that hit them. The driver hadn't been as fortunate.

The fragrant white flowers woven into her hair tickled his nose, and he turned his head so that his cheek rested against the top of her head. Tightening his hold on her, he savored the crush of her curves and soft skin against him. He stroked her back, her bare arms, the soft tumble of hair that escaped carefully placed bobby pins.

When she trembled, he absorbed the tremor, feeling an answering quake reverberate at his core. Jake closed his eyes and inhaled deeply, clearing his mind, focusing on the problem at hand. What the hell was he supposed to do with Paige? Where would they go? Considering he'd been lusting after her since Scofield had introduced his bride earlier that week, how could he survive the next few days with his sanity intact?

Adrenaline had his nerves jumping. But the press of her body against his spiked his blood pressure and had heat flashing over his skin. He'd barely had a chance to catch his breath since Trench Coat and his merry band of thugs had opened fire, and comforting Paige wasn't helping him focus.

As he fought down the desire that wound him tight, his thoughts jumped back to the scene at the church, and a shudder racked him. Jake had been part of a convoy in Iraq that was ambushed. The gun- and mortar fire had been deafening, the casualties high and the resulting chaos devastating to morale. But today's attack, with so many civilian lives at stake, had shaken Jake far worse. Against such lopsided odds, Jake had felt overwhelmed…and useless. An unsettling sensation for a man trained by the navy to be among the most deadly, the most effective, the most skilled.

When Paige's tears subsided to sniffles, she backed from his embrace and sent him a chagrined glance. "I'm sorry. I just…it's all so—"

He shook his head and twitched his lips in an dismissive grin. "Forget it." He rubbed the back of his neck and blew a deep breath from puffed cheeks. "I'll…give you a minute to change and pull yourself together. Then we need to make tracks."

She nodded, and he climbed out of the backseat, scanning the surrounding area for anything suspicious, anything helpful. A moment later, she opened the back door and stepped out, wearing a pair of formfitting blue jeans and a New Orleans Saints T-shirt. Sports-team apparel had never looked so good. Paige had taken the rest of the bobby pins from her hair, and raven ringlets hung around her shoulders. Finger-combing her hair back from her face, she gave him a quick nod. "I'm ready."

Before they left, Jake searched the dead driver, found the man's cell phone and dialed 911. He told the operator where to find the body, and when asked for his name, Jake set the phone on the front seat, line still open, and signaled for Paige to follow him.

She hoisted her suitcase, which he immediately took from her, and as they started toward the road, she gave the bullet-riddled, ribbon-and-paint-decorated honeymoon getaway car one last sad look before falling in step next to him.

For an instant, sympathy plucked at him. No one deserved to have their wedding day ruined, and Paige's disappointment was palpable.

Then the bigger picture reared its head, and he shook off the silly sentimental lapse.

National security. Well-armed terrorists. His client shot and bleeding.

What was a spoiled wedding compared to the life-and-death stakes they faced? He had no business letting emotion interfere with his duty to his job.

Keep the bead safe at all cost.

Jake hesitated.

Paige has what they want.

"Wait." He turned back to the limo. "Get the dress. Bring it with us."

Paige tipped her head, her gaze querying. "Don't you think it's a bit cumbersome to carry? Not to mention still as conspicuous in our arms as on me."

He frowned. "I'm not looking forward to dragging it with

us, but Brent said protect the *bead*. Your dress is covered in beading." He scowled. "I don't see how the beads on the dress could be what he wants protected, but after getting shot at because of this *bead* already, I'm not willing to take the chance that it's not one of the embellishments on your gown. How about you?"

Her shoulders slumped. "I see your point."

He grabbed the dress and slung it over his arm, bunching up the yards of flowing satin to keep from tripping over it as they headed toward the street.

She sent him a side glance that asked, "Now what?"

Good question. When he'd signed on to be Scofield's bodyguard, he'd imagined the job would be a cushy assignment, indulging an old friend's belief that he was being followed, that he needed protection. All Brent had told him was that a business deal had gone sour, and he suspected the other party might try to hurt him. Jake hadn't asked questions, dismissing Scofield's concern as paranoia. His first mistake.

And he'd never bargained for extended duty, guarding his client's bride, a woman whose guileless green eyes and body built for sin were distractions he didn't need if he wanted to keep them alive.

"We'll thumb a ride back to town," he said, answering her unspoken question and trying not to grimace when pain from his knee shot fiery bolts through his leg. "From there, we'll rent a car to get…wherever."

"Look, I…I have two tickets to Jamaica in my purse. The plane leaves in three hours. Why don't we use the tickets to get out of the country and—"

"No." Jake imagined Paige in a bikini on a white-sand beach with a fruity island drink in her hand, and another blast of heat slammed him in the gut. "Do you think those thugs don't know where you were headed on your honeymoon?"

She raised her chin, blinked, then frowned her consternation. "But that's—"

"I guarantee they also know where you live, what you drive, where you eat lunch with your girlfriends, where you buy your four-dollar coffee and what route you use to get to the office."

Her troubled look grew stormier, an edge of panic creeping into her gaze. Slowing her pace, Paige pressed a hand to her chest and wheezed, her breathing shallow.

"Hey, don't do that. You'll hyperventilate." Jake seized her arms and drilled her with a hard look. "I need you to keep it together for me, all right?"

She closed her eyes and nodded. Sucking in a few deep breaths, she flexed and balled her hands at her sides, and when she met his gaze again, she seemed in better control.

"I won't... I'm not going to fall apart on you. I promise. This is just all so overwhelming, so out of the blue. I don't understand any of it, and—" She cut herself off with another deep inhalation. "I'll be fine. Really."

The rumble of a car engine called his attention to the road, where a late-model sedan rolled past. He stepped toward the traffic lane and waved the car down.

"Are you sure hitching's the best idea? How do we know we can trust them?" she asked.

Jake nodded toward the elderly occupants of the car. "Look at them. What's not to trust? Besides, if grandma and grandpa do give us trouble, I can take them both down before they know what hit 'em."

The elderly driver slowed to a stop and rolled down his window. "You kids all right?"

"We could use a ride into town. We had a bit of car trouble a little ways back." He hitched his thumb down the road, and when the older man's gaze drifted to the wedding dress, the blood on Jake's shirt and the tear tracks on Paige's cheeks, Jake added, "Our honeymoon's not off to a very good start. I got a nosebleed and ruined my shirt, then the car broke down." He glanced at Paige, sending her a silent signal with his eyes, asking for her cooperation. "And my wife is convinced we're going to miss our flight to Jamaica."

The older man turned to Paige. "Don't cry, sweetheart.

We'll take you back to town, and if you call the airline, I bet they could reschedule you for a later flight."

Paige forced a smile. "I hope so. Everything else has gone wrong today. I'd hate to think we'll miss our plane."

Jake opened the back door for Paige, and she climbed into the car. Once they were settled in the sedan, Paige and Jake listened to the older couple regale them with stories of the mishaps from their wedding fifty-two years ago and many of the disagreements since.

As they approached town, their elderly driver turned from the main road onto a side street that led into a residential area.

"Henry, where are you going? This isn't the right way!" the woman fussed.

"It's a shortcut."

Henry's wife harrumphed. "Shortcut, my fanny. Shortcut is your term for lost. Turn around and go back to the highway."

Paige sent Jake a worried side glance, and he lifted a corner of his mouth in amusement before returning his attention to the middle-class houses they passed.

"I'm not lost. Stop worrying," Henry returned.

"That's what you always say. I'm telling you—"

"Wait a minute," Jake interrupted, spotting a for-sale sign in one of the front yards. "Stop here."

Henry stomped the brakes, and the sedan stopped with a lurch. "Something wrong?"

Paige gave Jake a curious look.

"I just remembered that a friend of mine lives on this street." He opened the car door and tugged on Paige's hand. "We'll go to his house, use his phone to call the airline, arrange for a tow truck and so forth." He tugged harder on his "bride's" hand, encouraging her compliance. "We appreciate the ride, folks."

"I can—" their driver started, then fumbled, as Jake hauled Paige's suitcase from the backseat. "Well, all right. Good luck, kids."

Jake gave the couple a friendly wave as they drove away, then faced Paige's confused scowl. "You don't have a friend in this neighborhood at all. Do you?"

"No."

"Then why did we get out?"

"Because I found a place for us to lay low until we can regroup and plan our next move." Jake lifted her suitcase and headed across the street to the small Acadian-style house with the Realtor's sign in the front yard.

Paige grabbed his arm. "Hang on a minute. Where are—?" Her gaze darted to the for-sale sign then back to him. He could see the wheels turning in her mind. "Whoa! You are not thinking about breaking into this house, are you?"

"That's exactly what I'm thinking. There are newspapers in the driveway, the grass hasn't been mowed. It's obvious the house is vacant."

He jogged to the backyard, and Paige stumbled to keep up. "I don't care if it's vacant! It's still breaking and entering. I won't do it!"

Pulling a small army knife from his pocket, Jake got to work jimmying the lock on the back door. "I don't think you're in a position to be picky about your accommodations, princess."

She grabbed his wrist as he worked, and he met her fiery glare. "Who died and made you boss of me?"

His jaw clenched. "Scofield."

Paige drew back with a gasp as if slapped. The wounded look in her eyes burrowed to his marrow.

"I'm sorry." He ducked his head and rubbed the back of his neck. "That was uncalled for." Jake squeezed her shoulder and drilled her with a stare that brooked no resistance. "I don't like the idea of breaking the law any more than you do, but this house is the safest cover we have right now. We're not here to rob it or deface it. In fact, we'll leave it better than we found it. We'll clean up the yard before we go, so it doesn't scream 'vacant' anymore."

With a last wiggle of his blade, the lock popped, and the door swung open. "After you."

Paige hesitated, glaring at him with righteous indignation. "This isn't right. We could go to a hotel."

Jake struggled to keep his cool. "Nothing about this situation is *right*. But we can't fix anything if we're dead and, for now, this house is our best chance to stay alive. By now, those thugs have every hotel within a hundred miles under surveillance or on their radar in some way. I'm not willing to risk being spotted at a hotel." He planted a hand at the small of her back and nudged her inside. "Now get in before the neighbors see us and call the cops."

Pressing her lips in a tight line of discontent, Paige stamped into the house. When she reached for the light switch, he caught her hand.

"A vacant house wouldn't have lights on. We can't give any indication we're here."

Beneath his fingers, her pulse fluttered at her wrist. Her gaze clashed with his, and he felt an answering kick of adrenaline in his veins. The anger sparking in her eyes and flushing her cheeks made her even more beautiful. He suppressed the urge to plow his fingers through the thick tresses of raven hair swirling around her shoulders.

"So we're just supposed to sit here in the dark?" She turned her attention to the empty room, then back to him. "There isn't even any furniture."

"Sorry, princess. Five-star accommodations aren't always possible when you're on the run."

"Stop calling me *princess* like that," she said through gritted teeth.

He arched an eyebrow, more amused by her temper than put off by it. "Like what?"

"Like you think I'm some pampered diva."

"Aren't you?"

She growled and snatched her wrist from his grip. "Can I at least use my cell phone to call my family and make sure they're safe? Let them know I'm all right?"

Jake rolled the tension from his shoulders, knowing how his answer wouldn't be received. "No. Cell phones can be tracked. In fact…give me your phone. We have to get rid of it."

Paige sputtered, her eyes wide. "Get rid— But all my contacts are on—"

He seized her shoulders and gave her a gentle shake. "Listen to me, and listen good. You saw what those men were capable of. This is no game. I can keep you alive and help you figure out what is going on, what you have that they want, but you have to trust me. You have to do what I tell you without question. All right?"

She opened her mouth, but immediately snapped it shut again. Fear and defeat crossed her face, and her muscles slackened beneath his hands. When she nodded her understanding, instead of feeling he'd won her cooperation, he felt a sense of loss.

"Where's your phone?"

She pointed to the floral suitcase. "In my purse. I packed it for safekeeping during the ceremony and reception."

He lay the suitcase flat on the floor and opened it. He handed her the handbag that had been tucked in one corner, and Paige fished her cell phone out. With an irritated huff, she handed the phone to him. He tucked the phone in his pocket and strode to the empty living room. After glancing out the front window, he lowered the blinds. "I'm going back out to get us a few things for tonight. Clothes for me. Food. Cash for later. I'll pick up a prepaid phone while I'm out, and you can use it to call your family. Okay?"

"Aren't you afraid you'll be seen?"

He scoffed. "Give me some credit. I'm a SEAL. I know how to avoid being spotted."

Paige wrapped her arms around herself and rubbed her bare elbows, despite the stuffy heat inside the house. "What am I supposed to do?"

"Stay out of sight. And try to think what you have, what Scofield might have given you or hidden in your suitcase that terrorists would want. Make a list of everything he's given you in the last few months. We have to figure out what the hell this *bead* is."

Paige stared at him, looking dazed, overwhelmed.

He crossed the room to her and cradled her chin in his palm. "Hey. You all right?"

"Guess I have to be. Don't have much choice." Ducking her head, she muttered, "As usual."

Jake frowned. "What's that supposed to mean?"

She shook her head. "Never mind. You go do what you have to."

He lingered another moment, debating whether he should press the issue, deciding whether he should insist she go with him. In the end, he decided he could move faster and more discreetly without her in tow. She'd be safer here, stashed in the vacant house until he got back. But, just in case, he pulled his pistol out from under his shirt at the small of his back and wrapped her hand around it. "Keep this with you. Only put your finger on the trigger if you intend to fire."

The color drained from her face. "I can't… I've never—"

"Just aim, two hands, and squeeze the trigger." He tweaked her chin and lifted a corner of his mouth in a grin intended to calm her. "Just be sure before you fire that it's not me coming back from my supply run. Got it?"

She gaped at the pistol as if it were a venomous snake and hurriedly set it on the kitchen counter.

He headed out the back door they'd come in through, brushing aside the small curtain on a side window to look out first and check for neighbors who might see him leaving.

"Jake?" she called, stopping him.

He faced her. "Yeah?"

She hesitated, her expression puzzled and her gaze fixed on the ring on her left hand. "Never mind. It will keep."

"What is it, Paige? Tell me."

She sighed. "Well, I was just wondering… Am I married… or not?"

Chapter 3

Paige thumbed the elaborate ring Brent had insisted she have, and nausea swirled in her belly. "I mean, we said our vows, but I never finished giving Brent his ring, and the minister never declared us man and wife."

She glanced up at Jake, who frowned, rolled his shoulders and shifted his weight. He'd been undaunted when they'd been under fire, running for their lives. So why did her simple question make him uncomfortable?

Then another, more ominous thought occurred to her. "I don't even know if Brent survived the attack. How do I know I'm not a widow?"

Jake jutted out his chin. "Don't borrow trouble or get hung up on worst-case scenarios. Until we know otherwise we're going to assume Brent is alive and will be fine. Got it?"

He jammed his restless hands in his pockets and narrowed his eyes. "Did you sign the marriage license?"

Her pulse tripped. A weight seemed to lift from her chest, and the tension screwing her muscles in knots loosened. "No.

We were supposed to do that after the ceremony, before the reception."

"Then I'd say, in the eyes of the law, you're not married."

He had a point. She nodded her agreement and exhaled silently, determined not to show him her relief.

"Why?"

She jerked her head up to meet his querying gaze. "What do you mean, *why?* Wouldn't you want to know if you were married or not?"

He shrugged. "Depends on if I really wanted to be married in the first place. Otherwise, the technical question of whether I'm married or not is moot." His incisive dark eyes scrutinized her. "Even without the legalities in place, your intentions to wed are still valid, your love for your fiancé is unchanged, the commitment you've made to each other is unbroken. Signing the license is a mere formality, in my view." He lifted an eyebrow and angled his head. "Right?"

Paige grabbed the edge of the counter behind her as her knees wobbled. "O-of course."

"But…" Jake stepped toward her as his knowing gaze homed in on her. "If, by some chance, you were having second thoughts about getting married, if you weren't as committed to your intended as you let everyone believe…"

Paige squared her shoulders and raised her chin. "Just what are you implying?"

He lifted a dismissive hand. "I'm not *implying* anything. I'm saying I saw your expression before Trench Coat busted in. I saw the doubt in your face. I saw your reluctance."

Nervous energy shot through Paige, and she suppressed a tremble. "Don't be ridiculous." When she heard the lack of conviction in her tone, she cleared her throat and added, "You saw nothing more than typical jitters over being in front of a crowd. Or a…a moment of…*reflection* as I considered the… importance of the day and—"

"Bull."

She gasped and shot him an affronted look.

"You can tell yourself that if you want, but I know what I

saw." His steady, keen gaze rattled her. "The SEALs trained me to read people, read body language, read subtle clues in facial expressions."

Paige swallowed hard and pressed a hand over the riot of acid in her gut. "You're wrong. I had every intention of marrying Brent before..." She flicked her hand, knowing he could fill in the blank.

He held her gaze for several unnerving seconds. The heat in his mahogany eyes turned her bones to dust and stirred a flutter in her belly. Just his proximity had her acutely aware of his height, his unflinching power and his ex-navy SEAL brawn. When they'd fled the church, he'd carried her to safety and still had the strength to run for the waiting limo. Even now, without him touching her, her skin flashed hot and tingled when she thought of his large hands in intimate places as he lifted her, shielded her, *saved her life.*

"I...I don't think I've thanked you yet...for what you did. Without you, I don't know if I'd have gotten out of the church alive."

The muscles in his square jaw twitched. "I did what I was trained to do. What I was hired to do. Besides...your fiancé is the one who knocked you out of the way when Trench Coat would have shot you. The one who took a bullet for you."

Paige's breath snagged in her lungs. She blinked back the sting of tears and choked down the bile that his reminder of Brent's sacrifice brought to her throat. Brent was dying, might even be dead, because he'd saved her from an assassin's gun.

"On the other hand," Jake continued, "your life would have never been at risk if not for the infamous *bead* Scofield had that Trench Coat wanted. We wouldn't be in danger now if not for him giving you the bead to protect. If he knew something about a threat to national security, how could he knowingly draw the woman he claims to love into the crosshairs of such dangerous men?"

Paige's leg wobbled, and she sank to the floor. The truth

behind Jake's assessment crushed her with a suffocating weight. "M-maybe Brent didn't realize the danger—"

"He knew. That's why he hired me to be his bodyguard."

She raised her bleary gaze to Jake. "Why didn't he want me to know? If he was in danger…"

How could Brent have hidden something so vital from her? She shook her head, unable to make sense of the bizarre twists the day had taken.

Jake squatted beside her and brushed her hair back from her cheek, tucking it behind her ear. "I don't know why he didn't tell you what was going on. I know for damn sure, though, if I were in love with a woman like you, I'd move heaven and earth to keep her safe. I'd never put her life in jeopardy the way Scofield did yours. It's not right."

A jab of loyalty to Brent compelled her to defend him, despite her misgivings about the strange situation. "I'm sure he had a good reason why—"

"No! There's *never* a good reason to put someone you love at risk." Jake's fingers curled into fists, and he clenched his jaw. Shoving to his feet, he stalked back to the door. "I have to go now. Keep this door locked and the gun within reach. I'll be back before dark."

"But what am I—?"

Before she could finish her question, Jake was gone. The silence in the vacant house was deafening. The stillness filled her with a terrifying sense of isolation.

Alone with her thoughts, Paige replayed the horrifying events of the afternoon, searching for some explanation for her frightening and senseless circumstances.

Her fiancé valued a bead over her life.

Brent was involved in something with national security repercussions.

She'd never signed the marriage license.

Paige bent her legs and, propping her arms on her knees, buried her face in her folded arms. Not knowing if Brent survived the attack or if her family was safe was maddening, terrifying. Fatigue, fear and confusion pounded inside her skull, but she refused to give in to the tears that threatened. She'd cried enough today.

We're going to assume Brent is alive.

The time had come to take back the control she'd lost over her life that afternoon. While Jake was gone, she had to figure out what Brent had given her that the terrorists wanted. She had to make a plan of action for getting out of this predicament, and she had to start rebuilding her shattered life—a life *without* Brent Scofield.

A mix of trepidation, guilt and relief for her decision spiraled through her, tangling around her heart. She didn't love Brent. Never really had. And today proved she didn't know him as well as she thought she had. Reason enough to reconsider her engagement. But as Jake pointed out, Brent had willingly put her in danger, set her up to be the target of terrorists. *Terrorists,* for crying out loud! Bitter anger blasted through her.

Until she thought of the way Brent had leaped in front of a bullet for her.

A leaden grief weighted her heart, made it hard to breathe. How could she ever sort this mess out?

An image of Jake wavered behind her closed eyes, and an odd reassurance settled over her like a warm blanket. When all hell had broken loose at the church, he'd saved her. When she'd been paralyzed by fear, he'd taken action. When she'd had her emotional meltdown in the limo, he'd been there with a warm embrace—and spared her empty platitudes.

Jake didn't waste time indulging her wishful thinking or misleading her with what she wanted to hear. He respected her enough to give her the hard-boiled truth. He gave orders and expected results. And he'd proven himself more than capable of protecting her from the threat Trench Coat—as Jake had called the lead terrorist—posed her.

Lifting her head to look around the empty house, Paige took a deep, centering breath. She owed Jake so much already. The least she could do before he returned was come up with something concrete they could work from. Organizing, analyzing and reasoning were what she did best. She'd been useless to Jake earlier because the unexpected, unexplainable chaos of this afternoon had left her completely out of her element.

Now, with a determination to put some order back in her life, Paige began dissecting the events of the past several days, searching for some clue to what the *bead* could be. As she fell into her familiar patterns of problem solving and rational thinking, a soothing balm flowed through her. She'd be fine—as soon as she solved the riddles she'd been presented by this afternoon's events.

After two hours alone, frantically searching her memories for answers, Paige was no closer to a solution when Jake returned with a few supplies and a rental car.

He set the new cell phones, a bag of fast food and other miscellany on the floor beside her and returned his gun to the waist of the new jeans he wore. His tux was nowhere in sight. "Any trouble while I was gone?"

"No. Nothing." Eager to hear from her family, Paige snatched up one of the phones. "Are these working? Have they been activated?"

"Yeah. But keep your call brief." He drilled her with a hard look that echoed the gravity in his tone. "And don't tell anyone anything about where we are. Someone could be listening on the other end."

Paige shivered, despite the stuffy house, and dialed her father's phone. After several rings, the call went to voice mail, and her stomach sank with disappointment and concern. What if her father had been hurt?

"Hi, Dad. It's Paige," she told his voice mail. "I'm safe. Shaken by what happened today but unhurt. I love you, and—" her voice cracked, and she paused to clear the emotion from her throat "—I'll call again when I can. Bye." She disconnected and immediately dialed her sister Holly's cell phone.

Holly answered on the first ring. "Hello?"

The stress and worry in her sister's voice sent fresh waves of panic and anxiety rippling through Paige. "It's me, Hol."

"Paige! Are you okay? Where are you? Oh, God, we've been so worried about you!"

"I'm fine. I'm with Jake McCall. How…how is Brent? Is he—?"

"He's alive, but he's critical."

Paige received the news with mixed feelings. Relief that he was alive, and grief for the severity of his condition. She clutched the phone like a lifeline to her family, and tears blossomed in her eyes.

"He lost a lot of blood, Paige. He's unresponsive, and I'm afraid it's still touch and go whether he'll make it through the night. We're at St. Mary's with him. How soon can you get here?"

"I—I don't think I can come." She glanced up at Jake for confirmation.

He shook his head. "Too dangerous."

She pulled the phone away from her mouth. "He's dying. I need to be there!"

"So you can die, too? Those men were willing to kill to get the bead. They saw me hustle you out of there, so I guarantee they know you have whatever it is they're looking for. You're their new target."

"Paige? Paige, are you sure you're all right? What do you mean you're not coming? Brent is your husband. He may not make it through the night."

"Technically, I don't think he *is* my husband. We never signed the marriage license." Paige frowned, hearing herself. Brent was dying, and she was arguing with Holly about the legality of her marriage? What was wrong with her?

Holly was conspicuously quiet, and guilt rolled through Paige. But Holly had a storybook marriage with her husband, Matt, and her stepchildren. How could she understand Paige's complicated feelings toward Brent? *She* didn't even understand her mixed emotions.

Paige raked the hair back from her face with her fingers

and sighed. "What about everybody else? Are Mom and Dad all right? Matt and the kids?"

"We're all shaken but not physically hurt. I think Mr. Garcia was shot in the leg, and I heard something about Fran Coulter being taken to the hospital. Lots of folks were treated at the scene for minor injuries and shock." Holly paused. "Mr. Diggle is dead, though."

"I know. I—"

Jake circled his finger in the air, signaling her to wrap up her call.

"Holly, I have to go. Tell everyone I love them. I'll try to call again when I can."

"Wait! Where are you? When are you coming home?"

"I don't know when I'll be home. Soon, I hope." She rubbed her eyes when moisture blurred her vision. "Jake thinks I'm still in danger. He thinks those men are still after me. Brent said I have something they want. He told Jake to hide me, protect me until—"

Jake yanked the phone from her. "She'll call later. Don't try to find us. Don't call the police. I'll keep her safe, but it's important that we lay low for a while. Goodbye."

With that, he snapped the phone closed and handed it back to her.

Paige glared at him. "What are you d—?"

"I said keep it short, and don't tell them too much. Her phone was probably bugged."

A tremor crawled up Paige's spine. "Bugged? I—" A new possibility occurred to her, and her breath snagged. "Do you think they'd go after my family to get to me? That they'd hurt them to bring me out of hiding?"

Jake gave her a blank, unreadable look. "It's possible. You should keep your contact with them to a minimum. Just in case."

Paige hugged herself, bending at the waist as fear for her family's safety knotted in her chest.

Jake placed a warm hand at the nape of her neck and gently rubbed her tense muscles. "The sooner we figure out what those men want and what we're supposed to do with it, the better—for everyone." He nudged the greasy sack of fast food toward her. "Eat something."

He toed off the tennis shoes that had replaced his wing tips since his trip out, and he settled beside her with his long legs stretched in front of him. "Did you make a list of the things that Brent has given you in the last several weeks?"

"Yes. But I'm no closer to figuring out what those men wanted." Twisting her mouth in frustration, she peered into the sack of burgers and fries he'd brought back with him, and her stomach growled. She hadn't eaten all day, having been too nervous for breakfast or lunch and worried about getting her dress to zip. But with the interrupted wedding behind her, what did it matter if she ate fried potatoes and red meat? Tonight she wanted comfort food.

"You can't think of *anything* he's given you, anything you packed for the honeymoon that might not be what it seemed?"

She pulled out a burger and handed it to him, then plucked a French fry from the sack and munched as she shook her head. "Nothing. At Christmas, he gave me tickets to the ballet in Chicago, and we flew up there for a weekend. The trip and a set of Waterford red-wine goblets were my Christmas presents." She ate another fry, then unwrapped a burger. "For Valentine's, he sent me two dozen roses—now dead and tossed out." She accounted for the items with her fingers as she listed them for Jake. "We bought an antique desk together that is at a dealer's being refurbished. He gave me a folder with life, car and home owner's insurance information to file a couple of weeks ago."

Jake's head came up. "Did you read the file? Are you sure that's what was in it?"

She nodded. "Read it and added the information to the spreadsheet I'd started for our finances. There was nothing unusual there."

Jake grunted, then, waving the hand with his burger, motioned for her to continue. "What else did he give you?"

She held up her hand, fingering the elaborate wedding band. "Well, my ring, obviously."

He arched an eyebrow as he glanced at the ring, then held out his hand. "Can I have a closer look?"

She slid the ring off and passed it to him.

He narrowed his gaze on the setting and whistled. "Wow. This is…" His expression said he was searching for a tactful term.

Paige sighed. "Gaudy? I know. I tried to tell him it was over-the-top, that all I wanted was a simple band to match my engagement ring, but he wouldn't hear of getting me something as mundane as a plain gold band." She felt a twinge of disloyalty for her complaint, but something compelled her to rationalize the showy ring to Jake. "I think he felt he needed to give me an expensive ring to prove he was worthy of me."

Jake raised an eyebrow as he tossed an amused side glance at her. "Think pretty highly of yourself, do you?"

She scowled and grunted. "That's not what I mean. Brent's the one who was intimidated by our family's money. He came from a family that had nothing. Through a lot of sacrifice and ambition, he worked his way up the ladder in Bancroft Industries in record time and was making good money. But I think he always felt like, with me, he was marrying up and had to prove to someone that he could compete with my family's wealth. He didn't need to, of course. But buying me an expensive wedding ring seemed so important to him, I didn't argue."

Jake turned the domed and jewel-encrusted band over, examining it from every angle. "Your wedding ring is a rather personal and significant item to compromise on. Do you make a habit of letting Brent bully you to get his way?"

Paige hiked her chin up and squared her shoulders defiantly. But her gut swirled, and her heart tapped an anxious rhythm. She refused to let Jake, a man who'd likely never compromised his wishes in his life, see how close to the truth he was. "My ring is just a *thing*. When you grow up surrounded by *things*, you learn how little *real* value and significance they have. Preserving Brent's pride was more important to me than what kind of ring I had." She snatched the ring back and jammed it on her finger. "If I can make someone happy by compromising on something trivial like a ring, then…so be it!"

She swallowed hard, hoping she hadn't overreacted and given herself away with her vehemence.

Jake only stared at her with his enigmatic dark eyes. She felt naked under his knowing scrutiny.

The SEALs trained me to read people, read body language, read subtle clues in facial expressions, Jake's words echoed in her mind.

She plucked another French fry from the bag and angled her body away from him. Nibbling on the cold fry, she forced her breathing to stay even, despite the flutter of nerves his scrutiny caused.

She heard the fast-food bag rattle as he dug into it. "Well, we can't rule out the ring, but keep thinking. What about computer files? Something he asked you to pack in your suitcase or hold in your purse?"

She fidgeted with her earring, then gasped and spun back toward Jake.

"His grandmother's earrings! He wanted me to wear them for the wedding—"

Jake's face lit up. "The ones you're wearing?"

Nodding, she put a hand behind her right earlobe and tipped her head to show him.

Leaning closer, Jake brushed her hair out of the way for a better view. When his fingertips skimmed her cheek, a tingle raced over her skin. She tensed, hyperalert to his nearness as he examined the simple gold dangling earrings. She held her breath, all too aware of the fact that in her entire relationship with Brent, her fiancé's caresses had never elicited half the electricity in her that Jake's accidental touch had. Her heartbeat kicked into overdrive when his mahogany eyes met hers at close range. "May I take it off?"

The deep, husky timbre of his voice stroked her, and she had to swallow hard before she could speak. "Sure."

She scrunched her eyes shut and gritted her teeth, certain she'd come out of her skin as he fumbled to remove the jewelry from her lobe, his warm fingers teasing the erogenous zone behind her ear. When he leaned back, his attention narrowed on the delicate earring, she drew a shaky breath, puzzled by her schoolgirl reaction to him.

He saved your life today. This giddy, blood-pumping response to him must be some form of emotional transference or hero worship. An adrenaline-based response to your brush with danger.

Appeased by her explanation, Paige turned her attention back to her hamburger but found she no longer had an appetite. She lifted her gaze to Jake, whose brows were furrowed in concentration.

"There are no gems on them," she offered, taking off the other earring to hand to him. "Nothing that could be called a bead. They're just hammered gold and a wire hook. They're not even all that pretty. But they're family heirlooms, and he asked me to wear them for the wedding." When he held out his hand for the second earring, she dropped it into his hand, careful not to touch him.

Chicken.

He shook his head and curled his fingers around the jewelry. "Damn. I thought we had something, but you're right. There's nothing to these things, nothing I see as suspicious. Nothing that'd make terrorists want 'em or threaten national security." He puffed out a frustrated breath and took another large bite of his sandwich. "What else?" he asked as he chewed.

She fingered the hem of her shirt and shrugged. "He had me keep the plane tickets for Jamaica in my purse. And… well, he gave me a corsage to wear at the rehearsal dinner last night. He gave—"

"Where's the corsage?" His eyes were bright with interest again.

"At my house, in the refrigerator. I was hoping it would stay fresh until I got back from the honeymoon." She sat straighter. "I don't remember anything beadlike added as embellishment. But I suppose— "

"It's not the corsage." Jake's jaw tightened. "The bead is important. Something he wanted protected, guarded. He wouldn't have put it in something you'd leave in your refrigerator while the two of you jetted off to the islands." He pressed his mouth in a thin line of consternation. "There has to be something else. Think!"

"I'm trying!" Her inability to decipher this puzzle grated on her logical, analytical nature. Jake's dissatisfaction with her help challenged her innate need to please, to prove herself, to excel. "We're assuming the term *bead* is literal. We don't know that what he gave me is *bead*like at all. What if *bead* is an acronym or a code name?"

"You're right. We shouldn't think so narrowly."

He shoved to his feet and grabbed her wedding dress from floor. "Have you gone over this to see if he hid something in the beading?"

"I didn't see anything unusual. Besides, Brent didn't give me the dress. He hadn't even seen it until today."

He continued probing the decorated folds of satin with a wrinkle in his brow. "Maybe he hid something in your suitcase without telling you. Have you searched it?"

"Yes. I didn't find anything I hadn't packed myself."

The house was rapidly growing dark as the sun set outside. Without the use of lights, which would call attention to their presence in the vacant house, they'd soon be left in an all-encompassing darkness. Paige shuddered at the thought, remembering the terrifying blast of gunfire and Trench Coat's menacing smirk.

She had something terrorists wanted. Something they'd happily kill her to retrieve.

The pressure to come up with an answer bore down on her. She curled her fingers into her hair, pressing her temples with the heels of her hands. "I don't know! I have no idea what those men were after or why Brent thinks I have it!" Her voice cracked, thick with defeat and fear. "I've gone over the last few weeks again and again, and I just can't—"

Jake captured her head between his hands, startling her. She hadn't noticed his approach, and his calmly commanding grasp stole her breath.

"It's all right, Paige." As soon as he had her attention, his hands gentled to a soothing stroke that settled at the base of her skull. His fingers tangled in her hair, and his gaze held hers. "Don't worry about it. We'll figure this out another way."

In the wake of all he'd sacrificed this afternoon to save her, her failure gnawed at her belly. "I'm sorry. I don't know what—"

"Shh." His thumbs caressed her jaw, and she saw a warmth and understanding that she'd never seen before in his chiseled face and military-hardened attitude. Her pulse stumbled, and heat flooded her cheeks where his thumbs grazed her skin. "Maybe we're going about this all wrong. Maybe a better plan would be to get a fix on what this bead is and why it is a national security risk."

With Jake's hands in her hair, his muscled body so close, her voice fled, but she managed a small nod.

His touch made her dizzy, and a heady thrill tripped through her veins. She indulged in a leisurely study of his full lips, his slightly crooked nose and his angular cheeks, where the first hints of evening stubble had grown.

Jake McCall, with his navy SEAL body, military bearing and ruggedly handsome face, exuded a masculinity that shook Paige to the core. He was nothing like the soft-in-the-middle, somewhat geeky, scientist-type men she'd dated. Nothing like the man she'd almost married.

Guilt bit hard on her conscience when she thought of Brent. How could she swoon like this over Jake's tantalizing touch and bedroom eyes while her fiancé was in the hospital dying?

No. Not her fiancé. She couldn't marry Brent now, not after he'd lied to her, put her in danger, proven how little she knew about him. Her chest tightened as she thought about how disappointed her father would be. He'd introduced her to Brent, encouraged the marriage, been so proud of her...

But she'd never had more than friendly affection for the man her father wanted her to marry. She'd believed the love would grow over the years, had believed passion was a fleeting thing only the fortunate few ever really had. Because marrying Brent made her father happy, because she knew how important Brent's role in Bancroft Industries was, Paige had been willing to enter a marriage based on platonic feelings and good business. She'd thought it would be enough for her.

Now, the extent of her relief that she'd not legally married Brent today told her just how wrong the marriage was. But how could she let her father down? How could she jeopardize her family's position at Bancroft Industries?

"Paige?" Jake's deep voice called her from her troubled thoughts and refocused her attention on their more immediate problem.

"H-how..." she croaked, then paused to clear her throat and lick her dry lips. "How are we supposed to find out what the bead is?"

Jake's gaze darted to her mouth, his pupils dilating, and she felt his grip tighten subtly.

"My sister said Brent's unresponsive, so we can't ask him about it."

When she mentioned Brent, Jake's expression shifted, hardened, and he withdrew his hands from her face. His movements stiff, he rose to his feet again and stalked across the floor.

"What about your father? Maybe he'd know something."

Paige blinked and shook her head, unsure she'd heard him correctly. "My father? Why would he know anything?"

"He's the head of the company, about to pass over the reins to Scofield. If this has anything to do with Bancroft Industries, there's a good chance he knows something."

"Who said Bancroft Industries was involved?"

"Brent said a business deal had gone sour. As a medical

research and development company, Bancroft Industries has the means to engineer something that could pose a national security risk." He shrugged. "Can you think of any other way Brent could have gotten involved with terrorists? He have any questionable hobbies, travel to exotic places?"

Paige's shoulders slumped. "No. The company is his life."

The idea that her father's business, a company her grandfather had built from the ground up, could have been infiltrated by terrorists made Paige nauseated.

Jake faced her, his body taut and poised for action. "In that case, our focus should be on Scofield's role at Bancroft Industries. Can you get me inside? I need to search Scofield's office, take a look at his computer."

"I...guess so. In the morning, I can—"

"No. Tonight." Jake stepped over to her and, with a hand under her elbow, hoisted her to her feet. "If national security is at risk, then the clock is ticking. We have to move on this. *Now.*"

Chapter 4

As they drove to Bancroft Industries in the nondescript Taurus Jake had rented on his last trip out, he briefed Paige on his search plan. "Remember, the place is likely being watched. We need to be as discreet and as quick as possible. Get in, get the files and get out. Stay close to me and follow my directions. Got it?"

Page sent him a worried look. "If those men are watching the office, how do you expect to get in without being seen?"

A buzz of energy flowed through Jake. After two years out of action, it felt good to be back in his element. "Trust me, okay? I once got a team of SEALs past thirty insurgents and inside an embassy building in Iraq without being noticed. I'm trained for this kind of thing."

He gave his aching knee a quick rub and tried to block out the reminder of his last mission, the ambush, his failure. He'd lost good men, most of his right kneecap and his career with the SEALs.

As he drove past the driveway to Bancroft Industries,

Paige cut a sharp glance across the front seat. "That was your turn."

"Not until we do a little surveillance of our own. Study the grounds carefully, and tell me if anything seems out of place, no matter how minor."

He cruised past the parking lot without slowing, giving her little time to study the grounds.

She grunted and cast him a withering look. "How am I supposed to tell anything if you don't slow down and give me a chance to look?"

"What would you think if you saw a car slow down as it drove past your house?"

She leaned back against the seat and sighed her resignation. "I'd think they were casing the property with ill intent. I'd find it suspicious."

"Did you get anything on that pass? Picture the scene in your head and analyze it."

Paige chewed her bottom lip and closed her eyes. "The parking lot was emptier than usual for this time of night, but that's probably because we let so many employees have today off for the wedding. There would only be a skeleton crew working." She scrunched her nose and, angling her head, met his gaze across the dark front seat. "And there were more security cars than usual. Two at the front gate instead of one, and I think I saw another near the main entrance. Why would—?" Her expression said she'd answered her own question.

"Apparently after what happened today at church, your dad saw the connection to Bancroft Industries, as well, and decided to beef up security."

A deep V creased her brow. "I should be with my family. This mess affects them and the business as much as me. Maybe my dad could help us figure out what the *bead* is. Even though he's not involved with whatever Brent has done, my dad knows Bancroft Industries inside out. He could—"

"How do you know he's not involved?"

"My father is not involved with terrorists!" Paige's jade eyes flashed with anger.

"Twenty-four hours ago you'd have said the same about Scofield."

"That's different. I know my father, and he's not—"

"All right." Jake raised a hand in concession. Now was not the time to argue that point. He just prayed they didn't find evidence in Scofield's files that implicated the senior Bancroft. He'd hate to see Paige disillusioned, heartbroken if her father had a hand in something illegal, even traitorous. "What else did you notice?"

She shook her head. "I didn't have time to see much else. Can you drive by again?"

"This car may be bland, but if we make another pass, we'll be noticed."

She frowned. "So that's it? One quick drive-by is your idea of reconnaissance?"

He quirked an eyebrow and gave her a smug grin. "If you're good, once is enough. And I'm very good," he said, his voice dipping.

He hadn't intended the seductive timbre, but the cant of her head and spark of intrigue that simmered in her gaze told him clearly that she'd heard the unspoken message in his tone.

"Let's hope so," she replied smoothly.

Jake shoved down the kick of libido that tightened his muscles. Sexual banter with the woman he was supposed to be guarding was just the kind of distraction that could get them killed. Gripping the steering wheel harder, he refocused the surge of energy toward finding a place to leave the car where they could make a quick getaway if needed.

Ten minutes later, they approached the Bancroft Industries property on foot, skirting the parking lot and staying hidden in the woods that bordered three sides of the facility. Jake did a quick scan of the area, noting the location of security cameras, parked cars and shadowed corners where someone could be hiding.

He took Paige's hand in his, then nodded toward the car nearest them in the parking lot. "That's our first stop. Stay low and keep up. Ready?"

"Is all this cloak-and-dagger stuff really necessary?" she whispered. "This is my family's company. I've worked here since I was an intern the summer after my high school graduation. I should be able to walk in the front door, without the spy games, and without anyone questioning me."

"Except that it's your wedding night, your fiancé is in the hospital and the same gunmen who opened fire at your ceremony would like nothing better than to see you walk through the front door so they can grab you and torture you until you tell them where the bead is."

Her eyes filled with fear. "I only meant—"

"We run on three." They didn't have time for her to lament what should have been. They could have already been spotted at the edge of the woods. He hiked onto his shoulder the empty backpack he'd brought to carry out their booty. "One. Two. Three."

Jake sprinted for the sedan at the corner of the lot, hauling Paige along behind him and ignoring the ache in his knee. He had a job to do and no time to waste on his bum knee.

When they reached the cover of the car, she crouched beside him, barely winded.

"You have your security card to get us inside?"

She gave a jerky nod and held up the electronic key pass. "The door on the back side of the building is closest to Brent's office, but it has more security cameras on it. I suggest we head to the second side entrance...there—" She pointed across the parking lot to a door near tall flowering shrubs. "The bushes will help give us cover until we can get inside."

Impressed with her reasoning, Jake nodded. "What's inside that door? We won't come in at a guard station or high-traffic restroom, will we?"

She gave him a how-stupid-do-I-look look. "That's the research hall. Mostly laboratories that should be empty tonight. We'll go down a short hall and take the first left.

There's a supply closet, first door on the right, where we can stop to regroup if we need to."

Jake lifted a corner of his mouth. "For someone who was complaining about the cloak-and-dagger approach earlier, you're pretty good at this."

"I just know we need a plan. You need to know where we are going, what we're up against, and we needed a contingency place to hide…just in case. I like to be prepared."

His grin tugged broader. "Prepared is good, but I'm used to playing things as they come."

"If we're downloading Brent's computer files, then we'll need a way to open the files later. Right?"

Jake arched an eyebrow. He'd already thought through this problem, but he was interested to hear her solution. "Go on."

"Well, my office is at the near end of the hall where we'll go in. Third door on the left. I have an old laptop stashed in the bottom of my desk that I haven't used since the company's last computer upgrade. It's a dinosaur, but it works."

Snagging her laptop while they were inside was a better idea than what he'd planned. "Perfect. We'll get it first, then head to Scofield's office. Good thinking, Paige."

She twitched her cheek in a grin.

"Ready to go?"

Paige jerked a nod. "On three?"

He winked. Counted. And they ran.

By the time they'd retrieved her laptop and reached Brent's office, Paige's heart rate was in the stratosphere. Shaking to her core, she plastered herself to the corridor wall, waiting for Jake to pick the lock on Brent's office door.

Her sister Zoey would have been far better suited to this kind of high-stakes errand. But Zoey was still who-knows-where with her loser boyfriend traveling from poker tournament to poker tournament and running headlong for a major heartache.

Paige's breath snagged. Her youngest sister had seen the

truth all along. Marrying Brent had been a misguided attempt to please her father. But Zoey lived her life to the fullest, chose what made her happy and pursued her dreams without fear.

Meanwhile, Paige's perfect wedding had become a perfect nightmare, and she'd never been more frightened and uncertain of her future in her life.

She heard the snick of the door lock, and Jake pushed the door open, swept the beam of his flashlight around the office and motioned her inside. After quietly closing the door behind them, he whispered, "I'll search the file cabinet. You get us into his computer records."

Paige wiped her sweaty palms on her jeans and dropped into Brent's chair. The faint aroma of Brent's aftershave hung in the room. The familiar scent had never been her favorite, but now it seemed cloying and made her stomach turn.

She powered on his PC and immediately encountered a password-protected sign in. She bit her thumbnail, unmindful of the salon manicure she'd had yesterday for the wedding. Tonight, in light of the day's turbulent events, her French manicure was of little importance. Paige closed her eyes, wondering if her life would ever resemble "normal" again.

She knew she had only three tries to get Brent's password correct or the office system would lock her out until the IT guys could reset his account.

Sucking in a deep breath, she typed *PAIGE*. Hit Enter.

The computer beeped and flashed an error message.

Jake flipped quickly through stacks of paperwork, making split-second assessments of whether various documents or folders might have vital information. Without pausing from his work, he whispered, "Keep trying. Sometimes passwords are the most obvious things, nothing secure at all."

She tried Brent's birth date.

Error.

She had one more guess. Pressing her hands to her cheeks, she leaned back in the chair and closed her eyes again. Searched her memory. What was important to Brent? What would he use as his private security code?

The company was the focus of all his time and energy. His upcoming promotion.

Hands shaking, Paige typed in *BICEO*.

Bancroft Industries Chief Executive Officer.

The screen blinked, then the hard drive purred to life.

She was in. Paige waited impatiently for the start-up procedure to finish, glancing across the room where Jake was shoving folders of documents into a backpack.

Her stomach whirled. She was helping a stranger steal company property. If her father knew…

Paige laced her fingers and pressed her thumbs together, trying to calm her jitters. She was doing all this to protect her father and the company. To help stop terrorists. To save herself and her family from the men who'd opened fire at the church today. But breaking and entering, stealing files, hiding like a fugitive rankled her safe, law-abiding and orderly instincts.

Once she was at Brent's desktop screen, she searched the icons for one that might guide her to the list of his most recent work files. Jake finished ransacking the file cabinets, stuffing the materials in his backpack, and stepped closer to hover over her shoulder.

She found another password-secured program and tried the code that had worked before.

BICEO.

Error.

Growling her frustration and impatience, she tried again, typing *PAIGE* and holding her breath.

Error.

Jake said nothing, but his presence unnerved her. He was counting on her to work fast, find what they needed and not let simple passwords stop her from getting results.

He swiped a hand down his jaw. "Want me to try?"

"I can do this. I know him better than you do."

"Try *VERONICA*."

Paige twisted on the chair to meet Jake's gaze. "What? Why?"

"Veronica Salley was the love of his life in high school.

I heard they got engaged in college. Don't know why they broke up, but I'm betting it wasn't his idea. He was crazy about her."

"He wouldn't—"

"Try it."

"But I only have one guess left. If you're wrong, the system will shut down."

"Try it."

Huffing out her disagreement, Paige pounded out *VERONICA*. Hit Enter.

The computer flashed to a list of saved documents.

Jealousy bit hard, and Paige gritted her teeth. Why she should care about an old girlfriend of a man she'd decided she didn't love and couldn't marry, she couldn't say.

Jake handed her a tiny USB flash drive. "Save them all to this. Hurry."

After plugging the device the size of a pack of gum into the computer, she hit a few keys to start the download.

A green bar popped onto the screen to track the progress of the files transfer. Ten-percent complete. Fifteen percent…

She angled her head toward Jake. "Is there anything else we should—"

A series of loud pops sounded down the hall.

Startled, Paige yelped, and Jake grabbed her arm, tugging her down from Brent's chair and behind the mammoth wooden desk. She recognized the noise far too quickly, had heard it too often already today.

Gunfire.

Jake reached behind him for the gun tucked in his jeans. "Listen to me. I'll hold them off as long as I can. Watch that download, and the second it is finished, pull the flash drive and stash it somewhere safe, somewhere you won't lose it if we have to run."

Paige's answering laugh was half irony, half panic. "*If* we have to run?"

With his free hand, Jake cupped her face and drilled a hard, yet oddly comforting gaze on her. He was calm, assured, in control of the situation. "I know this looks bad. I know you've been through a lot today, and this is frightening. But you have to keep it together for me. Just stay calm, do what I tell you, and we'll get through this."

More gunfire echoed in the corridor. Closer. Louder.

The download read sixty-five-percent complete.

Paige's pulse hiked higher. "But they have us cornered in here! How are we supposed to get out of this office?"

His grip on her face tightened slightly. "I'll find us another way out."

Jake's steady mahogany gaze penetrated the shroud of fear surrounding her. His confidence and skill bolstered her wavering courage. She trusted Jake. He'd already saved her, come through for her so many times today.

She gave a jerky nod of cooperation.

Jake smacked a quick kiss on her forehead and shoved to his feet. Dragging a chair below the air vent, he used a knife blade to quickly loosen the screws holding the cover in place.

Download seventy-eight-percent complete.

More gunfire.

Paige snapped her gaze to the door. Three men clad in dark clothes and wielding large guns burst into the office.

Jake dropped and rolled back behind the desk with her as a spray of bullets pelted the wall behind her.

She swallowed her scream, too terrified to muster the breath needed.

Download ninety-two-percent complete.

Snatching up his gun, Jake aimed his weapon at the intruders and dropped two of them with deadly accuracy. The third man swung back into the hall for cover, shouting, "They're in here!"

Jake grabbed her wrist and shoved the gun into her hand. "Cover me."

She gaped at him. "Wh-what?"

"Aim at the door and squeeze the trigger. Hold them off. I gotta get that vent open." With that, he scuttled back to the chair where he stood to pry the air duct cover from the vent.

The man at the door swung around from the hall and fired at Jake.

"Paige!"

Her heart leaped to her throat. Hands shaking, she pushed to her knees, propped her elbows on the desk and fired off two rounds at the man in the door. The man screamed and grabbed his arm.

Download ninety-nine-percent complete.

Jake popped the vent cover free and shoved the backpack stuffed with paper files inside the duct. "Paige, let's go!"

"C'mon, c'mon!" she begged the computer.

The gunman fumbled for his weapon with his left hand, his firing arm hanging loose at his side. Raising his gun, he aimed now at Paige. She gasped and ducked, just as two bullets whizzed past her head. The wood paneling behind her splintered.

"Paige!" Jake rushed back behind the desk with her and nudged her toward the vent. "Move it!"

Download complete. Thank heavens!

She snatched the portable storage device from the USB port and shoved it in her jeans pocket.

Taking the gun from her, Jake finished off the guy at the door, just as his backup arrived.

Holding her breath, Paige ran for the chair under the vent and scrambled to find a handhold. A large hand planted on her bottom, shoving her up and into the narrow vent. She wiggled and squeezed, hurrying to clear the way for Jake as a fresh round of gunfire blazed.

Darkness swallowed her inside the vent. The tight passage reminded her of a tomb, and she fought off a cloying claustrophobia. Breathing raggedly, her arms trembling, she felt her way hand over hand, inching forward. Her hand bumped the large backpack full of files Jake had salvaged, and she pushed it deeper into the air return. When she found a side outlet, she pulled herself around the right angle. The side vent was large enough for her to sit up and turn around. Dim light from the open end of the vent illuminated the path she'd just come through.

Jake wasn't behind her. Panic roiled in her gut, filling her mouth with bitter fear. "Jake!"

From the office, she heard muffled grunts, loud thumps and breaking glass.

Her heart in her throat, she crawled back toward the office. "Jake!"

"Don't wait for me! Go!"

Relief swamped her knowing he was alive, yet she hesitated. Go without Jake?

A face appeared at the vent opening. Glowering. Bleeding.

Not Jake's.

She saw the flash of metal as the man raised a gun to the vent opening. Then a spray of red as a bullet hit his head.

Gasping, Paige scuttled back awkwardly, bumping her head and jamming her elbow. Her pulse thundered wildly in her ears, a harsh counterpoint to the sounds of violence echoing through the metal cave.

Twisting around, she crawled back into the side vent, feeling for a means of escape. But the side tunnel led to a large fan, blocked off with a sturdy steel screen. A dead end.

Struggling to keep her breathing even and not give in to the clamoring fear squeezing her chest, Paige turned around and crawled back the way she had come.

Still no Jake. More thumps. More gunfire. More grunts of pain.

Acid sawed in her stomach. If anything happened to Jake…

Paige closed her eyes and sucked in slow, deep breaths. She had to fight the panic, had to keep it together if she wanted to be any use to Jake. If she wanted to survive this nightmare.

Brent's fault. She was in all this danger because of Brent, because of the bead.

Anger slashed through her. How could he have claimed to

love her, then put her in this position? How could she have ever believed she loved Brent?

She rolled to her belly as she went back into the first, smaller duct. Shimmying forward on her hands and stomach, she scrunched along the tight tunnel, pushing the backpack in front of her, only to find that the duct narrowed as she crawled farther back. There was no way Jake, with his broad shoulders, would fit in this restricted space. And Paige wasn't too keen on the idea of trying to squeeze through herself and risk getting stuck. The air-return tunnel wasn't going to provide an escape.

Swallowing her disappointment and a fresh wave of fear, she backed up. The hard floor of the metal duct bit into her knees and elbows as she wiggled toward the side outlet, where there was space to turn around. If they couldn't get out through the HVAC ducts, how—?

"Paige?" Jake's deep voice was sweet music to her ears. No other noises came from the office. The silence was chilling.

"J-Jake?" A hand grabbed her ankle, and she gasped, flinched.

"Easy. It's me."

"We can't get through that way. One duct is too small, and the other is blocked."

"Forget it. I handled the problem. I'll help you down." Jake positioned her foot on his shoulder. "Bring the backpack."

As she found her footing, he skimmed his hand up her leg to her waist to help her balance as she crawled backward out of the vent. "What happened to—?"

Her breath caught when she saw the carnage in Brent's office. No less than six men—all clearly dead—broken furniture, scattered files, shattered glass. And blood.

On the floor. On the walls. On Jake.

Icy horror swept through her, and she clutched the backpack to her chest as if it could shield her from the grisly scene. "Oh, my God! Are you all right? How... What—?"

"I'll be fine." He wiped his bloody lip on his shoulder then stooped to take a large gun from the hands of one of the dead men. Pulling the backpack from her hands, he shoved the assault rifle toward her. "Take this. We're not in the clear yet."

She stifled the question that sprang to her mind—how had he overpowered all those men? Judging by the noises she'd heard, the odd angle of some of their necks and Jake's obvious injuries, she didn't *want* to know what SEAL-trained techniques he'd employed. Paige shuddered and stared down at the assault weapon in her hands. "M-maybe we should… call in the police now. This is all too—"

"No." Jake threaded his arms through the straps of the backpack and edged toward the door. "Brent was very clear. He said Homeland Security had been compromised. If we call the local police about this, they'll be obligated to call in the Feds. Until we know who and what we are dealing with, who we can trust, we do this alone." He peered around the door frame and hitched his head. "Come on. We need to hurry."

Paige stepped over a burly man whose dark eyes stared sightlessly at her. The urge to cry, to curl up and fall apart was strong, but digging deep and gritting her teeth, she crushed the temptation to give in to her weakness. Jake needed her to be strong, think clearly, be ready to follow his directions.

He took her hand and led her down the hall at a jog. Jake was limping, favoring his right leg. They paused at the intersection, where there was another corridor, long enough for Jake to peek around the corner. When he gave her the all-clear nod, they set off again. At the end of the hall, the night guard's body lay sprawled in a pool of blood. Her stomach rebelled at the sight. She remembered hearing gunfire before the terrorists had arrived at Brent's office. Now she knew why. Jake's grip on her hand was tight to the point of being painful, but Paige didn't dare pull away. She was keenly aware how dependent she was on him to get out of the building—and this entire macabre situation—alive.

Chapter 5

When they reached the rental car, Paige dropped onto the passenger seat and closed her eyes. A shudder raced through her, and she mumbled a prayer of thanks that they'd made it out of the building in one piece. Most of Bancroft Industry's security force hadn't been as lucky, thanks to the terrorists. Whoever these people were, they played hardball and would ruthlessly kill anyone who stood in their way.

Jake climbed in the driver's side and cranked the engine, giving the area a searching glance before he pulled the car from the cover of the bushes where they'd parked. "Show me the flash drive."

Paige fished in her pocket and pulled out the tiny device. Jake nodded. They drove in silence for several blocks before he spoke again. "Hey, you did a good job in there."

She cast a blank stare at him as he pulled to a stop at a red light.

"How can you say that? I crawled into the vent and hid. You single-handedly took out six men!"

"Not all at once. And you slowed that one guy with a good shot to the arm."

She shrugged, not wanting to think about having to shoot at the man who was trying to kill Jake. "But you knew the password to Brent's files would be his ex-girlfriend's name." She huffed with disgust. "That stung. How silly of me to think he'd use *my* name as a password. I'm only his fiancée."

He turned his palm up from the steering wheel. "Well, maybe that's why he didn't use it. Maybe he thought it was too obvious, not safe enough. They tell you to avoid things like birthdays and children's names, because they're too easily guessed."

"Maybe." Paige rubbed her hands over her arms, still shivering in a post-adrenaline crash. "But his password was still another woman's name. I think that speaks volumes. Don't you?"

He hesitated, casting a hooded side glance to her. "Yeah. I think it says he's still in love with Veronica, and you were justified in your doubts about marrying him."

She opened her mouth to deny again that she'd been having second thoughts at the wedding, then snapped her mouth closed. His eyes were too incisive, and arguing seemed pointless. He was right, and the pretense she'd been living had blown up in her face.

With a sigh she leaned back against the headrest. "Guess it also says he was using me to impress my dad and get the inside track on the CEO job when Dad retires this fall."

"Brent was always ambitious."

She grunted and turned to stare out the side window. "Very. I just didn't realize I was nothing more than a rung in his climb up the ladder."

"He cares about you."

Her shoulders drooped. "Don't patronize me."

"I'm not. I saw it in his face when he talked about you at the rehearsal. It may not have been love, but he cared. He cared enough to step in front of a bullet for you."

She whipped her head around to face him. "A bullet that

would never have been aimed at me if not for his secret life as a spy or a terrorist or whatever the hell he's mixed up in!"

Jake drew a deep breath and scrubbed a hand over his face. "Yes, he *did* drag you into this firestorm…which leads us back to my original point. Considering how this was dumped on you and all you've been through today, you did a good job tonight."

He parked the car along a residential curb and cut the engine. She recognized the vacant house where they'd hidden earlier several houses down the street. Apparently the empty home was their base of operation for the time being.

"You've a right to be proud of yourself," he continued. "It might have been messy, but we got what we went in for. We got his files, so…mission accomplished. Good work, partner."

Lifting a corner of his mouth, he held his fist out to her.

She blinked. Frowned.

After a moment, Jake reached for her hand, curled her fingers into a ball and tapped his knuckles against hers. The awkward fist bump shouldn't have meant so much to her. But the simple congratulatory gesture, coupled with his praise, spun a frisson of warmth through her that burrowed beneath the chill of her fear, her disappointment, her disillusionment.

Knowing she'd done something, *anything,* worthy of Jake's approval pleased her. Brought a small grin to her lips. "Thanks. You deserve the credit, though. I didn't—"

He pressed a finger to her lips, cutting her off. His touch sizzled through her, backed up her breath in her lungs.

"You sell yourself short. You showed courage, intelligence, forethought… I was proud of you."

When he added a quick, lopsided grin to his compliment, her pulse scampered. Jake turned to climb out of the car, giving her time to collect herself and shove down her body's reaction to him. The last thing she needed was a telltale shiver or something in her expression giving away her schoolgirl attraction to him.

Jake ushered her to the back door of the vacant house and had her wait on the stoop until he'd swept through each room to be sure no one was lying in wait for them. Once inside, she dropped wearily to the floor of the living room, glad now for the cover of the darkness. Jake's skill in reading her thoughts and interpreting her body language unnerved her. Now that they were out of harm's way, she wasn't sure how much longer she could keep her emotions at bay.

She hugged herself as she watched Jake's shadowy movements. She recognized the sounds when he took his gun out and reloaded it—the rattle of the bullets in his hand, the click when he locked the magazine into place.

The rustle of the curtains when he brushed them back to check the yard. The crinkle of paper when he pulled a cold hamburger from the fast-food sack and peeled the wrapper back.

"Want half this burger?"

She shook her head, then, realizing he'd likely not seen the gesture in the dark, whispered, "No, thanks. I'm not hungry."

Folding her arm under her cheek, she lay down on her side and stared into the inky blackness. Fatigue sank to the bone, but images of the day's horrors paraded through her mind, keeping her from falling asleep. After several minutes, she sighed and tried to find a more comfortable position on the hard floor.

"Don't think about it," Jake said.

"About what?"

"Whatever's keeping you awake. Probably the violence you witnessed today."

She didn't bother asking how he knew. Even without his skills in reading people, the cause of her restlessness was pretty obvious. "It's kinda hard not to think about it."

"I know, but try to focus on something good, maybe a favorite memory. Like…the last time you had lunch with your sister Holly."

She sighed.

"We were at Brundle's Deli…planning my wedding." The happy memory made her voice crack.

If only she could go back to that day last week, before…

"Come here." Jake moved to lie at her side. He nudged her closer, cradling her in the crook of his arm and pulling her head down to his shoulder. "Try to sleep."

Paige turned on her side and rested her hand on his chest. His heart bumped a steady cadence under her palm, and the slow, sure beat soothed her ragged nerves.

When Jake strummed his fingers up and down her spine, the hypnotic stroking made her whole body tingle. A feral, musky scent clung to him and teased her senses. In his arms, she felt both serenely safe and on the precipice of some unknown but exhilarating danger. For tonight, she didn't want to examine the contradiction. Instead, she curled her fingers into the soft material of his T-shirt. Closing her eyes, she indulged the urge to snuggle closer to him and feel the raw strength of his hard body pressed along the length of hers.

She shouldn't be so wildly attracted to another man on the same day she'd been about to marry Brent. But she hadn't planned to be so drawn to Jake, and Brent had never evoked the sensual response from her that Jake did. Brent had deceived her and put her at risk. And today, she'd admitted to herself that she didn't love Brent, didn't want to marry him.

"I know what you saw today was frightening for you." His deep voice rumbled gently like distant thunder in the dark room. "But Brent asked me to keep you safe, and that is what I'm going to do."

Paige scoffed. "Correction, he told you to keep the *bead* safe. I was just a by-the-way. The unfortunate one who had the damnable bead when everything hit the fan." She didn't try to mask the resentment in her tone. "Clearly, my safety wasn't his greatest concern or he'd never have put me in this position."

Jake raked his fingers through her hair, capturing the base of her skull and angling her head so that she looked up at him. "Brent may not have considered you the priority, but I do. I'm making it my job to see that you get through this safe and sound. You have my word, Paige."

A sliver of light from a street lamp sliced through the window blinds and illuminated his face. The pale glow highlighted the rugged angles in his cheeks, the square cut of his jaw—and reflected the determination in his dark eyes.

She held his gaze, mesmerized by the intensity that vibrated from him. In a moment, his attention shifted to her mouth, and Paige felt his muscles tense. Her pulse quickened, and her gaze gravitated to Jake's lips.

The air between them charged, grew thick with palpable heat and tension.

She read Jake's internal battle in his twitching cheek as he gritted his teeth, the flaring of his nose as he sucked in a slow breath. His fight for restraint buzzed through the taut muscles of his arms and the increasing tempo of his heartbeat under her hand.

After a mind-numbing day of having danger thrown in her face, her life thrust in the line of fire, Paige had little patience for the careful thought and reason she typically relied on. In that moment, she wanted only to savor the tempting sensations Jake stirred in her. She wanted to flout caution, ignore the voice that warned her to go slowly.

Without analyzing the impulse, she tunneled her fingers into his hair, closed the distance between them and brushed her lips against his. With their bodies aligned, she absorbed the shudder that raced through Jake. A groan hummed from his throat as he anchored her head between his hands and deepened the kiss. Tingling sparks shot through her blood, taunting her, thrilling her.

He was endearingly tentative at first, as if asking permission to be bolder. Paige settled the question for him by sweeping her tongue along the seam of his lips and sliding her leg over his. Her thigh bumped the hard ridge under his fly, and knowing that she'd aroused him filled her with a confidence—and recklessness—she'd never experienced. A surge of crackling energy coursed through her, urging her to sate the growing hunger, gnawing deep inside.

Jake's tongue parried with hers, and his fingers kneaded

her bottom. He lifted her hips and scooted beneath her so that she lay intimately draped atop him. His hands mussed her hair as their kiss escalated, as their bodies heated and the rest of the world fell away.

Paige hooked her legs around Jake's, and her caresses roamed restlessly over his wide shoulders, rock-hard arms and muscled chest. And still she wanted more. She craved the escape, the sweet oblivion his body offered. She ground her hips against his, and her hands pulled impatiently at his T-shirt. She wanted to feel his skin on hers, wanted to draw him closer, wanted to blot out everything except the mind-numbing sensations he awoke in her.

When she reached for the button on his jeans, he caught her hand and broke their kiss.

"Jake…" she rasped, moving her mouth to nibble the line of his jaw.

"Paige, stop." He captured her face between his hands and angled her chin up so he could meet her gaze. "We have to stop."

"Why? We both want it," she whispered breathlessly, her head still muzzy and unfocused. "And heaven knows, after today we've earned the right to a little pleasure…"

He pulled her head down to his shoulder with one hand and hugged her close with his other arm. "First, because we don't have protection."

She jolted, her pulse kicking with the sobering reminder of how she'd lost her usually pragmatic senses.

"And second, because…I can't take advantage of you. We both want this for the wrong reasons." When she stiffened, he tightened his grip on her. "You're vulnerable tonight. Frightened. Confused. You don't want to complicate those feelings with sex you may regret in the morning."

The cold splash of reality doused the sizzle in her veins and, feeling suddenly awkward and embarrassed, Paige shoved away from Jake. The one time she'd tossed caution aside, she'd made a fool of herself, throwing herself at Jake.

"I'm sorry. I shouldn't have—"

"Wait." He refused to release her when she struggled. "I'm not saying I don't want you. I'd think it was pretty obvious how much I *do* want you."

"Jake, you don't have to—"

Without warning, he rolled over so that she was pinned beneath him. "Paige, listen. You are an extremely desirable woman. And yes, I want you. But I can't forget the danger we're in. I can't afford to be distracted."

She shivered, despite the heat of his body pressed against her.

Jake smoothed a hand along her cheek. "And I can't ignore the fact that this morning you were engaged to a man I'd been hired to guard. A man I failed to protect when he needed me most. Making love to you would feel like…a betrayal."

Paige caught her breath. Jake was right to stop them, but hearing him enumerate the many ways she'd abandoned her good judgment rubbed salt in the wounds she'd suffered today. She squeezed her eyes closed, fighting back the burn of tears and chastising herself for her lapse, for her recklessness. "You're right. And…it won't happen again. I'm sorry."

"Don't apologize." Jake rested his forehead lightly against hers and sighed. "You did nothing wrong."

Despite the reminders why indulging her attraction to Jake was a mistake, the gentle caress of his breath on her cheeks still stirred a flutter in her belly, still created a warmth and intimacy that wrapped comfortably around her heart.

His knuckles brushed her cheek, and he pressed a kiss to her temple. "Now get some sleep."

She nestled down, closer to him. How she'd fall asleep with the distraction of his body pressed to hers she didn't know.

But somehow she did, because the next thing she knew, bright yellow sun streamed through the gaps in the window blinds and roused her from sensuous dreams of Jake.

Squinting against the beam of buttery light that hit her face, she sat up and glanced about, finding herself alone on the living room floor. She rubbed her eyes and raked her hair away from her face, knowing she had to look a wreck. She prayed the hot water was still on in the house. She needed a reviving shower in the worst way. "Jake?"

"Mornin'."

She twisted at the waist and found Jake behind the kitchen counter with a stack of papers in his hands. Shoving to her feet, she ambled into the kitchen, yawning and casting a curious glance at the clutter of paperwork on the counter. "Brent's files?"

He nodded, then hitched his head toward the far end of the counter. "Breakfast. The coffee's probably pretty cold by now, but it's caffeine, if you're as addicted as I am."

Smiling her thanks, she popped the plastic lid off the insulated cup waiting for her. She wasn't a big coffee drinker, but his thoughtfulness touched her.

"Sugar and creamer are in the bag with the doughnuts. I wasn't sure how you took your coffee, so…" He let his sentence trail off as he turned his attention back to the scattered papers spread before him.

She sipped the coffee and raised her gaze to study her raven-haired protector.

He rubbed his chin as he read the open file, and the scratch of his morning beard against his fingers sent a rush of heat skittering through her.

Last night she'd been prepared to have sex with this man who knew so little about her, he didn't even know how she liked her coffee. No matter how sexy Jake was or how scared she'd been, there was no excuse for letting herself be so… emotional and rash.

Zoey was the impulsive sister—and look where it had gotten her. Traveling the country with a gambler, supporting his addiction and living hand to mouth off *Zoey's* life savings.

But, Paige, she's happy. She loves this guy. Who are we to judge how she lives her life if she's doing what feels right to her, what makes her happy? Holly had said, the last time Paige complained about Zoey's poor choices. Holly—the peacemaker, the nurturer, the blissfully-wedded idealist. She saw only the good in Zoey. In everyone.

Jake grunted, pulling her out of her drifting thoughts.

She stepped toward him to glance over his shoulder. "What? Did you find something?"

He waved a hand toward the file he was reading. "There's a lot in here about new drugs and vaccines Bancroft was developing."

"Makes sense. Research and Development is the largest and most profitable branch of the company. Besides, that's where Brent got his start. He's a research junkie at heart, though he set his sights on leading the company when Dad announced his retirement plans a couple years ago."

Jake glanced over his shoulder to her. "Any one project in particular that he talked about more than others? Something big in production that he was excited about?"

Paige sipped her coffee as she tried to recall what Brent had mentioned working on recently. "Nothing that stands out. He talked about meetings he had, contracts he'd signed. Mostly daily agenda stuff. To be honest, I was so preoccupied the last several months with wedding stuff, those plans were what we talked about most often."

"Did he mention trouble with any project, holdups or delays?"

"Every project has its delays and red tape. Backlogs for approval at the FDA, requests for new studies, data that has to be reanalyzed. Problems are common."

He grunted again as he turned his attention back to the file.

Paige plucked a doughnut from the sack and shook off the extra powdered sugar before taking a large bite and savoring the sweet treat. "What can I do to help?"

Jake glanced up and rubbed the back of his neck. "You could set up your laptop and take a look at the files on the USB. I was waiting for you to get up before I turned on your computer." He shrugged. "Felt like an invasion of your privacy to get on your computer without you."

She chuckled and shook her head. "Like breaking into

Brent's office and stealing his files wasn't an invasion of privacy?"

"Way I see it, Brent gave up the right to privacy when he put national security in jeopardy."

The sweet pastry in her mouth soured. *National security.* What on earth had Brent gotten her involved in?

After brushing sugar from her fingers, she retrieved the laptop from Jake's backpack and opened the top. She plugged in the power cord and took a seat on the floor while the computer started up.

"This is interesting." Jake picked up the file he'd been studying and moved to sit beside her, spreading the folder of papers on his lap. "I found a receipt stuck in here with all the paperwork on this project he called Superbug."

Paige cast him a curious glance. "A receipt for what?"

"Your wedding ring." He handed her the itemized jewelry-store printout. "Why would that be in the files of the company's research projects?"

"Are you kidding? Did you see his office when we were there? Clutter everywhere. Brent was brilliant, but he was disorganized. Messy." She glanced at the receipt then handed it back to Jake. "It was probably just misfiled."

He hummed an acknowledgment but continued to stare at the paper. "He had your ring specially designed. Built from scratch according to a design he gave the jeweler."

Statements, not questions. Yet Jake's expression said he felt an explanation was in order.

"Yeah. I told you that last night. Remember?" She slipped the wedding ring off and handed it to Jake. Why was she even still wearing it? "He wanted to give me a ring he called *unique* and *special*. I always took that to mean exorbitant and showy."

Her laptop finished loading programs, and she plugged the flash drive into a side port. While Jake turned the ring over, examining it again, she tapped her keyboard and began opening files uploaded from the flash drive. She found Brent's schedule spreadsheet with his appointments, meetings, names and phone numbers.

Holding her breath, Paige scanned the calendar, looking for anything that seemed out of place, unusual. Maybe a contact she'd never heard him mention.

"What if the receipt wasn't misfiled?"

She raised her gaze to Jake when he spoke. "Meaning?"

"What if this ring, the design he ordered, was relevant to the research outlined in these files?" He tossed the ring up and caught it. "Why would he be so determined to design the ring himself?"

She lifted a shoulder. "I always thought that was romantic, even if I didn't like his design. The thought that he wanted to create something especially for me was sweet."

Jake curled his fingers around the ring, and a thoughtful hum rumbled from his throat.

"You think there's more to it than that. You think the ring has the bead in it. Don't you?"

"It's the most likely scenario at this point." He extended the ring to her, and she hesitantly took it from him.

"What should I do with it? If this bead thing is dangerous, I don't want to wear it."

"I doubt it's dangerous as is. And wearing it is the best way to keep up with it."

Paige scowled and stared at the gaudy jewelry. She had the ring halfway on her left ring finger before she stopped, choosing to slide it onto her right hand instead. When she glanced up at Jake, he arched an eyebrow and sent her a knowing look.

Self-conscious heat crept up her neck as she returned her attention to her computer screen. "I found Brent's date book. Maybe something—"

"Shh!" Jake warned, jerking to attention and waving her silent. He cocked his head as if straining to hear something, then crept to the window. Pressing his back to the wall, he peered through the tiny gap between the blinds and the windowsill. And grumbled a scorching expletive.

"We have company. Clear out—fast!"

Chapter 6

Staying low, Jake hurried back to the counter and raked the scattered papers into a folder.

Paige's pulse skyrocketed, terror spiking in her with a full-body shudder. "Is it the terrorists?"

Visions of more gunfire, more blood, more death made her head swim. Trembling, she closed her laptop and jammed it in Jake's backpack.

He scooped up messy piles of paper, shoved the files in the pack with her computer and snatched the doughnut bag from the counter. "No. The Realtor is here with buyers. She's showing them the yard, the landscaping now. We'll go out the back."

Some of the tension in her chest loosened, but Jake's haste and concern still frazzled her.

"Get everything." He aimed a finger across the room where her suitcase and wedding dress lay on the floor. "We can't let anyone know we were here—unless you want B and E charges on your police record."

B and E. *Breaking and entering.*

Her breath stuttered. She'd almost forgotten they were trespassing.

Paige grabbed the dress, tossed it to Jake. With her coffee in one hand and her suitcase in the other, she followed Jake to the back door. Heart thundering, she waited while he checked the yard through the side window.

When the lock on the front door rattled, he opened the back door and rushed her out.

Paige gave the empty house a brief encompassing glance, double-checking that they'd gotten everything. On the living room floor next to the spot where they'd slept, she spotted Jake's gun.

She gasped. Pointed. "Jake!"

He turned to look and gritted out another curse.

"I'll get it. You go!" Dumping her wedding dress over her arm, he shoved her outside, directing her with a quick hand gesture. "Cut through that neighbor's driveway. Meet me on the next street."

Trying not to trip over the draping folds of her gown, Paige scurried down the back steps. Her suitcase bumped against her legs. She tried to be discreet, tried not to attract attention, but dragging a suitcase and wedding dress, she was hardly low profile.

Hurry, Jake!

When she reached the next residential street, she spotted a large recreational vehicle in a driveway and made a beeline for it. She crouched behind the behemoth, watching and waiting for Jake. Her thudding heartbeat counted the precious passing seconds. After two full minutes, more than enough time for him to nab the gun and meet her, Jake still hadn't shown.

What would she do if Jake had been seen? Detained? Arrested? She chewed her bottom lip, her anxiety growing as she considered what could be keeping him. A sheen of perspiration beaded on her forehead, and Paige began planning her next move. If Jake never came...

She had the ring. Her dress. Her suitcase. Which meant she probably still had the bead. Jake had said going to the police or FBI was risky, that Brent had indicated they couldn't be trusted for some reason.

Brent was in the hospital, weak, possibly dying.

Her father would help her. So would her sisters. But how could she draw any more danger back to her family? She swallowed against the knot forming in her throat.

Without Jake, she was alone. Despite the steamy Louisiana temperatures, a chill slithered through her. Where was Jake? What was keeping him?

Jake pressed himself against the back wall of the closet where he'd taken refuge and gritted his teeth in frustration. Rather than starting the home tour with the kitchen, just off the entry hall, the Realtor had brought the buyers straight back to the living room to enjoy the view of the backyard. He'd only had time to dash for the utility closet and prayed no one explored the storage options—yet. Getting caught didn't worry him. If discovered, he'd have no problem getting past the Realtor and her clients and getting away—but getting away unseen would be far better.

He hoped Paige had made tracks and cleared the backyard before the buyers reached the windows to admire the yard's amenities. For five full minutes, the Realtor gushed about the landscaping, the safe neighborhood, the wonderful school district and the underground sprinkler system.

"And wait until you see the oversize tub and walk-in closets in the master bathroom!" the Realtor cooed. Finally the thump of footsteps and drone of voices moved down the hall.

Jake cracked open the closet door and peered out, scanning the living room. All clear.

With the pantherlike stealth the SEALs had taught him, he crossed the floor and slid out the back door. He kept out of sight, using fences and shrubbery for cover as he made his way through the neighbor's yard and out to the next street. He scanned the road for Paige, and in the gap under a large motor home, he glimpsed a red suitcase, a white gown and two feet.

He made a point of scuffling his feet as he approached so that he didn't startle her. He didn't need her yelping and drawing more attention to them than their strange collection of cargo already did.

"Paige?" he called quietly, and she darted from behind the RV and threw herself into his arms.

"Jake, thank heavens! What took you so long?"

The distress in her wide green eyes made her look all the more vulnerable, fragile. Beautiful. A frisson of heat burrowed into him.

Earlier, when she'd strolled into the kitchen, rumpled from sleep, he'd almost jumped out of his skin. He'd had to draw on all his reserves not to let on how just the sight of her, tousled and free of makeup, roused carnal images. By keeping his eyes off her and his attention focused on Scofield's files, he'd brought his body's instant reaction to her under control. Barely.

He rubbed her back briefly and stepped away before the press of her curves fired a libido he'd had only a fingernail grip on since last night. "Just detained for a minute. No problem."

"No problem? What if you'd been caught?" Her voice quivered, and her eyes rounded.

He couldn't remember the last time he'd had someone who cared enough about him to worry for his well-being. That she cared enough to be concerned did strange things to his heart. Then again, she could have just been anxious for her own safety, not his.

"I might have been seen, but I wouldn't have been caught." He gave her a smug grin to cover the jumpy sensation her concern stirred in his chest. Their hasty getaway was a walk in the park for him, but he found the idea that Paige had worried about him unsettling. Foreign. Intoxicating.

"So now what do we do?" She sagged against the RV, and her shoulders slumped.

He rolled the strange tension from his shoulders and glanced around. "We find a new place to stay."

"No more vacant houses!" Passion and conviction fired her gaze. "I hate the idea of trespassing, of breaking into someone else's home. Even if it is vacant and for sale."

He nodded. Now that he'd had a little more time to plan their next move, he agreed that they needed to go another route this time.

"Can't we just go to a hotel?" Paige's eyes pleaded with him, and compunction tugged at him. "We could drive somewhere out of town, even out of state."

"How would we pay for it without leaving a paper trail? Do you have hundreds in cash with you?"

"Well, no, but I have enough for a couple nights, anyway."

Jake rubbed his cheek, turning the situation over in his head. Where could they stay that was out of the way, but still provided shelter and—

His gaze darted up to the RV Paige leaned against. He stepped closer and ran his hand down the side wall, kicked the tires. "That's it. An RV."

Paige jerked her head up, her eyes wide. "No, Jake. No way! You are *not* stealing this RV! I won't allow it! No more breaking the law. There has to be a way to do this without—"

He caught her chin in his hand and dropped a quick kiss on her mouth. "Not this one. I'm not a thief."

Paige stared at him, looking poleaxed. With her pupils wide and her bowed lips parted in surprise, she raised a hand to her mouth and drew a shaky breath. Jake had to call on every bit of his willpower to keep from kissing her again.

He cleared his throat and said, "We'll rent a camper."

Paige curled her lips in and closed her eyes. When she looked up at him again, her dubious expression spoke for her reluctance. "We're going to *camp?* Where?"

"A campground, of course." He paused. "Wait. Are you telling me you've never been camping?"

She flashed him a weak grin. "Does cheerleading camp count?"

"Did you stay in tents or cabins?"

"More like the dorms at the host college."

He snorted his dismissal and shook his head. "Darlin', you are overdue. You're going to love roughing it."

"Roughing it? Can't we get one of the RVs with the bathroom and kitchen and regular bed?"

He tugged up his cheek and winked at her. "We'll play it by ear, see what's for rent and how far our cash goes." He looped the backpack over his shoulder and picked up her suitcase. Nodding toward the wedding dress, he frowned. "Since Brent didn't give you the dress, I think we can safely assume that the bead isn't one of the sequins on your gown. Can we ditch the dress now?"

"Ditch it? Like leave it here?"

"You really want to keep hauling it around with us?"

"Jake, it's a Vera Wang! Do you know what it is worth?"

He gave her a disgruntled frown, then hesitated. "Do you know where there's a consignment shop or secondhand store where we can sell it? The extra cash would help us out a lot."

She pulled her shoulders back, sending him an appalled look that finally melted to resignation. "You're right. I don't need it anymore. If selling it will help us, then that's what we should do."

"It's from Vera Wang's spring collection. Only worn once, although…" Paige cringed and rearranged the folds of satin to show the consignment shop owner the dress's new flaw. Blood stains. "I'm afraid it's far from like-new quality."

She cast a side glance to Jake, who looked decidedly uncomfortable in the feminine shop, standing among the frilly prom dresses and lacy wedding gowns.

The older lady slid her reading glasses down her nose to examine the stain. "Is this red wine?"

Paige swallowed. "Um, no, ma'am. It's…blood."

The woman hummed a noncommital response and eyed

the stains more closely. "Should I ask how you got blood on your wedding gown?"

"No," Jake said flatly.

The woman gave Jake a curious look, then held the dress up. "Well, it is an exquisite gown. And since most of the blood is on the skirt, not the bodice, I think with a little creative tailoring, I can salvage the dress." She rummaged under the counter and pulled out a slim catalog. "Vera Wang, you say?"

Paige nodded and pointed in the catalog to the listing for her dress. "There it is."

Jake leaned closer, glancing at the listing. His eyes widened, and, making a funny choking sound, he sent Paige a stunned look. "Eight thousand dollars?" he mouthed.

The shop owner whistled. "I can't give you anywhere near retail, you understand. I'll have to deduct for the work I'll have to invest, plus a standard markdown since it is used."

Paige nodded. "I understand."

Five minutes later, they returned to the rental car with a hefty sum in Paige's purse.

"You know…" she said, giving her hand a considering scrutiny, "we could sell or pawn my engagement ring, too."

Jake settled in the driver's seat and cranked the engine. "You'd be willing to part with it? What about its sentimental value?"

Paige only leveled a stare at him.

When he caught her gaze, he grunted. "Okay, we can hock it if you're willing."

She shrugged. "I am. Its greatest value to me now is in how it can get us through the next several days. Heaven only knows what kind of expenses we'll run into, and if we can't use our credit cards, since the charges could help the wedding-crashing terrorists track us down, we're gonna need cash."

He narrowed his eyes. "You're sure?"

"Brent got us into this." She held up her hand and thumbed the diamond solitaire. "His ring is going to help get us out."

Jake backed out of the parking space, his expression deeply

thoughtful. "What if the bead he says you have is the diamond in your engagement ring? I'm not sure we should part with it until we know more about what we're dealing with."

"Yes, but I've had this ring for over two years. Why would the terrorists think Brent had the bead now if he gave me my engagement ring two years ago? Haven't we decided the bead has to have been hidden in something he's given me just in the last few weeks?"

Jake twisted his mouth as he drove. "I see your point. Brent told me the threat he'd needed protection from was due to a recent turn of events, a recent deal that went bad. So maybe we can eliminate the engagement ring." He scratched the two-day stubble on his chin and grunted. "Okay, we'll find a pawnshop first, then a camping store where we can get our new digs. I don't like being out like this where we can be spotted. Once we're settled at a campsite, we'll dive back into the rest of those files. Finding the bead is our priority. It's the key to this whole nightmare."

"It is important to park the camper on a level surface and secure the wheel braces before raising the top," Jake read from the manual that came with the pop-up tent-camper they'd rented at a sporting goods megastore with the money they got by selling her dress and engagement ring.

Paige stood beside him at the Shady Acres campground and shook her head in disbelief. "I don't get it. How are we supposed to camp in that little box?"

"Hang tight. It's not set up yet." He lowered his gaze to the manual again and continued setting up the pop-up camper, following the step-by-step instructions. "The top raises, and the sides slide out to make the beds. Believe it or not, there's even a stove, a table and seats in there." He scowled at the manual. "When I figure this out," he mumbled under his breath.

"But I—"

He raised his gaze to her again when she stopped abruptly. "But what?"

She squared her shoulders and gave him a forced smile. "Never mind. I trust you. I just have a steep learning curve here, seeing as how I've never—" She glanced around at the other wooded campsites where children played tag and their parents chatted amiably with neighboring campers from folding chairs. "—done this before."

Jake grinned. "Honey, this is four-star accommodations compared to some of the places I've slept while on missions in the Middle East."

But for Paige, who'd clearly led a rather pampered lifestyle, the canvas-walled, crank-top tent-camper was roughing it. Jake studied the skeptical shadows in her eyes. Although she'd kept her concerns to herself for the most part, he'd caught her nibbling her bottom lip several times since they hitched the trailer to the rental car that afternoon. Now, when she caught him studying her, she straightened her posture and flashed a tenuous smile.

Obviously, being outside of her comfort zone, not knowing what to expect, rankled her need for order and control. Her highly organized mind and impulse to analyze spun their wheels in the unknown territory she found herself in. He admired her for the grace she'd shown so far. She had to have a number of gripes with his choice to camp—the mosquitoes munching on them, the heat, the lack of private bathroom facilities—yet she'd not complained.

"Need some help?"

Jake glanced toward the balding man wearing a faded Atlanta Braves T-shirt who'd spoken. A woman with graying brown hair pulled back in a ponytail followed a step behind, smiling warmly.

"Uh, thanks, but I've—"

"Name's Pat Appelman. And this is my wife, Diane. We used to have a fold-down camper before we bought the monster over there." Pat hitched his thumb over his shoulder to the large RV parked in the next campsite.

Paige's face brightened politely, and she offered her hand to Pat and Diane. "Paige Ba—"

"Bailey," Jake interrupted, almost shouting the name.

Paige sent him a startled look, and he pasted on a grin as he divided a glance between Paige and the Appelmans.

"Paige and Jake *Bailey*. We're, uh…newlyweds, and she forgets to use her new married name sometimes." *Smooth, McCall. Real subtle.* Staying in character, he stepped up beside Paige and wrapped his arm around her waist, pulling her close to his side and kissing her temple. "Isn't that right, honey?"

"Um, right. Bailey…silly me." He felt the tremor that raced through her. Or was that his own shudder, a kick of lust for having her curves pressed close to him? A flash of memory teased him. Her body on his last night. Hot kisses. The spontaneous passion and heat…

Sweat beaded on his brow that had nothing to do with the Louisiana summer afternoon.

"So where are you folks from?" Diane asked, smiling pleasantly.

Paige looked up at him expectantly.

"Texas," he offered.

"Big state." Pat laughed. "Where about in Texas?"

"Amarillo." Paige sent him a smug grin, as if to say, *two can play this game.*

Diane nodded. "We're from Baton Rouge. We heard this part of the state had some nice camping, so we headed up here on a lark. We've made a lot of spontaneous trips since we became empty-nesters."

"Don't suppose you kids have any children yet, being newlyweds and all?" Pat asked.

Paige shook her head, smiling politely, but Jake felt the slight tensing of her muscles. The idea of having babies with Paige shot a surreal sensation, an odd longing through Jake that made his head buzz. Family was a concept he held at arm's length, a subject too intimate and raw to consider. Like staring into the sun, he had to look away quickly or risk the damaging effects.

"Listen, kids, later tonight we'll have a big campfire and

roast hot dogs and marshmallows." Diane motioned to them with a sweep of her arm. "Why don't you come over and join us? We have plenty!"

Jake groaned internally. Maybe camping had been a mistake. Clearly, slipping into the campground quietly and keeping a low profile was not an option. Not if all the neighbors were as outgoing and curious as the Appelmans.

A refusal was on the tip of his tongue when Paige piped in, "We don't have other plans for dinner, and that sounds like fun. Count us in. And thank you."

Pat glanced to the pop-up camper. "Sure you don't want a hand?"

Before Jake could answer, Pat was taking over. In minutes, their neighbor had the rented camper set up and was showing Jake all the features inside. The fold-down table, the slide-out beds, the tiny refrigerator and electricity hookup.

Finally their loquacious neighbors headed back to "the monster," leaving Jake and Paige to settle into the small camper.

Jake's gut tightened when he considered the coming days, sharing these cramped quarters with Paige. Twenty-four/seven contact. All-day and all-night exposure to her vulnerable green eyes and the sweet scent that clung to her.

Gritting his teeth, he focused on the job at hand. He only had to remind himself that national security was at risk to bring his libido under control. Almost.

He pulled out the stack of files from Scofield's office, eager to get to work after the day full of delays and distractions.

But Paige's restless movement around the tiny camper, her quiet sighs and nervous tongue clicks as she set up the laptop and logged on, kept him hyperaware of his roommate. He sat across from her at the tiny fold-up table. Doubling as the baseboard for one of the beds when folded down and laid between the two bench seats, the table barely had space for him to spread a file and for her to park the laptop. Beneath the table, her knees bumped his when she shifted, and Jake almost swallowed his tongue as an unexpected jolt of electricity crackled through him.

Curling his fingers into his palms, he struggled to focus on the dry reading in the files, but the deep breath he took to clear his mind was scented with Paige's shampoo, or her perfume, or whatever the source of the intoxicating floral aroma that swirled around her.

He cast a furtive glance in her direction. She studied the computer screen with rapt attention. If the brush of their knees had rattled her as much as it had him, she showed no sign of it. With one hand maneuvering the roller-ball mouse, Paige alternately chewed her manicured fingernail and tapped the polished nail on her teeth.

What did it say about him that he found her nervous habit endearing, mesmerizing?

Says you're way too easily distracted, pal. Get a grip!

"Hey, Jake, take a look at this." Paige waved a finger toward the computer screen, and her gaze shifted to meet his. "I'm looking through Brent's planning calendar, and the entry for tomorrow is kinda weird."

Jake turned the laptop to face him and read the entry.

June 13—Gates—3
18* 30' 0" N 77* 55' 0" W

"What do you suppose that means?" Paige waved a hand in query. "*Gates 3*. Is that like an airport gate number? Could the rest be an ID number or an account number or—?"

"No." Jake shook his head as he met her eyes. He knew the pattern of numbers well. "I'd say they're coordinates, GPS. Except it looks like he used an asterisk instead of the circle for degrees."

"Coordinates for what? For where?"

He lifted a shoulder, scratched his chin. "Ballpark guess would be somewhere in the Caribbean. Which, considering that's where you were honeymooning, makes sense, but doesn't help us out much. This could be the coordinates of an address where he had a meeting."

"Or of a restaurant he wanted to take me to, or of a landmark tourist attraction he wanted me to see." Her tone was somewhat defensive, and like the many other times she'd tried to defend or justify Scofield's motives or actions, Jake had to suppress a twist of frustration and…what?

He tightened his jaw and tried to decipher the secondary emotion that left a sour burn in his throat and had his muscles tensing. Jealousy?

He had no reason to be envious of Brent Scofield. He could easily compete with his old friend in most any aspect—appearance, physical ability, worldly experience, money. So why did Paige's loyalty to Scofield rankle him so much?

Jake quickly squelched the thought before it could fully form. Loyalty was a luxury that he'd learned could easily be snatched away. He had no use for something so fickle.

"Without a way to check these coordinates, there's no point speculating about the location."

Paige leaned back on the bench seat and crossed her arms under her breasts. He tried not to stare at the enticing way the gesture plumped her cleavage. And failed.

A man had his limits.

"Can't we plug the coordinates into the internet and find out where they're for?"

He jerked his gaze to her face when she spoke. "Yeah, but we have no cell-phone reception out here in the boonies, much less a Wi-Fi connection. But next time we're in town, we'll stop by the library or a coffee shop where we can get on the internet." He spun the laptop back around for Paige. "Meantime, keep looking. Maybe something else in there will give us a clue."

"So what are you finding?" She waved a finger at the papers he'd spread on the tabletop.

Besides how easily you distract me?

Jake cleared his throat and riffled through the papers. "Most of this seems pretty routine. Memos and forms related to research projects. Marketing reports…" He lifted a meaningful glance to her. "Your handiwork, I take it?"

She twitched a quick grin. "If I was writing marketing reports on a product, then it was out of development and on the market. Doesn't seem likely anything widely available would be what the terrorists are after."

"Yeah. That's what I'm thinking." Jake closed a couple of folders and shuffled them to the bottom of his stack. Tapping the file now on top with his pen, Jake caught Paige's gaze. "This *PMB-611* file, the one he calls Superbug, looks like the most recent study."

She tipped her head and lifted a shoulder. "It may be the one he started most recently, but we have multiple research projects ongoing at any time. Can you tell from what's there what the project was researching? What kind of drug was in development?"

Jake flipped back through the papers to find a report he'd read earlier. "Um, it says…'part of a progressive study to manufacture a vaccine for drug-resistant flu.'" He looked up from the page. "Drug-resistant-flu vaccine? Isn't that an oxymoron?"

She smiled. "In a way, I guess. But the flu strains that are currently resistant to drug therapy are the very ones we need most to find a vaccine or treatment for. New flu viruses show up every year. Older viruses mutate and adapt to the current treatments so that the drugs are less effective." She sighed. "It's a never-ending battle."

"Fortunately…for Bancroft Industries and other drug developers' pockets."

She frowned, lines of discontent pleating her forehead. "Bancroft's products save thousands—*hundreds of thousands*—of lives every year! Do you know how many people die from just the regular seasonal flu every year?" She paused briefly and arched a delicate eyebrow. "Thousands. Globally, the number could be as many as half a million."

Jake cocked his head, stunned. "Really? That many? I knew the number was high, but…"

"Yeah. And with the recent emergence of avian and swine flu, researchers are scrambling to find new vaccines for the new variants of the virus. A pandemic, like the one in 1918 that infected about five hundred million people and killed fifty million worldwide, could develop any day and spread in a matter of weeks." Passion and gravity for her subject blazed in her eyes.

"Yeah, I watch the news. I heard all this when the bird and swine flus showed up."

"So…Bancroft Industries is just doing its part to try to stop diseases like that from decimating the population." She paused. "Among other worthy projects."

Jake drank in the flush in her cheeks, the green fire in her eyes and the husky, authoritative undertones in her voice as she made her point.

Damn, but she was sexy when she got riled…

"But they also stand to make millions of dollars if their product is approved to fight one of these diseases." He lifted a corner of his mouth when her eyes widened in dismay. "I mean, come on, you're in marketing. It's always about the bottom line."

She shoved to her feet, her expression reflecting hurt and disgust. "Yes, the company makes money. Business is business. But my grandfather and my father did not pour their lives' work into Bancroft Industries just to get rich off the illness of others! They wanted to help stop illness and needless deaths. They wanted to contribute to society in a positive way. It's not all about the money!"

Jake leaned back as far as he could on the narrow bench seat and stacked his hands behind his head. "A little touchy about your family's wealth, Paige?"

"You brought it up! And you made it sound like I should be ashamed that my father's company is successful. That all his hard work and his contributions to medical research were based in greed. That Bancroft—"

"Whoa!" Jake whipped a hand out to cut her off. "I didn't mean any offense. Really."

Paige glared at him, her expression dubious and her arms akimbo. After a moment, he took one of her hands between his, rubbing the back with calming strokes of his thumb. "I'm sorry if anything I said insulted you or your family." Her expression softened, and he added, "Or Bancroft Industries."

She drew a deep breath and exhaled slowly. "Okay."

Before he released her hand, he brought it to his lips and pressed a chaste kiss to the back of it. His eyes held hers, and he watched her pupils widen, her eyes darken to the color of a deep lake. He felt himself sinking in that deep green water, drowning in the desire he saw reflected in her eyes. Reluctantly, he dropped her hand and tore his gaze away.

He leaned forward, hovering over the files from Brent's office, but his attention was shot. All he could think about was how much he wanted to pull Paige close and taste her sweet lips as he had mere hours ago.

And what would she think if he *did* kiss her? She wasn't as vulnerable today. She wasn't shaking with the shock of the carnage and gunfire at Scofield's office or reeling from her disrupted wedding as she had been last night. She'd had some time to collect herself, to know if kissing him was what she really wanted or just a gut response to an oversupply of adrenaline and life-threatening circumstances. Yet even with the luxury of a day's perspective, Paige's eyes warmed when he touched her. Her lips trembled when he held her gaze, and the air between them crackled the way the summer sky produced heat lightning.

Jake ducked his head, clenching his teeth until his jaw ached. Getting involved with his client's fiancée—even his client's ex-fiancée—was asking for trouble. They had big enough problems dealing with terrorists chasing them, some undefined threat to national security hanging over their heads and no solid leads to tell them what the hell they were mixed up in. His duty to protect Paige started with protecting her from himself. He knew without asking that she was not the one-night-stand type.

Paige was society weddings and Vera Wang dresses. She needed commitment, security, love.

He was a loner, black ops in third-world countries and dusty military fatigues. And he had nothing to offer her but his pledge to get her out of this debacle alive. Knowing this shouldn't bother him. He was used to keeping people at arm's length. So why did the prospect of walking away from Paige at the end of this assignment leave him feeling so…empty?

Chapter 7

Later that afternoon, Paige unzipped the canvas that covered the camper window and peeked outside.

Instantly, Jake jerked to attention. "What's wrong? Did you hear something?"

"It's a campground, Jake. I hear plenty of noise. Nothing to worry about." She flashed him a wry grin. "Unless that kid who has been blaring his rap music plans to keep his speakers on very late tonight."

Jake pulled a face. "I think if that happens, I could be convinced to remove his speakers from him. Permanently."

He stretched his arms over his head, and his T-shirt pulled taut across his broad, muscled chest.

Paige's mouth went dry, and she shoved to her feet from the narrow bench seat. "Actually, I was checking to see if our neighbors had their fire going yet. I'm beginning to crave a roasted hot dog."

After several hours huddled around the small camper table, searching Brent's files, Paige needed a break. Trying to ignore Jake, or rather, her magnetic attraction to Jake, was a bit like trying to ignore a rattlesnake coiled on the floor. And like a rattlesnake, Paige feared the powerful temptation Jake posed could come back to bite her if she didn't keep her guard up.

She knew her interest in Jake was purely physical—he had an elite soldier's body, a movie star's face and dark bedroom eyes she could get lost in. She knew her reaction to him was emotional—he'd saved her life, comforted her when she was falling apart and shown her nothing but kindness. And she knew even considering a relationship with Jake was impractical and illogical—she couldn't see anything they had in common, and the timing couldn't be worse, days after her doomed wedding, while running from dangerous thugs.

The way Paige saw it, emotionalism and physical attraction were poor reasons to fall for a man, and the absence of the two ingredients she looked for, practicality and logic, cinched the deal. Falling for Jake would be a huge mistake.

But knowing he was all wrong for her wasn't enough, apparently, to keep her nerves from tingling every time their knees brushed under the small table or her pulse from scampering when he held her hand and looked into her eyes. She'd nearly melted into a puddle of goo when he held her hand to apologize for his comments about Bancroft Industries profiting from the products they designed to fight disease.

Or maybe the reason her heart was racing had more to do with the implication that she, as a Bancroft, was spoiled. That her wealth somehow put her in an untouchable class that he resented.

Heaven knows, Brent always felt he had to strive toward a higher mark to be "good enough" for her. And she'd hated it. She wanted to be loved and accepted for who she was, not what she had. And she wanted the man she loved to know her affection was not tied to monetary worth or status in society.

Jake closed the paper files and rubbed his eyes. "Dinner does sound good, and I wasn't looking forward to the canned and packaged stuff we bought today."

Paige peeled back the corner of the zippered window

cover. Diane Appelman spotted her and waved from behind a crackling campfire. "I think they're ready for us." She smoothed a hand over the wrinkles in her cotton khaki shorts, a wasted effort. The manners her mother had bred into her from birth plucked her conscience. "I feel bad going empty-handed. Grab that can of corn. Can that be heated over a campfire?" she asked as she stepped back to give Jake room to scoot out from the table.

How were they supposed to share such tight quarters without going nuts?

"Sure. I bet the Appelmans have any number of ways to cook over an open fire." He picked out two cans of corn and two of baked beans to contribute to dinner and, after putting the cans in a plastic sack, ushered her outside.

A swarm of annoying bugs flew in her face the minute they stepped outside, and she swatted at them, swallowing the groan of disgust that rose in her throat. As much as she hated bugs, she hated the idea of the terrorists finding them more. If Jake thought camping was their best bet for staying hidden, she would play along without complaint.

She shuddered. Even if that meant sharing her legs with a cloud of hungry mosquitoes. She gritted her teeth and slapped at the pesky menaces nipping her calves.

"Come over here by the fire, honey!" Diane called to her. "The bugs hate the smoke. And I have bug repellent you can use."

Paige accepted the can of spray the woman handed her as they approached the neighboring campsite. "Diane, you're my new best friend."

The older woman chuckled. "When you've been doing this as long as we have, you learn to be prepared. Don't worry. The bugs are worst now, at dusk. In a minute, Pat will get the citronella torches going, and you'd be surprised how few bugs you'll see then."

Paige turned to Jake. "Make a note for our next trip for supplies. Citronella and bug repellent."

He massaged the base of her neck with his free hand. "Roger that, sweetheart."

Dry warmth from the campfire baked her face, while another sort of heat blasted through her from his touch. The endearment he'd addressed her with had been for show, part of the role of newlyweds they played for their neighbors, but a flutter of sweet longing tap-danced in her chest. Brent had always been so formal, had never used a pet name for her, so Jake's use of such an intimacy caught her off guard.

Jake passed the plastic bag to Diane. "Our contribution to dinner."

Diane peeked in the sack. "Why, thank you, honey. I'll get a pan and start these heatin'."

As Paige settled in the lawn chair Pat set up for her, she caught a movement in the shadows of her peripheral vision. Jumpy from the past couple days of insanity, she jerked her head toward the movement, searching the fading daylight near their camper for whatever had caught her attention.

A small black cat crept out from under the trailer hitch and inched nearer the campfire. Paige pressed a hand over her stumbling heart and exhaled with relief. A cat. It was just a cat. Not terrorists or assassins with automatic weapons.

Still, as her pulse eased back to a normal speed, she scooted her lawn chair closer to Jake's.

Pat passed her and Jake each an extra-long-handled fork and nodded to a platter of hot dogs on top of a nearby cooler. "Help yourself. The roasting is as much fun as the eating."

With a rumble of her stomach, Paige followed Jake's lead, and soon the smoky scent of their supper filled the air. The aroma brought the black cat out from the shadows to skirt the edge of the campsite, as well. He sniffed the air and eyed the cooking hot dogs with interest.

"Is that your cat?" Paige asked Pat, pointing.

Pat glanced up from the campfire. "Naw. He's a stray. He's been around here before, begging for scraps. And since Diane, the soft-heart, feeds him, we're a regular stop on his evening rounds now. She calls him Nate and had some convoluted explanation of how she came up with the name. Something about the fact that he has no tail, and she thought he was a girl at first and…" Pat waved a hand of dismissal. "Whatever."

No tail? A sympathetic pang speared her heart, and Paige tore off the tip of her hot dog and tossed it toward the cat. "Here ya go, Nate. Come on, kitty."

Nate looked wistfully at the meat, then blinked warily at the three humans huddled around the fire. Finally he trotted forward, gulped down the bite of hot dog, then scurried back to the shadows under the trailer hitch. Paige's heart broke for the skinny, maimed stray.

"Okay, veggies are heating," Diane announced as she came back out of their RV.

"We met Nate," Paige said as Diane took a seat beside her.

The woman smiled. "He's a sweet cat, but rather skittish. Doesn't quite know what to make of people…or if he can trust people not to hurt him."

Jake elbowed her in the ribs. "Hey, stop staring at the cat and watch your dog. It's on fire."

Paige gasped and pulled her charred wiener from the flames. Jake helped her blow out the fire, and they all chuckled over her mishap.

"Rookie," Jake teased with a warmth in his eyes that washed over her like a pleasant summer breeze.

She and Jake passed an enjoyable evening, chatting with the Appelmans, making s'mores and drinking iced tea.

After a couple of hours in front of the glowing campfire, Paige could wait no longer to use the restroom. She stood and glanced around the dark, wooded campground, uncertain where the facilities were. "Diane, which direction is the restroom?"

"It's through the trees, that way." The older woman aimed a finger over her shoulder. "Tell you what, I'll go with you."

Jake stood, a troubled look on his face. "No, I'll take her."

Pat and Diane gave him curious, amused looks, and Paige

chuckled awkwardly. "Um…*sweetheart,* I think I can go to the bathroom by myself."

He cleared his throat and leveled a stern stare at her. "*Sweetie,* maybe I need to use the facilities, too."

The Appelmans grinned, and Paige gave Jake a teasingly haughty look. "In that case, you can come with."

They thanked the Appelmans for sharing their dinner, their fire and their conversation and said good-nights as they left. Once they were out of earshot, swallowed by the darkness of the night, Paige leaned closer to Jake and muttered, "Do you really have to go, or was that an excuse to get away from our hosts? 'Cause I thought they were nice. I had fun tonight… despite the bugs."

Jake draped an arm around her shoulders as they walked. The gesture spun a mix of pleasure and security through her. She hadn't anticipated how dark the walk through the trees to the community bathhouse would be, and foreign sounds chirps, croaks and buzzing—filled the evening air.

"They seemed nice enough." Jake twitched a grin, visible only as a flash of white teeth in the thin moonlight that seeped through the trees. "Told ya you'd like camping."

She returned a mock scowl. "I said I had fun roasting hot dogs and chatting with the Appelmans. The jury is still out on camping."

He pulled on her shoulder, guiding her around a stump she hadn't seen until the last second. Clearly, his night vision was better than hers. Paige nestled closer, wrapping her arm around his waist. "Then why—"

"I came with you because it's my job to keep you safe."

His statement hung in the air for a moment as her heartbeat stumbled. She glanced around the black woods, wondering what threats—wild animals?—Jake knew about but wasn't telling her. "From what?"

"After the past two days, you have to ask?"

Despite the sultry summer temperature, a chill skittered down her spine. "You mean… But I thought we were camping out here, because it was a safe hideout! If you think—"

"Don't panic. I don't necessarily think there's a bogeyman waiting in the bathroom to grab you. But we have to be alert. They *could* track us here. I just want to be careful."

When she shivered, he rubbed his hand down her arm and gave her a quick squeeze.

"Look, we're probably safe here for now, but ..." They passed under a security light as they neared the bathhouse, and he paused, turning to her. With a hand on each of her shoulders and his mahogany eyes drilling into her, he said, "I want you to promise me you won't go anywhere without me. Not to the bathhouse, not for walks with Diane, not anywhere. Got it?"

"You're going to come with me every time I have to pee? When I shower?"

His pupils grew slightly, and a muscle in his jaw ticked. The idea of him joining her in the shower sent a rush of heat to her belly, and the desire that had been growing between them coiled tighter.

His nostrils flared as he took a deep breath and cleared his throat. "I want to check things out before you go into a building blind. We just don't know when or where Trench Coat's cohorts might show up."

The gravity of his warning burrowed deep inside her, scaring her more than the wild beasts she'd imagined moments ago. She'd take an encounter with a raccoon or even a coyote over a gun-wielding terrorist any day.

When she remained silent, grappling with the knowledge that even in this remote campground they were vulnerable to attack, Jake shook her slightly. "Do you understand?"

"I...yes." Her voice cracked, and she swallowed hard to moisten her suddenly dry throat.

"Promise me."

She nodded stiffly. "I promise."

"Okay." He guided her closer to the door of the ladies' bathroom. "You wait here while I have a look inside."

"What if there are other women in there? This is a community bathhouse, after all."

He glanced toward the door. "I know how to be discreet."

She arched an eyebrow and leaned back against the cinder block wall of the bathhouse to wait.

Jake stepped just inside the bathhouse door and cocked his head as if listening, then disappeared inside briefly.

While she waited, she scanned the dark woods. She'd never known how completely black it got at night outside the city, away from street lights and security lamps and car headlights. A stir of motion to her left sent her pulse scampering.

She pressed her back farther up against the rough concrete wall. Where was Jake, and why was it taking so long to check a few bathroom stalls?

Her mouth going a bit drier, she strained to see through the murky night. She heard a twig snap.

"Hello?"

No answer. Then the blur of motion separated from the dark woods, moving closer.

Nate, the black cat.

Paige exhaled sharply and shook her head at the cat. "Jeepers, Nate. You know how to scare a girl. That's twice tonight!"

He sat down several feet from her and blinked as if bored.

"Did you like your hot dog? Were you able to mooch more dinner off the other campers?"

"Who are you talking to?"

Paige jolted at the sound of Jake's voice behind her and whirled around. "Don't sneak up on me like that!"

He shrugged and tipped his head. "You should pay closer attention to your surroundings so no one can sneak up on you." He glanced past her and repeated, "Who were you talking to?"

She waved her hand toward the spot where Nate sat. "Uh, the cat from earlier was here. I guess you scared him off."

He hitched his head toward the bathroom. "All clear. You can go in."

Paige resisted the urge to roll her eyes. He had her best interests at heart, even if his measures seemed like overkill.

When they'd finished at the bathhouse, they picked their way back through the dark campground to the tent-camper.

When Jake flipped on the small light in the camper, Paige shook her head. "I never thought I took much for granted, but even having electricity in this glorified tent is…a blessing."

"Nothing but the best for my girl." Jake gave her an ironic smile, and a funny flutter stirred in her chest. She couldn't be sure if it was his "my girl" comment or the teasing edge to his voice that had her ruffled.

She was trying to be a good sport about camping, even though everything about the experience was foreign to her. Her family vacationed in luxury hotels in historic parts of Europe or exotic ports of call. But if Jake thought this camper, this campground, by virtue of its obscurity, was the safest place to hide until they figured out how to solve the mess they were in, then she'd cooperate fully, not complain.

She trusted Jake. But…

She paused, watching Jake climb onto one of the two beds situated on either side of the camper.

What if the terrorists did track them here? Then what would they do? The flimsy door lock and largely fabric walls of their rented home were far from secure if the bullets started flying and the wedding crashers wanted to get in and slit their throats in the middle of the night.

"Jake…"

Lying on his back with his hands stacked behind his head, he angled his face toward her. "Yeah?"

"What's our contingency plan?"

"What do you mean?"

"If we're found here. Then what?"

He sighed tiredly. "We…get the hell out of Dodge and do something else. I know this arrangement isn't your usual cup of tea, but I promise you we're safe here…for now."

"For now. But what happens when they do figure out where

we are? You said yourself these guys aren't just gonna go away."

He grunted. "If that happens, I'll figure something out. We've got a couple alternatives, but I prefer to keep things fluid. Play it by ear. Not get boxed in with a limited mind-set, but keep my options open."

Paige's gut clenched. "Play it by ear? Jake, our lives are at stake! And the security of our country, if Brent's to be believed. We need a concrete plan."

Jake scowled and turned to stare up at the tented ceiling over his berth. "Trust me, okay? This is my area of expertise. While you were earning your master's degree in marketing and helping the family business earn more millions, I was sleeping in foxholes and inserting my SEAL team behind enemy lines."

Paige tensed. He sounded…resentful. Judgmental.

"I'm not doubting your abilities, Jake. That's not my point. I just want to know we have a backup plan if—"

"I've got your back, Paige. I'm gonna keep you safe." His tone was calmer now. Warmer. "I promise."

His reassurances helped. Some. But she thrived on planning. Needed organization and structure to feel…safe. She blinked, pondering that realization.

She needed order, goals and a blueprint for action in order to feel secure. Why?

Her family had always loved and supported her. Her job had always fulfilled her professionally. She'd never wanted for anything in her life.

So why did she need structure and contingencies to feel secure?

She toed off her shoes and flipped the light off. After crawling under the sheet of her bed, a mirror image of the one across the camper where Jake slept, she closed her eyes and mulled that question.

She heard the rustle of cloth across the camper and heard a telltale swish and muted thump—the sound of jeans being stripped off and dumped on the camper floor.

She tried not to think about Jake, sleeping no more than ten feet away in his underwear.

Or in the buff. Was he naked?

An enticing sensation shimmered over her, coiling low in her belly. She fisted the sheet in her hands and gnawed her bottom lip. What was she going to do about her undeniable attraction to Jake? As if she needed any clearer message that he was all wrong for her and a sexual fling now would be reckless, his attitude toward her education, the family's money, the success of Bancroft Industries confirmed the differences between them.

That distance between where she stood and his opinion of her stung more than it should.

Paige stared into the complete blackness, listening to the lullaby of night sounds outside. But her mind was restless, and she couldn't sleep. She glanced toward Jake's bed, even though she could see nothing in the inky darkness. "Jake?"

"Hmm?" he rumbled groggily.

"You think I'm spoiled, don't you?"

He remained silent for so long, she thought he might have drifted off to sleep and wouldn't answer. Or his silence was an affirmation of her suspicion. Or—

"I've never said you were spoiled."

She sighed. "You didn't have to. I can tell."

"Well, you're wrong."

"Am I? When my family's money comes up, you tend to act so…" She searched for the right word.

"It's not the money," he said before she could finish her thought. "Well, maybe a little. I guess I'm wary of that kind of wealth. And maybe just a little jealous. But—"

His bed creaked as he stirred, and she waited for him to continue. When he didn't, she prodded, "I take it your family didn't have much money when you were growing up? Is that it?"

Another long silence followed, and then, "No, it was the family I didn't have. I, uh…grew up in foster homes. Six by the time I left high school to join the navy."

Paige's heart clenched. "Oh, Jake…"

"So when you talk about how close you are to your sisters, or how your parents must be worried about you, or—I guess I'm a little envious that you have so many people that care about you, people who'll stand by you no matter what. I've never really had that."

"What about the SEALs? I always heard the rigors of special-forces training and warfare bonded the members of special-forces teams like family."

He heaved a heavy sigh. "Yeah, that's what I used to think, too." Pause. "Until they kicked me out of the family."

"Kicked you out?"

"I messed up my knee real bad during a roadside bomb attack. You can't be a SEAL with a bum knee, so I got my walking papers."

"Just like that? Couldn't they reassign you to a desk job or noncombat—"

"I didn't want to be a desk jockey!"

The pain in his tone reverberated in the darkness, and the pressure in her chest twisted harder. "I'm sorry. I…"

"The SEALs had felt like a family to me. More than any foster family ever did. I always knew I was an outsider, taken into a foster home. Every home was temporary. I learned not to grow dependent on anyone in a foster home, because…I'd be moved on soon enough."

Paige heard clearly what Jake didn't say. It vibrated in the thick silence of the dark camper. He'd learned not to give his love or allow himself to form attachments to his foster families. He'd been hurt when he opened his heart, when he'd sought love and permanence. Pain clawed her, laying her heart open to the bitter wounds he'd suffered at such a young age.

"When I was a SEAL, I thought I'd found the place where I belonged. I trusted the other guys in my unit with my life, and they trusted me with theirs. We did have something like a family bond. But…" He huffed, sounding frustrated. "When the navy discharged me…"

Her throat was tight, clogged with emotion. "It felt like a betrayal?"

"Something like that."

"Don't you keep in touch with the guys form your SEAL team?"

Once again he stayed silent for long moments before answering. "I can't."

"Of course you can! Pick up the phone. Send an email. Write a let—"

"They're dead."

Paige gasped. Her stomach lurched.

"Most of my team was killed in that roadside bombing. Besides me, only two other guys lived. Tommy was killed a few weeks later in Baghdad, and Mark…" He hesitated. "He made it back stateside like I did, also booted from the navy because of his injuries."

Paige held her breath, fearing what would come next.

"He was killed by a drunk driver a few months ago."

Paige squeezed her eyes shut, aching for all of Jake's losses. "That's awful, Jake. I'm s—"

"*Hell,* why whitewash it? *He* was the drunk driver. He drowned himself in the bottle when he got home from Iraq and was wasted when he got behind the wheel. The freaking idiot!" Frustration and misery colored his tone. Jake bit out an expletive. "I don't know why I'm telling you all this. I've never—"

She swallowed hard, searching for her voice. "I'm glad you did. I think…maybe it was time you did tell someone. Keeping it cooped up inside—"

"Is what I should have done. Airing my dirty laundry serves no purpose, so don't hand me any psychoanalysis or some crap about 'sharing my feelings.'"

She winced and choked down the platitudes waiting on her tongue. Squeezing the sheet in her fist tighter, she angled her head to gaze blindly across the camper toward his bed. "Then why did you tell me?"

"You asked."

She chuckled softly. "I asked why you thought I was spoiled."

"And a bunch of other follow-up questions that…" He grunted. "Hell. I don't know."

He sounded charmingly embarrassed, and she grinned.

"It's dark in here," he said, and she heard his bed squeak again as he shifted his weight.

She pulled a face, knowing he couldn't see it. "Duh. So?"

"It's easier to be honest, to…spill your guts, when it's dark. When no one can look at you, and you don't have to see people's reactions. Or so I hear. Guess it must be true, since I—" A buzz of lips accompanied his exhaled breath. "Just forget I said anything, and go to sleep."

Paige rolled to her side, facing Jake in the darkness, and pillowed her hands under her cheek. She wouldn't push him. "Sure. Good night, Jake."

But she knew it would be a long time before she fell asleep. He'd given her far too much fodder for her restless thoughts and analytical mind.

Chapter 8

The next morning, Jake woke early after a restless night of little sleep. When he did manage to steal a few minutes of shut-eye, his dreams were vivid and disturbing—roadside bombings where he found Paige dead among the carnage, meetings with his child-services caseworker where she told him he had failed his duty as a SEAL, campfires where the flames leaped out to grab Paige while she cried, "Why didn't you plan for this?"

He woke in a sweat that had nothing to do with the humid June morning and the lack of air-conditioning in their camper. Keeping the sheet around his waist, he bent to collect his jeans from the floor. In the watery light of daybreak that seeped into the camper, Jake studied Paige's profile. She had her back to him, her curvy hip and trim waist draped by her sheet, and her long dark hair spread in a chocolate cascade against the white pillowcase.

Peaceful. Beautiful. Off-limits.

A fist of emotion blindsided him and squeezed his lungs. Last night had been a mistake. Lulled into a false sense of privacy and emotional security by the still, dark night and Paige's soft, reassuring voice, he'd told her things he'd never shared with anyone. He'd bared parts of his soul he rarely acknowledged even to himself. And what had he gotten for his honesty? An endless parade of nightmares and the prospect of her pitying looks today.

Hell. What had he been thinking?

He scrubbed his face and finger-combed his hair. If she mentioned his late-night ramblings, he could always downplay them, shrug them off as inconsequential.

He blew out a sleep-deprived sigh. Paige was smarter than that. He could only hope she'd respect his request to forget the conversation ever happened.

His stomach growled, and as quietly as he could, he rummaged through the bag of groceries they'd bought yesterday on the way to the campground. He selected a couple of granola bars and an apple, then set up the collapsible table to start working his way through Scofield's files again.

There had to be more clues to what the bead was, what Brent had gotten mixed up in, than what the research files he'd read yesterday indicated.

Flu vaccines. GPS coordinates in Brent's datebook. A jeweler's receipt. How did it all fit together? What was the bigger picture he was missing? Did Paige know something she didn't know she knew, something that might have seemed inconsequential to her when she first learned it?

He opted to take his turn reading through the files on Scofield's computer. Scofield likely thought his password-protected computer files were safe. He'd likely not kept a hard copy of anything truly incriminating.

He opened Paige's laptop and said a prayer that the battery lasted long enough for him to get something accomplished today. The low-wattage electric hookup the campsite provided wasn't sufficient to recharge the computer battery. Soon, he and Paige would have to go back into town and find an internet café where they could broaden their research and recharge the laptop.

But today, he wanted to lay low. Scour the files they had. Tap Paige's memory once more, now that she'd had time to look at her relationship with Brent from a fresh perspective.

The laptop beeped and chirped as it started up, and Paige stirred. She rolled to her back, then jerked her head to face him with a gasp. "Oh, it's you." She rubbed her eyes. "For a minute, I forgot where I was and—"

"Sorry I woke you. I was trying to be quiet." He held up a granola bar. "Breakfast?"

She laid her arm over her eyes and groaned groggily. "Later."

He turned his attention back to the computer, which awaited his next command. He logged in using Paige's password and started opening documents to read.

Sheets rustled, and Paige slid her feet to the floor and raked her tousled hair back from her face. He hazarded a glance at her.

Damn, but she was sexy in the morning, rumpled from sleep as if she'd just been thoroughly…

Jake dropped his gaze to the screen again and shoved the thought aside. For starters, Paige was not the sort to indulge in one-night stands or raucous sex. He knew that much about her after just a few days with her. She would *make love*. Emphasis on the emotion.

Which was all the reason he needed to keep his mind off Paige and any notion of sharing her bed.

He swallowed hard, fighting the temptation to peek up at her again as she smoothed out the sheets on her bed and managed, through some admirable contortions, to change shirts without ever being topless.

"Making love" doesn't preclude lusty, aerobic, thoroughly satisfying sex.

When the thought popped into his head, his hands shook so hard, he had to reenter a file name three times before he got it right.

She cleared her throat. "Um…Jake?"

Paige's voice sent a wave of heat over his skin, deep into

his belly. He clenched his teeth and kept his head bent over the computer. "Yeah?"

"I need to go to the bathhouse. I want to get a shower... among other things."

His eyes darted up to hers now. She had a towel over her arm, a bottle of shampoo in her hand, her bottom lip caught in her teeth.

Damn, he wished she wouldn't bite her mouth that way. It made him want to nibble that lip himself. And somehow the gesture made her green eyes look wider and more vulnerable.

"You said you wanted to go with me wherever I went. Even to the bathhouse."

He closed the computer and scooted it back. "Right." He slid out from the bench seat and jammed his feet in his shoes, praying his jeans didn't look as tight as they felt.

He'd been part of a lot of dangerous, top secret missions as a SEAL. But being Paige's bodyguard, sticking by her wherever she went, being near her 24/7, may well be the toughest assignment he'd ever undertaken.

Paige spent a hot, wearisome day cooped up in the tiny camper with Jake, going over Brent's files. Even after hours of tedious reading and note taking, they'd not learned more than what they knew yesterday. The bead was *probably* in her wedding ring. Brent's most recent project with R and D was for a new flu vaccine. To date, the vaccine was still in the works, nothing terrorists should be interested in.

Besides the strange GPS coordinates, Brent's datebook didn't mention any unexplained meetings or contacts that Paige didn't recognize. None of the older projects mentioned in his files could be construed as any threat to national security, including an attempt by Bancroft Industries to create a drug to treat erectile dysfunction.

When he discovered the notes on that development project, Jake sent her a hooded glance. "So maybe not all of your products are developed to save lives. Maybe this project was about cashing in?"

Paige sent him a patient glance. "Doesn't quality of life count for anything?"

"Mmm-hmm. Counts for $2.6 million in gross sales for the company, according to your market research."

She gave him a wry grin, then cocked her head. "Although I find your interest in the product...fascinating."

Jake's eyes widened, and color flushed his cheeks. "I don't—" he fumbled.

Paige chuckled, but her mind flashed back to that morning when Jake had stood from behind the table to escort her to the bathhouse. She'd seen for herself that Jake *didn't*. Not by a long shot...

Danger, her conscience screamed. Any consideration of Jake's virility was definitely a treacherous path for her. Working in such close proximity all day had been hard enough.

As the day passed, his wide shoulders seemed to fill more and more of the cramped space. When the heat of the day had led him to shed his shirt, she'd nearly swallowed her tongue. And the sexy, low rumble of his voice as they dissected Brent's reports, looking for useful information, had made her belly quiver on more than one occasion. His deep, throaty *mmm-hmms* as he reviewed new information reminded her of the gentle roll of thunder announcing a sultry summer storm. Or of a man savoring a good orgasm.

Now it was her turn to blush. She felt the sting of heat in her cheeks and covered her embarrassment by shoving to her feet and pacing to the other end of the camper—all of about six feet—to stretch the kinks from her back.

She hitched a thumb toward the door and stuttered, "I'm... gonna go—"

Jake started to slide out from the table, and she held up her hand.

"Down boy. I just want some fresh air. I won't leave our campsite."

He rolled his muscled shoulders and nodded once. "I'm gonna read the last few files we downloaded from Brent's computer before I call it quits for the day."

"Suit yourself."

"Later, if you'll help me gather up some wood, we'll have our own campfire tonight."

With a nod of agreement, she staggered out of the sweltering camper to the equally stifling outdoors. She sent an envious glance toward the Appelmans' RV, where a window air-conditioning unit purred quietly. That morning, the Appelmans had been pulling out of the campsite with fishing equipment loaded in the back of their truck when Jake and Paige had returned from the bathhouse.

She longed for just a couple minutes in front of the cool breeze of that window unit....

She glanced back toward their own rented camper and sighed. Maybe a cold shower would better suit her needs. Last week, if someone had told her she'd be so powerfully attracted to a man so ill-suited for her, she'd have laughed. But then, if that same someone had suggested Brent was involved in something nefarious and was wanted by terrorists, she'd have had a similar reaction. Preposterous!

But she was undeniably drawn to Jake. So she had to either figure out how to control her lusty urges or just have a fling with Jake and work the erotic longing out of her system. She dropped onto a large log that a previous enterprising camper had placed near their fire pit as a bench.

Have a sexual fling with Jake? Was she nuts?

Paige plowed her fingers into her sweat-dampened hair and groaned. Tempting as the notion was, that kind of recklessness was more Zoey's style. Paige couldn't commit to something so bold without considering the ramifications. For starters, although she was on the pill, using a condom, too, would provide additional protection. Before she slept with Jake, she'd have to buy—

Paige shook her head and scoffed. *Before she slept with Jake?* As if it were a done deal, an inevitability?

The heat was affecting her reasoning, her *sanity*. She and Jake were nothing alike. She wasn't even sure he liked her much. He seemed to resent the family's money.

It's not the money. Jake's whispered confession last night teased her memory, and her heart tripped. *I guess I'm a little envious that you have so many people that care about you.*

She squeezed her eyes shut, trying not to think about the pain that had filled Jake's voice last night when he'd told her about being bounced from one foster home to another and about the loss of his navy family. He'd been burned so many times.

Was there something she could do to prove to him that not everyone in his life would be so fickle?

Yet even as she had that thought, Brent's deception, the lies of their relationship ricocheted through her head. She'd faithfully kept her promises to Brent, even though she hadn't loved him, but her loyalty and commitment hadn't been enough to forge a meaningful, lasting relationship. Why was it her sisters, even flighty, irresponsible Zoey, could make relationships work, when she couldn't? What else did she need to do to prove herself? She wasn't above putting hard work into making a relationship work, but all her sacrifices with Brent had been for naught. What else—?

Jake stepped out of the camper, and Paige snapped her gaze up, losing her train of thought in an instant. Damn it, how did Jake do that? Around him, all rational thought fled, her concentration shattered and her hormones took control.

He met her inquiring gaze and shrugged. "So much for reading those last few files. The laptop died."

"We have an electric hookup. Can't we recharge the battery? Run it off the hookup?"

He shook his head. "Not enough juice here. We'll need to take it into town, find a low-profile place where we can hang out for a couple hours without attracting attention. Someplace with Wi-Fi would be good. I have a few questions I want to research on the net."

He strolled over and sat beside her on the log bench. His

slightly musky, somewhat woodsy, thoroughly sexy scent drifted to her on a stir of breeze. The masculine aroma danced along every nerve ending, firing all her senses. She'd never been so *aware* of a man in her life. The sound of his voice, the scent of his shampoo, the color of his eyes, the feel of his lips on hers...

Heat flashed through her, raising her already high body temperature. She lifted her face to the pitifully insufficient waft of humid air, looking for some shred of relief from the June heat wave.

"So three days in, and we really don't have much more to go on than when we started." She watched a boy toss a Frisbee to an energetic dog a few campsites away and sighed her frustration with their progress. "We still have no clue what the security threat is and what to do about it. Or how to get the gun-toting goons off our backs."

Chapter 9

The next day, after loading anything that could be relevant to their case in the rented Taurus, they headed back into Lagniappe to find an internet café. Near a large mall, they found a coffee shop that boasted Wi-Fi access that met their needs.

While Jake was occupied, she eased across the coffee shop, nearer to the order counter where she had a modicum of privacy. Using the prepaid cell phone Jake had bought her the first night they were in hiding, Paige punched in Holly's cell-phone number.

"Hello?" Holly sounded tired, uncertain, wary.

"It's me."

"Paige! How—?"

"I'm fine, but I don't have much time to talk. Are you still in Lagniappe? How are Mom and Dad? Have you heard anything from Zoey? Is Brent conscious yet?"

"Whoa. Slow down! And to answer your questions—yes, worried sick, no, and yes."

Paige performed a mental rewind to remember what

she'd asked and match the answers. When she reached the last answer, she blinked, gasped. "Brent's awake? He survived?"

Her heart hammered an expectant, hopeful rhythm. If she could get to St. Mary's hospital and talk to him…

"He woke up a couple hours ago, but he's weak," Holly replied. "The doctors are about to operate to fix some new complications that have come up. Something about damaged veins or arteries…. They say in his condition, it's risky surgery, but without the repair, the veins could tear at any time, and he'd die."

Brent was awake, but for how long? She bit down on her bottom lip and tried to squelch the trill of panic rising in her chest. She had to talk to him before he went into surgery. Brent had answers she and Jake needed. "Is he alert? Is he coherent?"

"Yes." Holly paused. "Paige, if you have…*things* you need to say to Brent, things to settle between you for your own peace of mind, you should come. You should be here when he goes into surgery and—"

Paige glanced across the coffee shop where Jake had his head down, his attention focused on the laptop. "I—I can't come, Hol. Those men are looking for us. It's too dangerous."

"Paige, Brent needs you! If the man I loved was dying, wild horses couldn't keep me away!"

Paige swallowed the bitter taste of guilt that rose in her throat. "Holly, I…I don't love Brent. I…never did." Silence screamed through the line, and Paige squeezed the phone tighter. "Holly?"

"I kinda wondered…before the wedding. I mean, you didn't seem happy. Not truly happy, like I am with Matt."

Not like I am with Jake.

The thought popped into her head unbidden, and Paige's pulse spiked.

Jake made her happy. Despite the mosquitoes, the fear of being found by Trench Coat's band of thugs, the total upheaval of the past several days, she was happy. She loved matching wits with Jake, loved his wry humor, loved his courage and sense of duty. She felt safe with him. She had an inner peace about Jake that she'd never known with Brent. An assurance that she was where she was meant to be.

I always knew I was an outsider.

The echo of Jake's words from the other night sent a sharp pain to her core. He still held himself apart, kept a distance between himself and others.

"Paige? Are you still there?"

"Yeah, I—" On the heels of the disappointment over Jake's isolationism, an impulse prodded Paige to act, to do something to show Jake they made a good team. She hadn't been much use to him so far, but she had a chance now to earn his respect, prove herself a valuable asset to the mission. "Holly, how long before Brent's surgery? Do I have time to come talk to him?"

"I thought you said it was too risky?"

She sighed, nibbling her bottom lip. "I'll have to disguise myself or something, but I need to talk to Brent. It's important."

Jake caught her gaze and scowled. He made a slashing motion across his throat.

She returned a nod and pressed the phone closer to her ear, as if she could be nearer her sister. "Hol, I have to go. If I talk too long, they might trace the call."

"Wait! What are you going to do? I'm worried about you."

"Bye, Hol. Love you." Folding the phone closed, she crossed the coffee shop and pulled her chair close to Jake's. She peered over his shoulder to the laptop screen.

"What did your sister say?" he said without looking up.

She didn't bother asking how he knew she was talking to her sister. It was a reasonable guess. "She said Brent was awake."

He didn't say anything, but his body tensed. The telltale muscle in his jaw twitched, giving away his consternation.

"Holly said the doctors have to operate. It's a risky procedure, and—"

"You can't go. They'll have men watching the hospital."

"Jake, if he can tell us—"

"No. Too dangerous. My first job is to keep you alive. Doing anything about this *bead* is ancillary to that objective."

Paige heaved a deep sigh, although she'd expected as much, even told Holly as much.

But even knowing the risk of visiting Brent in the hospital didn't ease the persistent drumbeat in her head that demanded answers.

Leaning closer to Jake, she studied the computer screen. "What did you find?"

"Well, I mapped out the GPS coordinates in Brent's planner, but they must be wrong. Or they relate to something other than an address. They're for a point ten miles off the coast of Jamaica."

Paige drew a slow breath, thinking. "Our honeymoon was supposed to be in Jamaica. Maybe he meant the coordinates to be someplace on the island. Like I said before, maybe he was planning a surprise for me on the island, like a special dinner or bike ride…"

"Why not use an address, then?" Jake drummed his fingers on the table, his brow creased as he thought. "Does Brent dive?"

"Dive?"

"Scuba dive. Maybe these are the coordinates of a shipwreck or coral reef he wanted to explore."

Paige shook her head. "He doesn't dive. At least, not that I know of." A memory tickled her mind. "Although…"

Jake turned an open expression to her, waiting.

"He talked about us going boating or deep-sea fishing one day while we were in Jamaica. I told him I get seasick even on small boats, but he was insistent. He told me I could stay back on the island and shop if I wanted, but he was hell-bent on going out fishing one day of our honeymoon."

Jake rocked his chair back on two legs. "Could mean something. Or it could just mean he really wanted to go fishing on his honeymoon. It was his vacation too, so—" He shrugged.

Paige leveled a flat stare on Jake. "We're talking about Brent. Brent doesn't fish. His idea of sport is a racquetball game on an air-conditioned court."

The more she thought about Brent's insistence on the fishing trip, the odder it seemed to her. Why was Brent so set on going? One more question she was itching to ask him.

If she could figure a way into the hospital to see him without being noticed.

Jake clicked a tab at the top of the screen to switch to another browser window he had open. "I also found an address for the jeweler who did the work on your ring. I plan on paying him a visit today and finding out what special instructions Brent may have given him." He clicked to open another web page. "And I found some interesting reading about flu vaccines and where research stands in stopping a pandemic. I'd like to find a place where I can print out this article and a few others to read more carefully later."

She tucked her hair behind her ear, mentally canvassing the neighborhood, trying to recall the local businesses. "There's a place a couple blocks over called Acme Copies. I think they have public-use printers."

"That's our next stop, then." Jake bookmarked the site, then closed the browser windows and shut down the laptop.

Donning the backpack, Paige followed Jake out to the Taurus. As she climbed into the car, she noticed a beauty shop across the street with a display of wigs in the front window. Blond wigs. Wigs the color of Holly's hair.

Holly could come and go from Brent's room without suspicion.

Maybe there was a way to visit Brent without being seen—if she could first get away from Jake.

* * *

If her plan was to work, she had to act fast. Jake wouldn't need long to print out the pages he'd bookmarked on the internet.

Paige slipped the ring off her finger and tucked it securely in a side pocket of Jake's backpack. If her plan didn't work and she was caught—she shuddered at the thought—at least the ring, the infamous bead, would be safe with Jake. Keeping her gaze on Jake, she moved quietly toward the door of the printing shop while he plugged the laptop to the printer and tapped the keys to bring up the web pages he wanted in hard copy. She backed farther from him, nearer the door. Opened the door quietly. And ran.

Clutching her purse to her chest, Paige darted down the block, back toward the beauty shop with the wigs. Under her breath she muttered a series of prayers. That Jake would forgive her. That her plan would work. That she wouldn't be too late to see Brent.

That she wouldn't be caught. Killed.

By the time she reached the beauty shop, she was out of breath and could barely talk. But she had no time to waste. She grabbed the blond wig she wanted from the display in the front window and jogged to the counter to pay for it.

One of the hairdressers stepped over to the register. "Can I help you?"

"Just need...to pay...for this," she gasped and slapped the wig on the counter, adding a pair of sunglasses and a silk scarf from a display by the register.

The hairdresser frowned. "Are you all right?"

Paige nodded. "Just out...of breath. I...ran here."

With a dubious look, the hairdresser rang up the wig. "Someone chasing you?"

"I—" Paige hesitated and considered telling the woman she was running from a violent and vindictive ex-boyfriend, but lying was anathema to her. She'd already skirted the line between right and wrong enough in recent days. "I'm just in a hurry."

After handing the woman enough cash to cover her purchase, and without waiting for change, Paige scurried to the door and contemplated how she was to get to the hospital. As disguises went, her wig-scarf-shades combo wasn't much cover, but under the circumstances and with her being in a hurry, she prayed it would suffice. She studied the street for a moment, wishing a taxi would drop out of the sky, when a city bus chugged by and stopped at the next corner. She wasn't sure where the bus was headed, but it was going in the general direction of the hospital. And away from Jake.

She'd just pushed open the beauty shop door and stepped onto the street when the roar of an engine eclipsed the noise of the other traffic. Her heart in her throat, Paige jerked her gaze down the block toward the print shop. Jake was rocketing up the street toward her.

In an instant, she darted back inside the beauty shop and hid behind a large plant near the door.

She watched Jake whiz by, his head swiveling back and forth as he scanned both sides of the street looking for her. Guilt plucked at her, and she fought the temptation to run out to the sidewalk and flag him down. She had to talk to Brent, had to know what made the bead a threat to national security, had to know how Brent had become involved with terrorists and how she could put an end to the danger they were all in.

Jake cruised past the beauty parlor again, slowing in front of the coffee shop to give the interior a longer look, then sped down the street.

The bus at the corner chugged, and the brake lights blinked off. Paige shoved through the front door of the beauty shop and raced to the bus as it began pulling away from the curb. She banged on the door and waved to the driver.

He scowled but stopped and opened the door for her.

"How near to St. Mary's hospital do you run?"

"Closest stop is at the corner of Eighth and Cherry, near the courthouse."

Paige did a mental calculation. The parish courthouse was about a half mile from the hospital. Walking distance.

With a nod, she took a seat and dug the prepaid phone out of her purse. She hit redial and waited for Holly to answer.

"I have a plan," she said without preamble when her sister picked up. "Can you meet me in the ladies' restroom by the information desk on the first floor of the hospital?"

"Trade clothes with me," Paige ordered Holly after exchanging hugs and tearful greetings.

Holly pulled a face. "Do what?"

Paige removed the sunglasses and silk scarf she'd worn over her hair. "I want to see Brent before his surgery, but I can't go up to his room as me. Jake is certain the terrorists, whoever they are, are watching Brent's room, expecting me to come by."

Holly shook her head and wrinkled her nose. "And?"

Paige took a deep breath, searching for patience. Her jitters weren't Holly's fault, and her sense of urgency would have to wait until Holly understood the risks. "And they think I have something they want. They'll grab me or kill me to get what they're after." Holly's face reflected a growing horror, but she let Paige finish. "So I have to go up to see Brent as you. You've already been there today, in those clothes, so that's how I have to look when I go upstairs."

Holly shook her head slowly. "How did you get involved in something like this?"

"That's what I intend to find out from Brent. This is something he did." At Holly's incredulous look, Paige sighed. "You should know, I'm not going to marry Brent. I never should have said yes when he proposed. I didn't love him. I thought I was doing the right thing for the family, for Bancroft Industries, and…for Dad. I knew our engagement made him so happy. But I—"

Holly caught her sister's shoulders. "You don't have to explain yourself. You did what you thought was right at the time. Now you know differently, and you have a chance to correct matters." She pulled her sister into a tight hug. "All I want for you is to be happy. Listen to your heart. Trust it. Don't let your head think you out of something wonderful because it doesn't look right on the surface. Sometimes life's greatest happiness is found in unexpected places."

Paige squeezed her eyes closed, and an image of Jake shimmered behind her eyelids.

Holly pulled away and started unbuttoning her blouse. "I'll trade clothes with you, but…I'm not sure we're the same size anymore."

Paige began undressing, as well. "But we've been the same size, traded clothes back and forth our whole lives."

Holly pulled her loose top back and curved a hand around a tiny bump at her belly. "That was before I got pregnant, though."

Paige paused, blinked. Squealed. "Oh, my gosh! Holly, really? Why didn't you say anything?"

"I was going to—when you got back from your honeymoon. I didn't want to steal your thunder. Your wedding had been in the works for almost two years, and I felt selfish stealing the spotlight."

Tears of joy prickled Paige's eyes. "I'm so happy for you. And Matt, of course. And…oh, wow! When are you due?"

"Around Christmas. Perfect, huh? I might get to share a birthday with my baby!"

Paige's mind spun in myriad directions. Anticipation of her niece or nephew's birth at the holidays. A fresh determination to keep her sisters safe from whatever threat Brent had entangled her in. Wondering whether she'd ever find someone to have children with.

What kind of father would Jake be? Protective, for sure. Thoughtful. But could he get past the hurts of his childhood and open his heart to a child of his own?

First he had to let down his guard long enough to let a woman close. Paige longed to be the one to find a way into Jake's heart, the one he trusted enough to let beyond his protective defenses.

"Paige? Yoo-hoo. Hello?" Holly waved a hand in front of her, snagging her attention back to the present. "Where'd you go just then?"

Paige blinked and shook off the daydream. "Just thinking."

Holly chuckled. "I figured as much with you. Thinking, dissecting...they are your hallmarks."

She knew Holly meant no ill will with her comment. She *had* always been the analytical sister. But lately she'd come to envy Zoey's free spirit, Holly's nurturing optimism. If she didn't think everything to death, could she find the kind of happiness and love her sisters had?

A buzzer of some sort sounded in the hall outside the restroom, prodding Paige to action. She didn't have the luxury of the time she wanted to spend planning with Holly for the birth of her sister's baby. Brent was heading to surgery soon. Jake would be looking for her. The terrorist were watching... waiting to strike. Time was critical.

She hastily peeled off the rest of her clothes and handed them to Holly, who gave her her clothes in return. Holly's clothes were loose but not enough to be noticed. Holly, on the other hand, couldn't snap Paige's jeans closed and just pulled her shirt down to cover the gap.

As Holly helped Paige tuck her long, dark hair under the blond wig, Paige met her sister's gaze in the mirror over the sink. "You'll have to wait here. We can't have two Hollys walking around the hospital."

Her sister nodded her understanding and gave her another hug for luck and safety. "Be careful."

After promising she'd take care, Paige slipped out of the bathroom and headed upstairs to Brent's room.

She kept a wary watch as she made her way through the busy hospital corridors, but had to admit to herself she had no idea what she was looking for. The terrorists would be smart enough to have their operative blend in. Whoever was watching Brent's room wouldn't be visibly toting a large gun, wearing suspicious black garb, or have a sign around their neck.

Keeping her head down and trying not to attract attention, Paige forced herself to walk, not run, to Brent's room. Stepping into the private room, she flinched when she saw the numerous tubes and wires hooked up to him, his paler than normal complexion, the dark shadows beneath his eyes.

Her gasp roused him, drew his gaze. A frown dented his forehead as he studied her. "Holly?"

Seeing for herself that he was alive, Paige sighed with relief. She stepped closer, brushing the bangs of the wig back from her eyes. "No. It's me. Paige."

Brent's nostrils flared around the nasal cannula feeding him oxygen, and he pressed his mouth in a firm line of discontent. "You shouldn't have come. It's too dangerous!" His voice was scratchy, little more than a whisper. "Jake's supposed to be protecting you! Why did he—"

"Jake doesn't know I'm here. He wouldn't approve, but—" Paige pulled a chair to the bedside and leaned close to Brent, keeping her voice low. "I had to see you, had to talk to you. You have to explain this to me. What happened at the church? Who are these people, and why—"

"I'm sorry, Paige. So sorry. I never meant—"

"To put my life in jeopardy by secretly giving me some… *thing* that puts our nation at risk? It's too late for sorry, Brent. Now you have to make things right. Help me understand what Jake and I are up against."

He sighed and lowered his eyes. "It was only for a few days. I was going to retrieve the bead once we were in Jamaica. Switch the rings." His gaze dropped to her hand, and his eyes rounded. "Where is it? Where's your wedding ring?"

Paige blew out a satisfied breath. "We figured the bead you were talking about had to be in the ring." She gritted her teeth and glared daggers at him. "So much for it being a token of your affection, huh?"

"Paige, I—" He glanced away, his expression guilty, before returning an urgent look to her. "Where is it?"

"With Jake. Now you answer a few questions. First, *what* is the *bead?* Why is it a threat to national security? Why do those men want it?"

"That's three questions." Brent lifted his cheek weakly in a feeble grin.

Paige's returned stare held no humor. "Answer me, Brent. You owe me the truth."

He nodded, then winced and brought a hand to his neck. "You're right."

She noted the heavy white bandage on his throat, remembering the bone-chilling minutes when Brent had been shot and blood had seeped from his wound. Paige averted her eyes, steeling herself for what she knew would be difficult to hear.

Brent closed his eyes and curled his fingers into the hospital blanket covering him. "The bead is a nano-size capsule, a nanotube, that contains a sample of a virus we created to aid in our research and development of a super-flu vaccine."

"Nano-size," Paige repeated, dredging up her college science to put the term in context.

"Yeah. Meaning it is in the scale of a nanometer. One billionth of a meter."

"Billionth? With a *b?* It's hard to imagine something so small." She shook her head and tried to wrap her brain around the concept.

Brent filled in the blank for her. "A human hair is typically about one hundred thousand nanometers wide. A typical virus is about one thousand nanometers. You need an atomic force microscope to see something that small, but nanotechnology is the future of science and medicine. There are tremendous strides being made every day to find new treatments for disease, new compounds to improve quality of life…"

When he paused for a breath, she interrupted. "I've read about the science and the aspirations to apply nanotech to many areas of life and research. I just didn't know Bancroft was conducting any nanotechnological research."

He met her eyes, but hesitated. "We…purposely kept it on the down low."

"Who is 'we'? Did my dad know?"

"Not in depth. He only knew we were doing sensitive, landmark research. He trusted me to handle the details until we had something…viable."

"Meaning?" Paige leaned closer, her stomach bunching in dread.

Brent visibly swallowed, then licked his cracked lips. "We were trying to develop a potent, deadly strain of flu—strictly in the laboratory—so we'd have a way to test the viability of the vaccine we were working on. The recent scares with swine flu and avian flu brought home to the public what medical researchers have known for years. We need an effective way to stop a super-virus. The company that developed and sold the vaccine that could prevent a pandemic stood to make a fortune."

"You created a super-virus? The very kind of disease that could cause said pandemic?"

He nodded. "Except…my super-virus is even more deadly that the Spanish flu that caused the 1918 pandemic."

She goggled at the idea. While she understood the concept in theory, the idea of creating what you hope to destroy seemed…sickly ironic. "What if this super-virus were to get out of the laboratory somehow? What if you started a pandemic with the disease you created before you found the vaccine you wanted?"

"Come on, Paige. You know medical research well enough to know how carefully laboratory materials and specimens are handled. Extreme precautions are taken to avoid accidentally releasing bio-threats. Our man-made virus was perfectly safe in the lab. We needed it for our research."

Paige's spine tingled as she keyed in on his choice of words. "*Was* safe? Past tense."

Brent stiffened and cut his gaze away again. The passion that had lit his face as he explained and defended the volatile research drained from his face, leaving him wan and pasty-looking. "Word of our man-made virus leaked out, and…I started getting calls."

"Go on." Icy fingers closed around Paige's throat.

"Other companies wanted to buy our virus for similar research. We were sitting on a gold mine of potential revenue. I scrambled to file for the patent. Meanwhile, the offers I was getting…began to change. The sums grew. The buyers…" He sent a desperate, frantic look to her. "Foreign governments, leaders of private militia…the offers were staggering. But I knew these people didn't want PMB-611 for medical research. They wanted to use it as a weapon. They wanted it for bioterrorism."

Paige was letting Brent's revelation take hold when the initials he'd used snagged her attention. "PMB-611. That's what you named the virus?"

A telltale flush tinted Brent's cheeks. "I—" He sighed. "Yeah."

"My initials are *PMB*."

"Yeah."

"And 611?"

"Our wedding date. June 11."

Paige's laugh held no humor. "You named your deadly super-virus after *me* and our *wedding date?*"

He raised a hand. "I meant it as an homage to you, not an insult. I thought the virus would help Bancroft Industries become a leader in medical research, help us develop a vaccine that would save the world from a lethal pandemic. I thought it would earn the company more money than you'd ever dreamed. More money than your father ever imagined."

Paige sat back. She struggled to draw air into her suddenly leaden lungs. Brent used an ex-girlfriend's name as a password on his computer. But her initials, her wedding date…she was immortalized with the name of a deadly germ that could start a catastrophic plague. Now she knew how Typhoid Mary felt.

She forced enough moisture into her mouth so she could

swallow. She lifted a scowl to Brent. "You sure know how to sweep a girl off her feet."

"Paige, you don't understand. The vaccine we were working on—"

"Forget it." She gentled her tone. Stressing him more than this conversation already would couldn't be good for his condition. "My feelings about the way you named your super-virus don't matter in the grand scheme. Tell me about the bead. The nanotube."

Jake pulled the Taurus into a parking space near the print shop and killed the engine. Where the hell was Paige?

His gut clenched. He feared the worst. Had the wedding crashers managed to grab her while he had his back turned? He found it hard to imagine they'd been able to walk in, nab Paige and get out of the store without him hearing or sensing anything.

His hands tightened on the steering wheel as the only other logical scenario repeated in his head. She'd ditched him. He was loath to examine why that truth left such a hollow, achy feeling in his chest, why her abandonment felt like a betrayal, why Paige had the power to elicit such a strong gut reaction from him in the first place. Protecting her was a job like any other he'd been assigned. Why couldn't he do his job without complicating things, letting things get personal?

Exhaling sharply, he tried to focus on the problem at hand. He'd failed again. He'd let his guard down for seconds, and Paige had disappeared.

Where would she have gone, alone, without transportation, without money?

Without cover or protection. Damn it!

The obvious answer left him in a cold sweat.

The hospital. To see Scofield. Double damn it!

Didn't she know how vulnerable and exposed she was there? The thugs who'd busted up her wedding would be crawling all over the hospital, waiting for her. Even if the police or Paige's family had added guards at Scofield's door, they could have already gotten to Brent by now.

He slammed a hand through his wind-mussed hair and muttered a blazing curse under his breath. After shouldering open the car door, he stormed back into the print shop to pick up the hard copies of the pages he'd ordered. He paid cash for the copies and jammed them into his backpack with the laptop. Striding back to the sidewalk, he scanned the street, hoping, praying Paige would scurry up to him with a smile and a story about how she'd just gotten hungry and stepped into the bakery next door for a bran muffin.

But she was nowhere in sight. He gritted his teeth so hard they hurt. Mad at himself for letting her give him the slip, furious with Paige for putting herself at risk and terrified that her disappearance meant she'd been kidnapped, Jake debated his options.

The hospital remained the best place to start. He needed to find a way to get to Scofield's room and get Paige out without being noticed. A clandestine insertion was a cakewalk for him. He'd entered heavily guarded buildings and extracted persons of interest more times than he could count. But those missions had been well-planned, timed to the second. He could hear his commanding officer's voice berating him, telling him that going in half-cocked could get him killed. Jake's fly-by-the-seat-of-his-pants approach had given his CO more than one reason to ream him out.

And while going into the hospital unprepared was dangerous, Paige had left him no option. He had to get her out… and pray he wasn't too late.

Chapter 10

"Like I said, the nanotube has a viable sample of PMB-611. Enough to infect several hundred people, say a room full of people at a concert or on a subway or airplane. The disease progresses fairly quickly and is contagious within hours of exposure."

"Long enough for the unknowing victims to start the global spread of the disease if dispersed on a key international flight." Paige gnawed her lip. "Is…is the nanotube safe? C-can it break and infect me and Jake?"

Brent shook his head. "Not as long as it is embedded in the ring. I had it encapsulated in the faux diamond."

She arched an eyebrow. "Faux diamond? The hunk of rock isn't real?"

Another slight head shake. "It's a special cut glass. An expert could tell the difference quite easily, but I only needed to disguise the nanotube, hide it in the fake ring for a few days. I had planned to—" He paused and swallowed hard.

"Please continue," she said with a hard glare. "What had you planned?"

"I was meeting someone. Passing the nanotube off to them while we were in the Caribbean."

"A terrorist?" She couldn't hide the scathing tone of accusation.

He blanched. "No. I had a contact within CDC. After I swapped the decoy ring with your real ring, we picked a safe location to meet, to transfer the decoy, with the nanotube and sample to him, and—"

"This location… Was it at sea? Were you meeting by boat?"

He blinked as if stunned she knew. "How did you—?"

"I saw the GPS coordinates in your planner." If he was curious how she'd gotten his planner, he didn't show it. "And I remembered you'd been insistent about deep-sea fishing on our honeymoon."

Brent turned up a palm, his expression pleading for understanding. "I knew how dangerous the situation had become, and I wanted the sample in safe hands in case…"

She shuddered. "In case certain terrorists caught up to you and demanded the bead?"

She interpreted his guilty look as a *yes*. "Who are they, Brent? How did they know about the bead and that you'd have it at the wedding?"

"I don't know what terror group they are with. Only that they are dangerous and well-funded, and they mean business."

Paige leaned closer, hardly believing her ears. "Why in the world would you get involved with people like that, Brent? What were you thinking!"

"I didn't know they were terrorists at first! I…I'd arranged to sell them the virus before I smelled a rat. When I started getting cold feet and questioning them, the arrangements turned ugly fast. They threatened me, ransacked my house, started following me. They…grabbed me once. Late at night. I'd been at the office working, and…" He shivered visibly and closed his eyes. "Let's just say, they demonstrated their lethal potential."

"Why didn't you tell me? How could all this have happened to you without me knowing?" she asked.

Opening his eyes, he found her gaze. "I made sure you didn't find out. To protect you and…because I was ashamed. I—I lied to you, covered my tracks and…planning the wedding kept you busy, distracted."

Paige rubbed her temple. "So how did they first contact you?"

"They had posed as buyers for the Department of Defense, for our government, the military. I thought it was my civic duty to cooperate with the DOD. And I thought about how the money would set us up for life. They offered a hell of a lot of money for the sample, and…I saw a chance to—"

"Get rich quick?" she offered when he let his words trail off.

A muscle in his jaw twitched, and he sent her a scornful glance. "What if I did want to make a fast buck? A lot of bucks? I was doing it for you!"

Paige shot up from her chair, her hands fisted at her sides. "For me? Don't you dare try to lay this at my feet! I don't care about money. I wasn't marrying you for your bank account. You know that!"

"No, you were marrying me to make Daddy happy, weren't you?"

She gasped. "I—"

"Don't try to deny it, Paige," he said softly. "I know it wasn't because you loved me. I could see that much in your eyes."

She opened her mouth to deny his claim, but no sound came out. It was the truth, after all. But she hated the pain in his face.

"Tell me something. If those men hadn't arrived and interrupted the service—" His expression was bleak. "Would you have gone through with it? Would you have married me?"

"Of course! I'd made a commitment to you. I—"

"I saw your reluctance. Heard the hesitation in your voice."
He sighed. "The truth, Paige. What would you have done?"

She blinked back the burn of tears. "I...don't know."

"And now?" he asked in little more than a whisper. "What
are you going to do now? What happens to us?"

Her chest twisted at the forlorn look in his eyes, the dim
hope that flickered across his face. Could he really have had
feelings for her? Did he still?

"There is no *us*, Brent. Not now. Not after all that's hap-
pened." She swiped at the moisture that dampened her cheek.
"I'm sorry. I should never have promised to marry you when
I knew deep in my heart it was a mis—"

When she hesitated, looking for a word that wouldn't hurt
his feelings, he said, "Mistake?"

"A...misrepresentation of my feelings for you. I misled you
to believe—"

He laughed without humor. "Come off it, Paige. I'm smarter
than that. I knew you didn't love me. You aren't that good
of an actress. I knew what we had was an arrangement of
convenience."

"And that was enough for you? Don't you want more for
yourself?" She thought about the arguments she'd had in the
past with Zoey on this subject, the happiness she saw between
Holly and Matt. The confusing feelings Jake evoked in her
and the temptations she'd faced around him the past few days.
"What about passion and romance and the real, deep-down joy
of being with a person who makes you feel alive and whole
and..."

Paige dropped heavily back into her seat, realizing what
she was saying. Jake made her feel...feminine, alive. For the
first time in years, she woke with an excited contentment about
what the day to come might hold. She was falling in love with
Jake.

"Paige?" Brent's voice jerked her attention back to the
hospital room. "What is it? You look upset."

She shook her head, as if doing so would clear away her
tangled feelings toward Jake. Her issues with Jake could wait.

Right now, she needed answers. Needed to get out of the hospital and back to the campground before someone saw her and recognized her.

"Never mind what I was thinking. What's important now—besides you getting well, getting back on your feet—is that you tell me everything I need to know about your contact at the CDC and what Jake and I are supposed to do with the nanotube. How do we get these terrorists off our backs?"

Ten minutes later, much longer than Paige had felt it was safe to spend with Brent, she had detailed information about Brent's CDC contact, what little information he knew about the terrorists who'd contacted him and a general plan in mind to bring this whole nightmare to an end.

Holly had been waiting for her in the women's restroom for almost thirty minutes now, and Paige was anxious to trade clothes again, don the scarf and sunglasses and slip out a back door of the hospital. She glanced nervously down the corridor outside Brent's room before she headed toward the elevator. She made it halfway to the nurses' station, saw nothing suspicious.

Then a strong arm seized her from behind....

Covering her mouth with a wide hand, her captor pulled her into a supply closet.

Icy terror balled in her stomach. A scream formed in her throat, but the smothering hand kept her from drawing the air she needed to voice it.

"Be quiet, and don't panic," a low, familiar voice rumbled in her ear. "I'm not going to hurt you, Holly."

When his grip loosened, Paige spun around, landing a punch on Jake's arm. "That's for scaring ten years off my life!" She raised her chin and glared at him. "And it's not Holly. It's me."

Jake did a double take, lifting a wisp of the wig for closer examination. He wore hospital scrubs a size too small for him and a surgical mask, which he jerked down to talk. "Paige?" Then hotly, "How about the scare you gave me?" He returned a dark glare and lowered his volume again. "Jeez, Paige, I thought you'd been kidnapped by those goons! I've been going crazy for the last hour!"

She held up a hand to cut him off. "Save the lecture. I know you said you thought it was too dangerous, but I've been careful." She poked him in the chest. "Even you thought I was Holly."

He scowled. "Because I only saw you from the back." He gave her clothes and wig a more thorough scrutiny. "Not bad though. Those her clothes?"

"Yes. And she's waiting for me in the downstairs restroom as we speak, so…can this argument wait until we get back to the campground?"

A muscle jumped in his jaw, giving away his continued frustration with her. She had a lot to make up to him for worrying him. But the information she'd gotten from Brent should go a long way toward that end.

He gave a tight nod. "Let's go. I've got the car in the rear parking lot." He started for the closet door, then sent a guarded look over his shoulder to her. "You go first. We shouldn't be seen together. But I'll be right behind you. In case of trouble."

Her heart still thumping double-time thanks to Jake's grab, Paige eased back out into the hall and walked quickly, but not so fast that she drew attention, to the elevator. The car arrived and just before the door closed, scrubs-clad Jake slipped in with her.

"Was Brent awake? Did you learn anything?" he asked.

"Yes and yes. It's worse than we thought. We were right that the bead is in my wedding ring. The bead has a nanotube inside that contains a deadly virus."

Without looking at her, he shushed her under his breath. "Not here."

"You asked!"

"A yes or no question. We'll get into the details later where it's safe."

The elevator dinged as they reached the bottom floor. With

a huff of frustration, Paige stepped off, glanced around the lobby, then headed for the ladies' room where Holly waited.

Her sister rushed over when she entered. "About time! How did it go?"

"We alone?" Paige asked, glancing toward the empty stalls.

"Yeah."

Paige started unbuttoning the blouse to return to Holly. "Jake's waiting for me outside. I have to go back into hiding with him until…until this mess gets resolved. Tell Mom and Dad that I'm safe. I'm with Jake, and…this should all be over soon."

"I hate this, Paige! We're worried sick about you! It's bad enough that Zoey's flitting around the country, incommunicado."

Paige handed the blouse and stretchy pants back to Holly. "I'm sorry. I don't really have a choice. Please, be safe. These men could try to hurt you to get to me."

Holly's brow furrowed. "Dad's hired extra security since the wedding. Both at Bancroft and at the house."

Paige nodded as she pulled on the last of her own clothes and the scarf-and-shades combo to hide her face. "Good." She pulled her sister into a hug. "I love you. Take care of my new niece." She laid a gentle hand on her sister's abdomen.

"Or nephew…"

Paige smiled, tears filling her eyes. "No. It's a girl. Another Bancroft woman to carry on our tradition."

Holly wiped a tear from her own face. "Be safe. I love you, too."

Paige emerged from the bathroom in her own clothes. Jake hustled her down the hospital corridor, his gaze sweeping the length of the hall, keeping a vigilant watch for suspicious activity. Heat blasted them as they stepped outside and crossed the blacktop parking lot to the rental car.

He unlocked and opened the door for Paige, who gave him a satisfied look as she settled in the passenger seat.

He cocked an eyebrow. "What?"

"I did it. I got in to see Brent, questioned him about the head and we got out without anyone seeing us or shooting at us."

He pressed his lips in a thin line. "Don't get cocky. We're not in the clear yet." Jake closed her door and scanned the parking area as he circled to the driver's side of the Taurus. The interior of the car had become an oven in the summer sun, and sweat popped out on his face within seconds of climbing inside. He cranked the engine and shot Paige a glance as he checked over his shoulder to back out.

She yanked the silk scarf from her head and tousled her thick dark hair. "Jeez, this thing is hot." She returned Jake's stare with a wide-eyed expression. "I have so much to tell you. I know what the security threat is and what our next move has to be."

Jake's gut tightened. As much as he wanted to know everything right then, he knew their higher priority was getting out of sight. "Save it. We'll go over everything back at the campground."

As he pulled out of the parking lot and merged into the downtown traffic, Paige turned the air-conditioning on full power, high fan.

"I learned something else today, too. About my sister." A broad smile lit her face, and she sighed contentedly. "I'm going to be an aunt! Holly is pregnant with her first child!"

Jake gave Paige the requisite grin, although the idea of children stirred uneasily in his gut. Family, kids, a white picket fence were all foreign concepts for him. Seeing how happy Paige was for her sister told him all he had to know about Paige's own wish for that kind of domestic bliss. The uneasy roil in his gut became a hollow ache.

Knowing he couldn't give Paige what she wanted, couldn't be the man she needed, hurt more than he cared to admit. When had he started thinking beyond the end of this mission? His job was to keep Paige safe and protect the bead to contain the national security threat. So why was he thinking in terms of any future for them past that?

He mulled that point fruitlessly, the empty pit in his chest growing deeper, until they reached the edge of town and headed for the highway back to the campground. To distract himself from that unsettling line of thought, he rolled his shoulders and sent her a puzzled look. "How is this Holly's first baby? I thought she and her husband had two kids."

As he returned his attention to the road, he glimpsed a blue sedan gaining on them quickly. *Two sedans,* he amended when the second car pulled forward into view.

"They do. They're Matt's kids from his first marriage. She's adopting them, but this is her first biological baby. The first Bancroft grandbaby by blood."

"Mm," he hummed in acknowledgment, but his focus was on the identical sedans. A prickle of alarm nipped his neck.

Jake sped up, looking for an exit. The sedans caught up to them but didn't pass. Grinding his back teeth, Jake took the next exit. Checked his mirrors.

The blue sedans followed.

He muttered an earthy curse word and squeezed the steering wheel.

"What?" Paiged asked, sending him a worried look.

"We have company. Hang on."

Paige twisted toward the back window as Jake took the first right turn he got to, then a left. The two blue cars stayed on their tail. He sped up, and the sedans matched his speed.

"They're still there!" Paige cried.

"Not only are they still there, they're not trying to hide the fact they're there." Acid churned in his gut. "Get my gun out of the glove compartment."

She did, and passed it to him. For several more blocks, Jake tried in vain to lose their pursuers.

Finally, the first sedan seemed to tire of the chase and raced ahead of them.

"Are they leaving?" Paige's voice held surprise and hope.

Jake knew better, and his body tensed even tighter. He

didn't have a chance to answer her wishful thinking before the first sedan jerked to a stop at an angle mere feet in front of them.

Jake braked hard to avoid hitting them, then slammed the rental car into Reverse. But the second car pulled up to the back bumper of their rental, boxing them in.

The doors of the first car flew open, and two armed men climbed out.

"Lock your door," he told her, knowing how little the move would mean if the goons wanted to get inside. If they started shooting...

"Get down. On the floor. Stay there until I tell you otherwise." He wrapped his fingers around his SIG Sauer, and with his free hand, he cut the wheels sharply. He backed up, crashing into the second car, then shifted back into Drive. He'd intended to drive off the shoulder, cross-country if needed, to get away. But one of the armed men was already at Paige's door.

He smashed her window with the butt of his gun. She screamed. Glass rained down on her.

Jake leveled his weapon on the barrel-chested goon at the passenger door. "Stand back!"

The driver's window shattered, and the cold kiss of steel touched his temple.

"Drop your weapon, or I'll drop you," a high-pitched male voice grated behind him.

"Do it!" the goon at Paige's door echoed.

Jake hesitated. His gun was all he had to defend Paige. If he put it down...

A sharp blow slammed into his skull, and the edges of his vision dimmed.

"Paige," he rasped, reaching for her.

And then...nothing.

Chapter 11

"Jake!" Paige screamed as his eyes rolled back and he slumped on the seat. She scrambled to reach him, tears filling her eyes. Instantly, the passenger door was yanked open, and a burly man grabbed her upper arm.

"No!" She flailed and fought, but against his brawn she stood no chance. He hauled her out of the car and shoved her toward the waiting blue sedan.

If you get in the car you're as good as dead. She remembered a self-defense video that she'd watched with Zoey a couple years ago that instructed women to fight with all they had for release.

And she fought. She clawed, she struggled, she jerked.

Until the beefy guy with his paw clamped on her arm and stuck a gun in her face. Icy, instinctive fear washed through her. Froze her.

"Get in the car."

She tried to scream again, but even her throat seemed paralyzed.

Jake! Jake! Help! her brain screamed.

The goon shoved her roughly into the backseat, and before the door closed, she cut a glance toward the rental car.

Jake hadn't moved.

Bile surged into her throat. Oh, God! Was he dead? What had they done to him?

"Get the boyfriend. Bring him, too," the driver shouted.

The beefy guy took two steps back toward the rental car then stopped. "We got company. Forget the guy. Let's move!" He climbed in next to her and gave her a leering grin. "We got what we need."

The second man, who'd hurt Jake, joined them on the backseat, frowning.

With a thud, the back door closed, and the sedan screeched away.

If you get in the car, you're as good as dead.

Paige's chest squeezed, and tears burned her eyes. She was dead.

Jake blinked. Black spots swam before his eyes, and nausea roiled in his gut. When he raised his head, lightning shot through his skull.

Squinting against the pain, he peered through the windshield in time to see Paige shoved into the blue sedan. A big ape of a man followed her in and slammed the door.

No! Alarms blared in his head. *No!*

He glanced desperately around the front seat, searching for his gun.

The squeal of tires cut his search for his SIG Sauer short. He glanced up just as the blue sedan pedaled away. The second car followed.

Jake's heart clenched, and a sinking sense of failure settled over him like a boulder in his chest.

His head throbbing, Jake blinked the world into focus. A fresh shot of adrenaline cleared the last remnants of haze from his brain.

He hadn't lost her yet. As long as he kept the blue sedan in sight, he had a chance to rescue Paige.

Jamming the car into gear and battling the headache from hell, he tore after the sedan.

Paige scuttled across the backseat, moving as far away from the beefy man as she could. She shook to her core, terrified of what they might do to her and worried sick about Jake.

Please, God, let Jake be all right!

"Wh-who are you? What do you want?" she demanded, although she knew what they wanted. She rubbed her fingers, almost involuntarily, and only then remembered she wasn't wearing the ring. She'd put it in Jake's backpack for safekeeping.

"We'll ask the questions. If you cooperate, we may even let you live." The beefy man snaked a hand out to stroke her cheek, and she flinched. "The world needs pretty women like you."

His leering expression made her stomach turn. The gun he held loosely in his hand sent a shiver to her bones. She didn't doubt for a minute that these men would shoot her if she didn't give them what they wanted.

But she didn't have what they wanted.

Jake did.

A fresh wave of icy fear washed through her. Not only could she not turn over the ring to save her life, telling the men where the ring was would put Jake's life in grave danger. Again.

Because Jake would surely resist, and these men would have no qualms about killing him. Acid puddled in her stomach, and her lunch seesawed and rebelled.

"Where is the bead with Scofield's nanotube?" the second man in the backseat growled, getting in her face. She recognized him now as one of the men who'd crashed her wedding with Trench Coat. Apparently, this man was now the ringleader.

"I—" she started, her voice cracking. "I don't—"

"And before you tell us you don't know what we're talking about, know this. We know you were at the hospital. We know you talked to Scofield. We know Scofield claims to have passed the bead to you at some point. Considering that you and your new boyfriend were in Scofield's office the other night, we know you are working with Scofield to keep us from getting the nanotube with the virus." He waved his gun in front of her. "So answer very carefully."

Paige's mouth grew dry, knowing her answers could put people she cared about in grave danger. If she gave up the location of the nanotube to these goons, they could use the virus in a weapon and start a terrible flu epidemic, costing thousands, even millions of people their lives.

She shuddered. But if she didn't give these men something, she'd be killed, pretty or not.

Think, Paige, think!

Ringleader had only said he knew that she'd been at the hospital, not that he'd heard any of her conversation with Brent.

Paige curled her fingers into a fist, digging her fingernails into her palm. And reasoning out her options. She had to tread lightly. If she lied, and they caught her in the lie, because they had been listening in Brent's hospital room...

"I—I only learned the truth about the bead and the virus in it today...when I saw Brent at the hospital."

That much was true.

"Go on." Ringleader gestured with the gun for her to proceed.

Their driver took a corner at a high speed, and Paige was thrown against the beefy thug who'd grabbed her. The sour smell that clung to him made her stomach roil harder.

Where were they going? It would behoove her to pay attention to where they were. In case she got free and had to tell someone—Jake, the cops, her father—where she was.

She craned her neck to see out the window, and Ringleader jabbed her in the ribs with his weapon.

"Stop stalling! What did Scofield say? Where is the damn bead!"

Paige shivered as her captor's voice elevated, sounding

more taut and angry with every word. She had to give him something to earn his trust, had to let him think she was cooperating, even if…

"He said he put the bead in…m-my ring." Her heart clenched as the words spilled out, but a heartbeat later, inspiration struck, and her hopes soared. "In my engagement ring."

Ringleader narrowed his eyes on her as if debating whether to believe her, then shot his cohort an inquiring glance.

"Could be done. He coulda hid that nanotube in about anything."

"He had a special glass bead made to look like a diamond. He…switched rings on me one night when I had my engagement ring off washing dishes. I never suspected anything." The lies rolled off her tongue, and she prayed she could be convincing and also not paint herself into a box that would trap her.

Ringleader arched a dark eyebrow, and his gaze darted to her left hand. With a rough grab, he jerked her hand up to study her fingers.

"Where is it? Where's the ring?"

"Well, see…here's the thing…I didn't know what he'd done. I didn't know about the nanotube, and—" The dark glare Ringleader narrowed on her almost tripped her up.

She swallowed hard as bile clambered up her throat. Once she'd calmed the sick roll in her gut, she offered them another tiny truth that would buy her and Jake more time. "I pawned it. For the cash. I sold it, a—" Her heart stumbled as she made a split-second decision. "And my wedding ring." Her pulse kicked higher as she prattled on, hoping to convince them of her story. "I was mad at Brent, knew I wasn't going to marry him after he'd betrayed me like this, and the money was—"

"Bull." Turning to his cohort, he barked, "She's got it somewhere. Search her."

Paige gasped, and her stomach roiled as she was subjected

to a rough, thorough and intimate search. "Stop it! I pawned it," she cried, battling Beefy Guy's hands. "I swear! I sold —"

"Where?" Ringleader cut her off. "What pawnshop?"

"I...don't remember the name of the shop."

Beefy Guy cocked his gun and angled it toward her. "Try harder."

Paige gasped and divided a frantic look between the scowling men. "I...think it had initials... like ABC Pawn or AAA Pawn or EZ Pawn. I know it was on the south side of town near the airport."

Along with dozens of other pawnshops. Maybe the sheer volume of pawnshops on the south side of town would keep these goons searching for a day or two.

She and Jake needed just twenty-four to forty-eight hours to find Brent's contact in the CDC, arrange to meet him and pass over the nanotube. She wished they could just go to the FBI or police, but Brent had repeated his warning not to. He had reason to believe the terrorists had help from someone within Homeland Security.

Ringleader still looked unconvinced, but he leaned forward and barked to the driver, "Head south. Call Bern and tell him to work up a list of every pawnshop in the city, listing the ones in the southern part of the city first." He glanced back to Paige with a suspicious scowl. "We're going shopping."

Jake kept the blue sedans in his sights but, by keeping several cars between him and his target, stayed far enough back not to be spotted.

Though pain pounded in his head, guilt hammered harder. He'd blown it again. He'd asked Paige to trust him to keep her safe, and he'd let her down.

He'd let her get snatched from the seat beside him. *Hell.*

Whatever it took, he would get Paige back. He would save her before those slime bags had a chance to—

A sharp ache reverberated in his skull. He could have a concussion. The pain made his eyes tear, and he clenched his teeth, fighting to stay conscious. When he touched his fingers to the goose egg on his head, he found a small bleeding cut.

Didn't matter. All that mattered was getting to Paige, getting her away from the terrorists before they could hurt her.

Ahead of him, the first blue sedan jerked a hard right-hand turn. The second sedan didn't.

Jake blinked as his vision swam, making sure he'd seen correctly. The blue sedans were splitting up?

A chill prickled Jake's nape. If he were two men, he'd follow the second car to see where it went. Maybe he'd find out more about who was behind the terrorist group and what they were after.

But he was only one man, and his priority, his only *real* goal, was Paige's safety.

Gripping the steering wheel so tightly his skin blanched, Jake shook off another wave of nearly blinding pain.

I'm sorry, Paige. I'm so sorry. Hang on. I'm coming.

When he reached the side street where the first car had turned, Jake followed.

"Tabor and Henchcliff can take the first half of the list, and we'll do the second half." Ringleader had gotten on his cell phone as soon as Paige told him about the pawnshop, and in short order, he had his minions scouring the city for her ring.

Her heart sank. She'd hoped the tidbit she'd given him would keep him busy for days, buying her time. Apparently, Ringleader had enough guys on his payroll to start a miniature dragnet combing the city's southside shops.

"The ring is an emerald-cut diamond solitaire set in white gold. It would have been brought in in the last three days by a pretty brunette." He sent her another side glance that made her stomach do serious flip-flops. "If anyone asks, it's an heirloom and the poor jilted darling hadn't known the family history. Got it?"

Ringleader snapped the cell phone closed and jammed it

in his shirt pocket. On his lap, his hand flexed and closed around his handgun.

Paige took a deep breath for courage. "Look, I told you what you wanted to know. Can't you let me go now?"

A muscle jumped in Ringleader's jaw, and his icy blue eyes narrowed on her. "Not until we have the ring and confirm that the nanotube is in it and intact." He leaned closer, and a fresh jolt of fear spilled more acid into her stomach. "If you and your new boyfriend have done anything to damage the bead…" His glare darkened. "It won't go well for you."

Trembling to her core, Paige squeezed her eyes shut and tried to slow her ragged breathing. Instead, behind closed eyes, she saw Jake slumping forward after he was smacked in the head. She heard Brent saying, "The super-virus is even more deadly than the Spanish flu that caused the 1918 pandemic." She smelled the blood that had splattered the walls the night she and Jake had been cornered in Brent's office. And a familiar, unsettling feeling crept over her…

When Paige was fourteen years old, her family had visited a theme park, and she'd gamely climbed on the biggest roller coaster. If ten-year-old Zoey could ride the Green Monster, so could she. But when the ride had crested the top of the first hill, a paralyzing fear had washed through Paige. Not because of the speed of the train or the height of the hill, but because she'd felt completely helpless. She'd known she had absolutely no control over the roller coaster and had been terrified. Since that day at the theme park, whenever she'd felt a complete loss of control over her life, Paige did the same thing she'd done on the Green Monster.

She threw up.

Now, scrunched between two armed men, hurtling down the highway, with the responsibility of keeping her country safe from the deadly virus her ex-fiancé created, control over her circumstances once again dangled beyond her reach. Her gut surged with the same nausea and panic she'd known when she'd seen the steep and undulating track that lay ahead for the roller coaster.

"Um…" She paused to swallow the bitter taste already climbing her throat. "We need to pull over."

"What?" Ringleader snarled.

"I think I'm…gonna be sick."

Her captor glowered at her, his expression pure suspicion. "Like hell."

"I don't know, Steward." Beefy Guy angled his head to study her, leaned closer. "She don't look so good. Kinda pale and—"

The sour smell surrounding Beefy Guy was the last straw. Paige's lunch rose in her throat in a violent wave. In the last seconds of coherent thought, before she gave herself over to abject misery and humiliation, she knew she could use her moment of weakness as a weapon. A tool.

Or else her split-second decision would backfire in the worse possible way.

Turning her head and throwing her shoulders forward, she aimed for Ringleader's lap, his hand. His gun.

"What the hell?" Ringleader bellowed, his face twisting in disgust. "Oh, my God! You bitch!" He shoved her away with a none-too-gentle thrust and yelled to their driver. "Pull over! Now!" After taking one look at his soiled gun, he flung his weapon on the floor of the car and wiped the mess from his hand on the backseat.

As the car jerked to the side of the road, Paige was tossed against Beefy Guy, who shrank away from her as if she carried the plague.

A second wave of nausea built to a roiling crescendo in her gut, and she pressed one hand to her mouth while gesturing wildly with the other.

Beefy Guy frantically fumbled to open the door.

She scrambled to climb over him and get out of the car. Again, she took advantage of her opportunity and purposely drove her knee into Beefy Guy's groin as she clambered across his lap to the shoulder of the road.

He hollered in pain and doubled over.

Despite the heat, despite the sick pitching in her stomach,

despite the odds against success, Paige knew she might never get a chance like this again. While Ringleader and Beefy Guy reeled from her unpleasant surprise attack, Paige ran.

Chapter 12

Jake tensed when the blue sedan abruptly stopped at the side of the road. This part of Lagniappe had few buildings, mostly offices for blue-collar businesses—plumbers, pest control a mom-and-pop grocery—spread out along a two-lane road amid numerous empty lots and weed-infested fields. Had he been spotted? Did the Wedding Crashers know he'd followed them?

Jake gritted his teeth and did what he did best—think on his feet, make snap decisions in high-stakes moments. Rather than pull over and wait the situation out, Jake saw what may be his only chance to act, to overtake the blue sedan and get Paige back.

He was outmanned and unarmed now—unless…

Jake fumbled on the floor under the driver's seat. His fingers closed around the familiar grip of his P226. *Thank God!*

He snatched the pistol off the floor, where he'd dropped it when he'd been knocked out, and sped forward. As he approached the blue sedan, the passenger-side back door flew open, and Paige stumbled out.

Jake's heart missed a beat. She was alive, appeared unharmed.

He didn't question, only reacted.

As Paige ran from the sedan, Jake wheeled the rental car in front of her and slammed on the brakes. With a scream, she came up short and sent a frightened, disoriented look through the windshield.

"Get in!" he yelled to her, making his head throb in protest.

"Jake!" She hesitated one startled second before sprinting to the passenger door and quickly climbing in. "How did you—I thought—"

He stomped the gas pedal before she could finish, before she even had the door closed. She fought to hang on and shut her door as they peeled away.

When they passed the blue sedan, Jake aimed his SIG Sauer at the rear tire, fired and hit his mark. "Buckle in. This could get dicey."

"Get dicey?" She barked a humorless laugh, then clamped a hand over her mouth. "Oh, man. I'm gonna be sick again."

As he rocketed down the narrow two-lane street, thankful the traffic was sparse, he shot her a glance. "Sick?"

She nodded and leaned her head back. "That's how I got away. I…threw up on Ringleader."

Jake chortled. "Oh, that's rich! Brilliant!"

"I tend to do that when I get really upset, really stressed out." She glared at him, apparently not seeing the humor in the situation that he did. "They pulled over so I could finish my business on the side of the road, and I saw my chance—"

Jake slapped the steering wheel and tamed his laughter to a broad grin. "Darling, that is a prime example of the kind of in-the-moment, tactical strategizing that would have made my CO in the SEALs proud. You worked with what you had and used it to your advantage. Simply brilliant!"

She gaped at him as if he'd lost his mind. "I didn't plan to get sick! I couldn't help it! That's how I respond to having my life threatened!"

"My point exactly. You can't plan for the unexpected. You have to know how to go with your gut…" He cut a sly glance and a wry grin toward her. "No pun intended."

She returned a sour smile.

He checked his rearview mirror and saw no sign of the blue sedan behind him. The grip of anxiety squeezing his chest loosened, and the drumbeat of pain in his head eased. But he knew better than to assume they were in the clear.

Rather than head straight back to the campground and risk an unseen tail following them, Jake headed toward the city limits, out to the countryside where long stretches of flat farmland allowed a clear view of the traffic behind him for many miles. Only when he was certain they had no one tailing them would he head back to the opposite side of town and their campsite.

Paige fell silent, and she rode with her eyes shut, her complexion pale, her breathing deep. He gave her the time she needed to calm her ragged nerves and work past the stress-induced nausea.

Pride swelled in his chest for her quick thinking, whether she could see the significance of her actions or not. For someone who claimed to be all about planning and organization and contingencies, she'd shown she could handle herself under fire.

He set the rental car's cruise control and settled back, rolling the tension from his shoulders and realizing the sharp throb in his skull had subsided to a dull ache. Progress.

With a lingering side glance, Jake drank in the image of Paige beside him. With her tangled hair, rumpled shirt and makeup-free face, she reminded him more of a wild adventuress than the pressed-and-pleated society bride he'd met last week. He liked this Paige. She had a raw sensuality about her that she kept hidden with her buttoned-down shirts and stiff formalities.

"Jake?" she said without opening her eyes, and he wondered briefly if she had felt his scrutinizing gaze.

"Yeah?"

She had more color in her cheeks now, and he took that as a good sign. Her breathing had steadied, but new worry lines creased her forehead.

"I told them…that the bead was hidden in my engagement ring." She opened her eyes now and angled her head toward him. Her troubled green gaze arrowed through him.

"I had to tell them something, and…"

"Your *engagement* ring, not the wedding ring?"

She nodded. "But when they saw I wasn't wearing it, I told them we'd also pawned the engagement ring. That's probably where they're headed now. They were making a list of all the pawnshops in town to start searching."

"You didn't tell them which shop we used?"

"I couldn't remember which shop we used. I was flustered and trying to give them something to appease them without selling out my country or putting you at risk."

"Me?"

She winced and nodded. "I put the wedding ring in your backpack before I left for the hospital. For safekeeping…in case I—" She didn't finish the thought, only sighed and turned her face away. "I told them we pawned my wedding ring, too. At the time it seemed like the right move. If I'd been mad enough at Brent to pawn my engagement ring for the cash, it seemed logical to me that I'd have also hocked the wedding ring. I figured they'd see that logic, too, so…"

"Makes sense. What's the problem?"

"Well, think about it. What happens when they find the right pawnshop and get my engagement ring?"

"Nothing. You said in the elevator at the hospital that Scofield confirmed the bead was in your *wedding* ring."

"But they're bound to ask for the wedding ring, too. To cover their bases. They'd be stupid not to. And these thugs may be vicious, but I doubt they're stupid."

He connected the dots and sighed. "And when the pawnshop

tells them you *didn't* pawn another ring, they'll know you lied about the wedding ring and put two and two together…"

"And get four." She held up four fingers. "Four words. *Bead in wedding ring.* And they'll be right back on our trail, except now they'll know what they're after."

Jake clenched his teeth, and immediately regretted it when another bolt of pain streaked through his skull. He pinched the bridge of his nose, wishing he had a couple of ibuprofen tablets for his headache. "You did what you thought you had to. Don't get worked up about it."

"I all but told them where the nanotube is hidden!"

He winced when she raised her voice. "But—" He raised his palm, signaling her to hold her volume down. "First they have to find us. We've shaken their tail, and we'll go back to the campground and lay low until we figure out our next move."

Her face brightened, and she pivoted on the seat to face him. "I know our next move. Brent gave me a name. He had a guy in the Centers for Disease Control with whom he'd arranged a clandestine meeting. He was going to give this guy the nanotube, ensuring the virus would be safe within the strict regulations and security measures of the CDC."

Jake frowned. "How do we know we can trust this guy?"

"Brent trusted him. He said he'd vetted him and knew his reputation."

Jake lifted a palm in agreement. "Works for me."

"He told me how to get in touch with this William Gates and give him the wedding ring. Gates would know how to extract the nanotube and recover the virus safely for future testing."

"And the rest of the virus has been destroyed? You know, all of this is for nothing if the Wedding Crashers can get the virus some other way."

"Steward."

Jake pulled a face. "Excuse me?"

"I think the ringleader's name is Steward. I heard Beefy Guy call him that once."

Jake nodded and filed that tidbit of information away.

"And, yes, the rest of the virus is gone. He told me today that one night at the Bancroft laboratory, when he'd known the terrorists were closing in on him, he'd incinerated everything except what was put in the nanotube." She pulled her bottom lip into her teeth, and her shoulders slumped. "But what's in that nanotube is still enough to start a global pandemic if it were properly weaponized."

Jake's chest tightened. He'd seen the effects of biowarfare both in the flesh and in training films. "So this is no ordinary flu we're talking about, I take it."

"Worse than the Spanish flu of 1918."

"That killed fifty million people."

"Yeah."

Jake squeezed the steering wheel harder and muttered a curse.

Behind them, the sun sank low over the horizon, and power poles cast long shadows across the endless rows of farmers' crops they drove past. Time to head back to the campground.

He sent Paige a hard look and braced himself. "Okay, tell me everything Scofield said about getting the ring to this Gates guy."

As they drove back to the campground, Jake listened silently while Paige relayed everything she'd learned from Brent, everything they'd discussed. Everything. His expression remained stony as she revealed how Brent had gotten caught up in the lure of money, how he'd only belatedly realized the buyers posing as federal officials weren't who they'd said. She repeated Brent's instructions on how to contact William Gates, his contact within the CDC.

Whether Jake was simply overwhelmed by the information, as she had been, or if he was mentally dissecting the news and making strategic plans as she now was, she couldn't be certain. His inscrutable face remained hard, his eyes distant.

Was he even listening? How could he hear they were in

possession of a monumentally deadly, incredibly tiny virus sample that terrorists wanted to weaponize and show no outward emotion or reaction at all?

Or maybe he was just as tired from the day's events, as stunned by the ramifications of Brent's research, as boggled by their responsibility to protect the virus as she was. She sighed and leaned back against the headrest.

"I also told Brent it was over, that I didn't love him and couldn't marry him."

Now Jake's head whipped toward her, his face registering intrigue. "You did? How did he take it?"

"He wasn't surprised. He seemed to be expecting it."

Jake said nothing, but he fixed a penetrating gaze on her for several seconds before returning his attention to the road.

"Sad, huh?" She studied his profile in the warm light of the setting sun. "Until a couple days ago, everyone knew I didn't love Brent, that our marriage was a mistake, except me. And my dad. He was so happy to see me marrying Brent. I let my dad's enthusiasm blind me."

"Why, do you think?"

She chortled in disbelief. "Why did I want my dad to approve of my choice of husband? Why did I want my dad to be happy?" She shook her head as if the answer should be obvious. "He's my dad, Jake. I love him."

"So that means his happiness is more important than your own?"

"No! I didn't say that."

"But that's what you were doing, isn't it? Putting your dad's wishes, his needs and happiness, before your own?"

She bristled defensively. "Of course not. I liked Brent well enough. Marrying him seemed logical and practical. We were well matched, and he was the heir apparent to take over the company from my dad, and—"

"Do you hear yourself?" Jake interrupted. His tone vibrated with an edge of anger or frustration that startled Paige.

She blinked at Jake, unsure how to respond.

He dragged a hand over his face and shot her a side glance

that teemed with energy and emotion. The contrast to his earlier stoicism left her breathless.

"You *liked* Brent *well enough?* Marrying him was *practical?*" He snorted in derision. "Paige, you buy a car or a computer because it's *practical.* And saying you liked Brent *well enough* reeks of settling for less than you deserve."

She gaped at him. "I—"

"You don't pick your husband according to your *dad's* choice to run the company. The man you marry should be—"

"Someone who makes *me* happy." She sighed and rolled her eyes. "Yeah, yeah. I've gotten this speech before from Zoey."

"Well, Zoey was right. But I was gonna say he should be someone who gets you hot and bothered, who makes you—"

"Horny? Is that the word you're looking for?" She scoffed, but even discussing sex with Jake made her skin feel too tight, hot and prickly. "'Cause there's a lot more to a marriage than sex, Jake."

He shot her a scowl. "I know that. And, yeah, *horny* works for me. That's part of what I'm saying, but not everything."

Her nerves jangling, Paige let her gaze roam over his hard, square jaw, his large hands gripping the steering wheel, his taut muscles that seemed as tightly wound as hers. Looking at Jake, she remembered her high-school physics class, and the term "potential energy" sprang to mind. He was pure strength, raw power and high-octane fuel ready to ignite. For days she'd felt the sizzle of attraction sparking between them. He'd have to have been dead to have missed it.

Her mouth dried. What would it be like to have all of his energy and intensity focused on her during sex? The thought lit a sensation like firecrackers in her blood.

Jake turned dark, hooded eyes toward her as if he'd read her thoughts. He opened his mouth, then closed it again and frowned before returning his gaze to the road. "The man you marry should be someone who loves you. You deserve that,

Paige. You deserve love and devotion and all that happily-ever-after stuff. The house with the picket fence."

Another pause. "And respect. And friendship. And, yeah… passion. Not just in sex, but…for life. You say you and Brent were the same, but sometimes *same* equals boring. As smart as you are, you should have someone who challenges you, someone you can fight with, someone who'll keep you on your toes and make your life interesting."

She harrumphed. "Maybe I don't want to fight with my husband. Maybe I like boring. Sometimes boring equals security and order. Maybe those things are more important to me than whether I have a great sex life." She gritted her teeth, wondering how they'd gotten on such a personal subject. Wondering why she was so uncomfortable defending her position to Jake.

Wondering if maybe she was getting a glimpse of Jake's deepest yearnings cleverly disguised as a dissection of *her* life.

Paige drew her bottom lip between her teeth, mulling that possibility. "And maybe that's what *you're* looking for in a wife. Someone passionate and interesting and spontaneous." All things she wasn't. With that realization, her heart sank. They might have sparks between them, but she and Jake had vast differences that made any future together impossible.

"I'm not marriage material, so that's a moot point."

He was shutting her out again, and after the intimate examination of her choices, his retreat raised her temper. "What does that mean, not marriage material? You think because you didn't have a traditional family growing up, because the navy released you from combat duty, that somehow you're unwanted or unworthy of a family?"

"Leave it alone, Paige." He pinched the bridge of his nose and squeezed his eyes shut as if in pain.

She remembered his head injury, and her irritation fled, replaced with concern. "Is your head okay? Should we take you to the E.R.?"

He gave his head a small shake. "Naw, I'll be fine. I've got a goose egg, maybe a cut, but it doesn't hurt that bad. If I start showing symptoms of a concussion, I'll let you know."

She stared at him skeptically. "Promise? You're not just being the tough guy, playing through the pain?"

He sent her a quick, stiff grin. "I'm fine. And we have more important matters to discuss than my reasons for not marrying. Like how to get that nanotube to Gates."

He narrowed his eyes and firmed his mouth. "Walking into the CDC offices and just handing it to him is not an option. Security at the CDC offices, the terrorists on our tail, the history of this case make that pretty obvious. I mean, Scofield had a rendezvous off the Jamaican coast set up for the transfer. And we don't have the luxury of time to make the kind of intricate arrangements Scofield was planning." Jake shifted restlessly on the front seat as he drove, and a tingle of apprehension nipped Paige's spine.

"But we can't go off half-cocked either. We have to make a workable plan. Including contingencies." The urgency she'd hoped to put in her tone sounded tremulous, more like fear. Yet she couldn't deny Jake's fly-by-the-seat-of-your-pants approach was more than a little worrisome to her.

Jake sent her a side glance. "Ever hear the expression, 'Man plans, God laughs'? As you discovered today for yourself, you can't plan for every possible twist of fate. It's better to play it by ear." He squared his shoulders, and a muscle in his jaw twitched. "I know I failed Brent at the wedding. I know I failed you today when those goons grabbed you. But if you'll trust me with this, I promise I will do whatever it takes to protect the nanotube from the terrorists. And I would die before I let them hurt you."

A chill slithered down her back. "I believe you."

But Jake dying in the course of this mission was exactly what she feared.

Chapter 13

That evening, Paige and Jake built their own campfire and shared a meal of tuna sandwiches and potato chips from the nonperishable supply of food Jake had bought earlier. As meals went, tuna was hardly gourmet, chips not exactly healthy, but Paige savored every bite of her dinner. Being kidnapped, facing death and losing her lunch had left her starving and more appreciative of simple things.

Eating beside the glowing campfire with Jake made the food feel special, romantic.

Until she thought of his declaration that afternoon. *I'm not marriage material.*

She'd known as much about Jake, yet the reminder plucked at her, left her off balance and feeling empty. She shifted on the hard log-bench, but her discomfort had more to do with her conversation with Jake about the qualifications of her husband-to-be.

"We should get a new rental car. The Wedding Crashers have seen this one—" Jake hitched his head toward the Taurus. "—and will be looking for it."

His comment snapped her out of her musings and back to the more pressing issue that faced them. For all his talk of playing things by ear, Jake was clearly in strategy mode. He sat on the ground with his legs crossed and his back propped against the fat log where she sat. His gaze was distant, meditative, as he stared into the fire.

"Wouldn't it be faster to fly to Atlanta? We still have some cash from the engagement ring for airline tickets." She glanced at him then poked idly at the fire with a stick she'd found and intended to use to roast marshmallows later.

"Airport's probably being watched. Atlanta is only a day's drive, and this way we have our own transportation, more control over our situation."

Paige nodded her agreement. The more control they had over the transfer of the ring, the nanotube, the virus, the better.

A movement in her peripheral vision startled Paige, made her heart jump. She jerked her head toward the edge of their campsite and spotted Nate, the stray black cat.

Paige took a cleansing breath. She'd been jumpy ever since they got back. Though Jake had assured her they hadn't been followed, she didn't feel as safe tonight as she had previous nights at the campground.

She watched Nate creep forward, sniffing the air. His gaze zeroed in on her tuna sandwich, and he meowed plaintively.

"Hey, Nate, ole boy. You want some of this tuna, don't you?" she cooed softly.

Jake snorted. "Is the Pope Catholic?"

Paige shoved to her feet, went inside the camper to retrieve a paper plate and another can of tuna. After opening the can and dumping the contents on the plate, she carried her offering to Nate outside.

The cat scurried back a few steps when she approached, although his nose twitched and his eyes were bright with anticipation.

Paige set the plate down and stepped back. Nate blinked at her, then cautiously crept forward to eat. She backed away quietly, careful not to spook their dinner guest, and rejoined Jake by the fire. "The poor thing is starved."

Jake glanced toward the cat, who wolfed down the canned tuna. "I'm sure he finds plenty of scraps around here in the trash. And a wild cat like that is bound to be a good hunter."

"Maybe. I still feel sorry for him."

"Because you have a soft heart." Jake wrapped his hand around hers and stroked her wrist with his thumb. The delicate caress stirred her pulse and sent heady sensations humming through her.

The crackling of the fire, the chirping of the summer frogs and the sough of a light breeze in the leaves sang a lulling harmony. If she didn't know better, she could almost believe that nothing existed outside the bubble of light created by their campfire. Almost.

She watched Nate gobbling his dinner and savored the quiet moment. After wolfing down most of the food, the cat sat up, licking his lips, and regarded her with a satisfied look on his face.

"He seems like such a sweet cat. He'd have made someone a good pet if he hadn't been abandoned out here."

Jake's only response was a grunt of acknowledgment, and when she turned to study his profile in the flickering light from the fire, she realized how much Nate and Jake had in common.

Alone in the world. No family. No real home. Clearly needing the affection she had to offer but too scarred by their pasts to risk letting her get close. So much potential for love lost to a greater fear of getting hurt.

"Heartbreaking…" she murmured.

"He'll be fine." Jake dropped her hand to pick up a stick and poke at the glowing coals. "He'll have a tougher life than a pampered house cat, but he'll be okay."

Paige swallowed hard to clear the lump from her throat. "Will he?"

Leaning back against the log-bench and stacking his

hands behind his head, Jake met her gaze. "Sure he will. 'Cause there'll always be another softy like you through the campground who'll feed him and look out for him, even if they can't turn him into a pet."

Paige felt her eyes water, and she jerked her gaze away.

Nate stood and stretched his lithe body before giving a soft meow and trotting off into the night. *There'll always be another softy.*

But, *damn it,* what if she didn't want him drifting from one soft heart to the next, rambling through life? Rootless. Searching. Never giving real love a chance.

Maybe she wanted to be the one to tame him, give him a home, give him her heart.

Paige bit her bottom lip and watched the cat disappear into the black shadows, realizing the one she wanted so desperately to share her love with…wasn't Nate.

It was Jake.

Jake woke abruptly in the wee hours of the night with a pervading sense that something was not right. He strained to listen, thinking that maybe a suspicious sound had roused him.

The crickets chirped. The frogs sang. A mosquito buzzed near his ear. All else was quiet. Still.

Too quiet.

And he knew what had woken him. Not a new sound, but the absence of Paige's quiet snoring.

He sat up and strained to peer through the dark camper to Paige's bed. He perked his ears, listening for the light rasp of her breathing. Nothing.

His pulse hammered, and he swung his legs off the bed and crept across the shadowed camper. "Paige?" he whispered harshly.

No answer. Her bed was empty.

Paige was gone.

Every muscle in his body tensed. The panic that had consumed him earlier in the day when he'd seen Paige grabbed and thrown into the blue car swamped him again. Except a sharper fear sliced through him. This afternoon, he'd seen who took Paige, had been able to follow the car, had known he'd get Paige back somehow...whatever it took. Now, he had no leads. He'd slept through her disappearance. He'd failed her when she needed him.

Pain ripped through his chest. Guilt and recriminations gnawed his gut. Fisting his hands, he began pacing the tiny floor of the camper. He had to do something, had to find her, had to—

Jake paused and dropped his chin to his chest. *Slow down. Think. Don't let your emotions run away and blind you.*

Damn it, that was the problem. Where Paige was concerned, he'd been letting his emotions get in the way, distract him from the job he had to do. He swallowed hard, clearing his mind and gritting his teeth. She'd promised not to go anywhere without him, but...maybe she'd just stepped outside for a minute. Maybe she'd just gone to the bathroom, or...

He flipped his wrist and checked his watch. Three o'clock.

Would Paige have really gone anywhere in the dark woods in the middle of the night alone? Not likely, but he had to check.

Wasting no time, he grabbed a flashlight and his gun and bolted from the camper.

"Paige?" he called, not caring who he woke. He swept the beam of light around the dark campground as he hurried toward the bathhouse. His head throbbed, his bad knee ached, but he ignored the pain. Rocks and sticks jabbed the soles of his bare feet, but he wouldn't take the time shoes required. Those seconds could be the difference between finding Paige in time or...not.

"Paige?" He startled a deer grazing at the edge of the camping area. His own pulse staggered, and he quickened his step. "Paige!"

As he neared the bathhouse, he heard two unmistakable noises. Water running...a shower.

And a low moaning,

Heart in his throat, Jake burst into the women's bathhouse, following the noises. "Paige!"

A gasp. "Jake?"

He darted toward the shower stalls, gun up, ready.

With a sweep of his hand, he shoved back the curtain of the first stall.

Nothing. The second. Empty.

The third.

Paige screamed. Her eyes flew to the gun.

"Do you mind?" she grated, her eyes flashing angrily.

She was alone. Unharmed. Safe.

Relief flowed through him so hard and fast it left his knees weak. He braced a hand on the tile wall, catching his breath. He set the gun and flashlight on the bench in the dressing area of the shower stall and tried to hide the tremble in his hands.

Then anger flooded him as the fear receded.

"Of all the stupid..." He aimed a finger at her, his rage tightening his muscles and making his head throb.

"Jake, get out!"

"I told you not to go anywhere without me! After today, I'd have thought the reason why would be painfully clear!"

Her gaze returned the daggers he shot her. "Jake! Get. Out!"

"Hell, Paige, do you have any idea what I thought when I woke up and you were gone?" He jammed a hand through his hair, while the mix of postpanic adrenaline and gut-grinding frustration seesawed sickly in his stomach.

"I'm sorry I worried you," she grated through clenched teeth, not sounding the slightest bit repentant. "Now, get the hell out of my shower!"

He drew a breath to fling another accusing assault at her, but stopped. Like a dousing with icy water, her shouted command finally penetrated the red haze of anger and fear that had tied him in knots since he woke up minutes ago. He stiffened. Took a step back.

And looked at her. Really looked at her.

Her eyes were red and puffy from crying—the moaning sound he'd heard. He absorbed the misery in her eyes like a kick in the chest. What had made her cry? Why—?

"Please, Jake…" She glared at him, but her pink-cheeked expression held something else…

And then he dared to let his gaze drift from her face.

Like a stunned child stating the obvious, his brain registered what he should have recognized sooner. If he hadn't been so wrapped up in his fear and subsequent fury.

She was showering. She was…naked.

Paige had her arms crossed over her chest and her lower body turned ninety degrees, giving him a profile view. A sultry, curvy, mouth-drying view.

His entire body tensed, and he stood paralyzed, mesmerized. Thrumming.

He followed the rivulets of water that coursed from her wet hair, slicked to her scalp and hanging in thick ropes around her shoulders. The hot shower spray pounded her pale skin, the heat leaving her ivory complexion tinted with a rosy hue. Billows of steam swirled around her, creating a dreamlike quality to the erotic image she cast.

Pounding desire stirred in his belly and spread fiery tongues through his blood.

An alarm screamed in his head, warning him away, but his feet were rooted, his attention locked on the vision straight out of his sexiest fantasies.

"Jake?"

The trembling, quizzical quality of Paige's voice, more than the sound of his name, brought his gaze back to hers.

A puzzled frown knit the bridge of her nose, and her jade eyes searched his.

Worried. Curious. Wanting…

As he studied her face, trying to decipher the myriad emotions swirling in her eyes, her gaze gave him the same slow, measured scrutiny he'd given her. His bare feet, bare chest, boxer briefs that did little to hide his state of arousal.

Damn. In his panic, in his rush to find her, he'd not so much as pulled on his jeans before bolting from the camper into the night. He was as good as naked himself. In a steamy shower. With a woman whose vulnerable green eyes and sensual lips had been tempting him for days.

Double damn.

"You've been crying," he said inanely, his voice thick. *Again with the childlike stating of the obvious. Good job, McCall. Brilliant.*

"I…kept thinking about…today when…well, I c-couldn't sleep and…I didn't want to wake you." Her chin trembled slightly before she bit her bottom lip to stop it.

Her eyes teared up again, and his heart squeezed until he couldn't breathe.

"I'm sorry, Jake." He could barely hear her whisper over the whoosh of the water. "I d-didn't mean to scare you."

He couldn't answer. His mouth was too dry, his throat too tight.

Her eyes flickered down his body again. Her pupils grew to large, dark pools, and desire glowed in their fathomless depths.

Where before he couldn't make his feet move, now he couldn't stop himself from closing the distance between them. The shower spray soaked him as he slid a hand to the nape of her neck and drew her to him. He dipped his head and captured her lips.

And he was lost.

The touch of Jake's lips sent the third shock in as many minutes to her overtaxed nerves—his sudden armed appearance in her shower, the realization that he, too, was virtually naked…and highly aroused. And now the electrifying jolt as his lips seized hers. The surge of energy, the crackling sensation that swamped her, short-circuited any semblance of reason or clear thinking. They must have. Why else would she be wrapping her arms around his neck and pressing the full length of her body against the hot, hard length of his?

She curled her fingers into his hair, angling her head to deepen the kiss. Shimmering sparks shot through her and coalesced low in her belly. Her hips canted forward, straining toward his as the hot, pulsing need in her grew.

A pleasured moan rumbled from her throat, and Jake answered in kind. She met the thrust of his tongue with an eager parry. A muddle of lust left her light-headed and blissfully muzzy. When her legs trembled, he folded her into his embrace, one hand sliding over her bottom to anchor her, the other splayed on her thigh.

And still they weren't close enough for her. She clambered to rise on her toes, to hook her leg around his hip. Sinking his fingers into her bottom, Jake scooted her against the tile wall and lifted her so that her hips were in perfect alignment with his. She rode the thick ridge of his arousal and gasped as powerful shock waves ripped through her.

They were in a public shower. But instead of deterring her, knowing they could be caught was exciting, enticing…slightly scandalous. Highly erotic.

They had terrorists after them. But instead of sobering her, the element of danger, the fear she'd already survived heightened her senses, made the moment sharper, clearer, more intense.

Jake was the wrong man for her in so many ways…though at the moment her overwhelmed brain couldn't conjure one. All Paige knew was the flood of fiery sensation flowing through her.

Need clawed her. Desire sizzled through her blood. Reason was tossed aside as the chaotic frenzy in her body shouted down rational thought.

She tightened the grip her legs had around his hips and, secure in the solid strength of his arms, she leaned back, giving him access to her breasts. Jake's hungry mouth descended on one tautly budded nipple while the warm shower spray lashed the other. The gentle tug of his lips, light scrape of his teeth and erotic flick of his tongue battered her with tingling heat. The urgency pounding inside her ramped to the edge of control.

"Jake," she rasped, arching her throat. Feeling the first quiver of climax.

But she didn't want to shatter yet. She wanted him with her. Inside her. "Please…"

She raked her fingers down his back to grab the wet fabric of his briefs. Awkwardly, she tugged them down, fighting them past the grip of her legs, the bulge of his erection. Finally, with a quick swipe of his hand, Jake shoved the briefs down his thighs.

Admiring the masculine beauty of him, Paige stroked her fingers along the length and heat of him. Jake bucked and tensed, making a strangled sounding moan.

"Oh, Paige…that. Feels. So. Good." He shuddered as if barely containing himself, and the pure pleasure on his face infused her with a sense of empowerment and joy, a carnal freedom that sweetened what was already shockingly satisfying.

His gaze locked with hers. Hot. Dark. Penetrating.

And dismayed. His jaw tightened.

"We don't have protection," he rasped, his voice deep and full of frustration.

She blinked, nodded. "I'm on the pill."

The relief that washed over his face would have been comical had she not been so tightly wound, so ready to come apart. Impatient for the climax hovering just beyond her grasp, Paige wrapped her arms around his neck and pulled herself up. And sank onto him.

He filled her, stretched her, stroked her in just the right way. A feeling of completion that had nothing to do with the mind-numbing physical sensations zinging through her body settled in her heart. She felt whole in a way she never had before. The joining of their bodies felt cosmically ordained.

And intensely stimulating.

As Jake thrust deeper, the tidal wave of sensations stole her breath. He pistoned his hips, driving deeper and pushing her closer to the edge. She arched her neck, and he pressed hot, openmouthed kisses along the curve of her throat. A low growl vibrated in his chest, swelling to a roar of satisfaction as his body shuddered and his grip tightened. His lusty groan sent her crashing into her own sweet oblivion. The powerful throb of her body matched the thundering beat in her chest.

She held Jake tightly, resting her face against his shoulder and mentally staggering under the assault of emotions she'd never known before. With her logical mind turned off, her heart screamed what she'd tried to deny before now.

She loved Jake.

She never wanted to be without him. Would do anything to make him happy. Wanted to give herself over to him, not only physically but spiritually, emotionally…completely. That was the wholeness she'd experienced when they'd joined their bodies, the sense that she'd found her soul mate.

This was the fulfilling joy and deep affection that had assured Holly that Matt was her future. The kind of passion and devotion that led Zoey to leave home and follow her boyfriend around the country.

The kind of happiness and ardor she'd never felt for Brent. When stripped of her defenses and the protests of her analytical brain, the depth of her feelings for Jake couldn't be ignored.

Recognizing her feelings for what they were should have given her a sense of peace. Instead, her gut clenched, and her strategic mind whispered, *"So you love him. What are you going to do about it?"*

For that question, she had no answer.

Jake wore the beach towel Paige had taken to the shower around his waist as they hurried back through the dark grounds to their camper. Once safely ensconced inside, he ripped the towel off and drew her back into his arms.

"Just so you know, before I left the hospital after the bombing in Iraq, I was tested for just about everything you can imagine. There's been no one since then. You're safe with me." She hadn't asked, had trusted him at the bathhouse, but he wanted her to know, to be certain.

Paige blinked at him, then let her gaze skim down his naked body, her eyes darkening with desire again. "No one? In...how long ago did you leave the SEALs?"

"Couple years now." He smoothed a hand along her cheek, dropped a kiss on her forehead. "Let's just say...I had other priorities in recent months. And the idea of one-night stands left me cold."

She tipped her head, opened her mouth as if she wanted to comment on his confession, but she snapped her mouth closed again, and her brow furrowed thoughtfully. "Mm. And I've only been with Brent. So you're safe with me, too."

He stiffened when she mentioned Scofield's name but tried to hide his guilty reaction. Scofield had hired Jake to protect him, then given him the charge of keeping Paige safe. Jake gritted his teeth. He'd done neither.

What he *had* done was ravish his client's fiancée mere days after taking over her protection. *Ex-fiancée,* a voice in his head corrected. Although what difference did it make, really? She was off-limits.

Some bodyguard he made. He couldn't even protect Paige from himself.

Sobering, he stepped back from her and balled his hands at his sides. "I'm sorry about... I shouldn't have..." He huffed his frustration. Who was he kidding? He wasn't a bit sorry. Making love to Paige had been pure nirvana, an experience he'd cherish in the lonely days and months to come.

Paige lifted a delicate eyebrow and stepped closer. "Did I complain?" She trailed a finger down his chest, and his nerve endings fired like live wires. "We both wanted it."

He drew a deep breath, trying to steel himself to the effect of her skin brushing his as she shed her bathrobe and pressed herself more fully against him. "That doesn't make it any less of a mistake."

She frowned and lifted wounded eyes to his. "Why is it a mistake?"

He gripped her arms to push her away but couldn't bring himself to move her back. She felt too good, fit too perfectly against him. Holding her felt too…right.

He shook his head to clear his thoughts. "Sex muddies the picture. Blurs the lines between us. And I…I can't give you the commitment you need."

She tilted her head back, a wrinkle at the bridge of her nose. "Did I ask for a commitment? I'm willing to wait for you, to give you time…"

He sighed. "I don't want to hurt you, Paige."

"Then don't." She rose on her toes to press a kiss to his lips. A rush of heat swept through him.

Rallying his defenses, he tightened his grip on her arms and met her gaze with a hard stare. "Paige, look at me and tell me that you're not, even as we speak, forming emotional attachments to me, telling yourself how your feelings for me have deepened because of what just happened. Tell me you're not thinking that things are different between us now."

Her eyes glistened with tears. "Things *are* different now, Jake."

He shook his head. "No. Nothing's changed. We're still the same people we were two hours ago—with different paths, different lives, different needs. Don't convince yourself you're falling in love. Believing you have feelings for me will only lead to heartache, Paige."

She pressed her mouth in a firm line and stepped back. "Earlier today, you told me different was good. That it would keep me on my toes and make my life interesting. That I needed someone with passion in order to be happy."

"I know, but I meant—"

"You make me happy, Jake." She reached for him again and raked cool fingers through his damp hair. "You can't deny we have passion together…in spades. We just proved that. And if you give me a chance, I'll prove to you how much I *do* love you."

His gut clenched, and a viselike pressure squeezed his heart. "Paige, don't…"

Her arms circled his neck, and she trailed butterfly kisses along his jaw, stealing his breath. "Don't shut me out, Jake. I know you've been hurt but, please…let me love you."

Gritting his teeth, he fought down the swell of pain in his chest. He'd heard similar requests before. From foster mothers asking him to trust. Only to betray him and send him away when he reached out.

By SEAL officers demanding his best, his commitment. Only to cut him loose after he'd sacrificed everything for his country.

How could he justify risking his heart with Paige? If he let himself love her, then lost her—

He didn't finish the thought. Just the suggestion revived the horror and sickening panic that had seized him when she'd been grabbed this afternoon. When he'd failed to keep her safe. What if—

With shattering clarity, the truth raked through him. What if he took the risk of loving Paige and failed her in some way? If he couldn't make her happy, if he couldn't keep her safe, if he couldn't give her the kind of life she deserved.

If she left him…

He shuddered, and Paige hugged him tighter. "Give me a chance to prove to you how much I care," she said, her voice cracking.

Jake buried his face in her hair, inhaling the sweet scent of her shampoo. He wanted to memorize her scent, the way she felt in his arms, the way her breath caressed his skin.

"Make love to me again, Jake," she whispered and tugged him toward her bed.

The air caught in his lungs. He wanted her so much it hurt, but how could he make love to her and not lose another piece of himself to her?

"Please, Jake. Trust me…." She nibbled the sensitive spot on his throat, and blood whooshed past his ears, left his head buzzing.

Maybe he couldn't give her a future, but he had the chance

tonight to show her what she meant to him. He could give her one night.

And he'd store up the memories of their passion for the cold and empty days to come.

Chapter 14

The jostling of the camper bed woke Paige early the next morning, and she rubbed bleary eyes to bring the day into focus. A sweet ache in her muscles revived memories of hours spent last night, her body twined with Jake's. Her heart swelled until she thought it might burst.

She touched a tender spot on her neck where Jake's unshaven chin had gently abraded her, and she smiled. Last night, Jake had been tender, and patient, and thorough.

Then demanding, and thrilling, and intense.

They'd probably woken their neighbors with their noise, but she didn't care. Making love to Jake had been better each time. Beyond her wildest dreams.

She propped on her elbow, letting the sheet slide low on her breasts, and watched Jake move around the tiny camper.

"Good morning, hot stuff." She gave him a coy grin to match her singsong tone.

He turned from shoving his spare clothes into his backpack and regarded her with a serious expression. Too serious.

"Morning," he mumbled. And turned away to continue stuffing the backpack.

She shoved down the niggling concern over his behavior and folded back the corner of the sheet. "Wanna come back to bed for a while?"

When he glanced over his shoulder, she waggled her eyebrows suggestively.

Jake's jaw tensed, and a muscle twitched in his cheek. "Can't. We gotta go. We're leaving as soon as we can get packed up."

More than the finality of his announcement, his brusque tone sent a shiver to her marrow. Where was the man whose deep, lulling voice had whispered sweet nothings as he'd joined their bodies just hours ago? Where was the warmth and affection that had been in every touch, every look, every kiss?

"Why the rush? Has something happened?"

"Nothing new. I just want to get on the road. Atlanta is at least eight hours away, and the sooner we get near a cell tower so we can call Gates, the better," he said without looking at her.

Paige tugged the sheet back up, clutching it under her chin, feeling self-conscious in the wake of Jake's cool attitude this morning. She gnawed her bottom lip, reviewing everything that had been said last night. What had caused his withdrawal?

He'd tried to distance himself after they'd made love in the shower, but she'd thought they'd moved beyond his fears and doubts when they'd spent the rest of the night in each other's arms. Was he having second thoughts? Regrets? A relapse of his commitment fears?

A heavy, cold ball of dread settled in her stomach. Hadn't last night shown him how much she cared? What else did she need to do to prove her feelings to him?

Paige knew they had more pressing issues facing them today, matters of national security, desperate terrorists on their tail, a deadly virus to keep safe. But how could she face

Jake, face her future, if she didn't find a way to work things out between them?

"Jake, about last night—"

"You better get dressed. It shouldn't take more than a half hour or so to get the camper folded down and hitched up to the Taurus. We can eat breakfast on the road."

Paige clenched her teeth when he interrupted. Clearly he thought last night was a closed subject. He was wrong.

Wrapping the sheet around her, she swung her feet over the side of the bed and nailed him with a hard stare. "What's wrong with you? Why are you being so abrupt and distant this morning?"

"Nothing's wrong. I just want to trade out the rental car for one the terrorists haven't seen and get on the road. The sooner we get the ring to Gates, the sooner we put this nightmare behind us."

"And then what?"

He paused and sent her a confused look. "What do you mean?"

"What happens to us after we give the ring to Gates?"

Jake shrugged. "Well, the Wedding Crashers will have no real reason to come after us. We won't have the virus anymore." He paused and frowned, adding, "Except that we can identify them to the authorities...hell. Well, we'll cross that bridge later."

A chill slithered down Paige's back. Even when this was over, it might not be *over* over. Would the terrorists come after them to silence them? Paige shook her head and shoved that frightening thought aside. One problem at a time.

"No, I mean what about *us?* What happens to you and me, our relationship? Last night was—"

"Great." He forced a smile. "Is that what you want to hear? Last night was fantastic. The best. But like I told you, there is no *us.* Not now, not when this is over."

Paige squeezed the sheet in her hand until her knuckles were bloodless. Her head reeled dizzily. "But last night—"

"See? This is why I said it was a mistake. You're reading

more into what happened than there was. It's distracting you from the bigger picture of getting that nanotube to Scofield's guy at the CDC. That is our one and only job. Got it?"

So that's how he wanted it, huh? The heat of anger and frustration swirled through her, mixing with the weight of hurt crushing her chest. She yanked the sheet back and stomped to her suitcase to find something clean to wear. With her jaw taut and her motions jerky, Paige dressed silently, occasionally shooting a dark look toward Jake. Though she resented being treated so coldly, especially after the deep intimacy they'd shared last night, she knew better than to push the issue of their future with him. He was preoccupied with delivering the ring to Brent's CDC contact. Surely, once the virus was safely transferred to the CDC, she'd get the chance to prove her love to Jake, and they'd get past his commitment issues. Wouldn't they?

Last night, she'd been certain they could. She'd tasted the kind of happiness Holly had with Matt, and Paige had seen the life she wanted with Jake.

But in light of Jake's withdrawal this morning, a tremor of uncertainty and a cold frisson of fear clouded her bright outlook.

As she threw her dirty clothes into her suitcase and zipped it closed, her lungs tightened until she could barely breathe. All her life she'd dealt with trouble by analyzing and problem solving. But her relationship with Jake wasn't an issue that could be critically dissected and solved through logic and elbow grease. This was a matter of the heart, of her soul, of her emotions. She was out of her league, didn't know if she could find the resolution and the happy ending she wanted so desperately. This emotional minefield scared her more than the Wedding Crashers or deadly viruses.

Because she could lose Jake.

Jake turned on his prepaid cell phone and checked the reception as soon as they hit the main highway into town. Service was still questionable, and since he didn't want to risk the call being dropped, he decided to wait a few minutes before trying to call William Gates. He handed the phone to Paige. "Keep an eye on the reception. When we have all the bars, I'll call Gates."

"*I* can call Gates."

Her tone was churlish, but he couldn't blame her. His behavior this morning had to have hurt her. But he couldn't let her see what last night had meant to him. He needed to make a clean break from her, and any mixed messages from him would only make their inevitable separation harder for her.

He rubbed a hot spot on his chest, but the ache, the gnawing pain wasn't a surface injury. The hurt was deep. Internal. Agonizing.

Because his heart was breaking.

He hadn't wanted to get involved with Paige, hating the idea of hurting her. But he'd never considered how much an ill-advised tryst with Paige would wound him. He'd let his emotions get in the way of what he knew was right and distract him from his assignment.

Protect the nanotube. And protect Paige.

The best way to accomplish the first goal was to shove down the nagging heartache that consumed him when he thought of leaving Paige. Focus on getting to Atlanta undetected and transferring Paige's wedding ring to William Gates.

The second goal…

His brain rebelled. He hated even considering what Paige's best interest meant for him. But Paige needed a man who could give her stability, family, long-term happiness. His life, to date, had been anything but stable. He knew nothing about building a family. And he had serious doubts about keeping a well-bred, wealthy career woman like Paige happy—outside the bedroom, that is—when he knew nothing of the lifestyle she was accustomed to. Hell, she hadn't even been *camping* before this week with him. They had almost nothing in common.

You told me different was good. That it would keep me on my toes and make my life interesting. Paige's accusation from last night haunted him. He'd believed what he'd told her when he said it. But he'd never imagined he could be the one to shake up Paige's staid, regimented life, challenge her, help her see that her own happiness wasn't based on pleasing others.

Paige's prepaid cell phone rang, jarring Jake from his thoughts. He sent her a quizzical look. "Did you give your number to anyone?"

"Not…exactly. But…" She checked the phone's screen. "Holly apparently got the number from her caller ID when I talked to her earlier."

Jake sighed. "Make it quick. Don't tell her where we're going…in case someone is listening."

Paige's green eyes still held shades of anger and hurt, and now, as she punched the button to answer her sister's call, wary concern darkened her gaze. She spoke briefly with her sister, assuring her she was safe, listening with increasing consternation to whatever report Holly gave, then hung up and turned to him. "Brent came through his surgery fine. They kept him sedated the rest of the evening, but when he woke up this morning, he asked to see my dad. Holly says Brent and Dad talked for over an hour, and when Dad came out, all he would say is, 'Call Paige and check on her. I have arrangements to handle.' She wanted to know if I knew what kind of arrangements Dad could have meant." She pressed her fingers to her eyes and drew a shaky breath. "You don't think Brent would have told my dad what is going on, do you? He'd been so secretive about the nanotube and the virus before…" She dropped her hands to her lap and sent him a wide-eyed look shimmering with fear. "Jake, what if Brent has involved my dad in this mess? If he put my dad in danger, put him on the terrorists' radar with some errand or sensitive information, I'll…I'll kill him myself!"

Jake bit down so hard on his back teeth his jaw ached. Having Neil Bancroft involved with this assignment could throw a monkey wrench into things. God only knew what Brent had told Bancroft to do, and Jake hated surprises. But he wouldn't put it past Scofield to panic, call in reserves, whether those reserves were qualified to handle the situation or not. And in Bancroft's case, most likely not.

"If the terrorists go after my family to manipulate me—" Paige's voice trembled, choked with tears.

He stretched a hand toward Paige to soothe her agitation, but quickly thought better of touching her. Sitting this close to her, smelling her shampoo and hearing her quaking sighs made it hard enough to keep his mind off her and the way they'd passed the late hours of the night. He snatched his hand back and squeezed the steering wheel. "Let's not borrow trouble. Your dad is a smart man. He knows something dangerous is happening. He saw what happened at the church. By now he's heard about the break-in and bodies in Brent's office. I guarantee he's hired extra protection for the family, alerted the police, done everything in his power to lock down the company."

Paige nodded. "Holly mentioned something about that when we talked yesterday." She frowned. "But I didn't see anyone guarding her at the hospital."

"They were there. I saw them."

"You did?"

"I've learned to spot so-called undercover protection. It's possible Holly didn't even know she was being watched. These guys were good, but I recognized them for what they were."

"How do you know they weren't with the terrorists?"

He sighed. "I just knew. I have enough training, enough hands-on experience to just…*know.* There were telltale signs. For instance, after I found you, while you traded back clothes with Holly, there was a guy near the restroom with a bulge under his scrubs who lingered too long writing in a chart. He checked his cell a couple times, glanced at me and clearly recognized me, but did nothing. Meaning he was on our side."

"Why didn't you tell me any of this earlier?"

He shrugged. "Maybe I should have, but if you'll remember, not long after that you were grabbed, and later…"

"And later?"

He scowled. "Why can't you trust me? Trust that I'm doing what I have to to keep you and the nanotube safe? If I don't explain every step, every detail to you, it's because I don't see where it is important for you to know."

"It's not important for me to know my family is being protected?" Exasperation and sarcasm saturated her tone.

"I didn't say that, and…could we not argue the point?"

"Oh, but I need someone to fight with." She crossed her arms over her chest. "Or don't you remember that element of your perfect man for me?"

Jake squeezed the steering wheel tighter. "Paige, I'm not—"

"Yeah, you've made that point perfectly clear." She huffed angrily. "Just…forget it."

When he glanced at her, her chin was trembling, but she quickly firmed her mouth and turned toward the passenger window. Her rigid silence sliced deep into his heart.

And Jake knew the pain might never go away.

Several times over the next six hours, Jake tried to call William Gates to set up a meeting, but Brent's CDC contact didn't answer either of the phone numbers Brent had given her. Paige could tell the inability to reach Gates was wearing on Jake as much as it frayed her own jittery nerves.

Still, she gave Jake the silent treatment for the majority of the trip to Atlanta. Not because she didn't have plenty she wanted tell him, but because every time she tried to bring up issues she felt were unresolved between them, her throat would clog with emotion. She didn't want Jake to know how deeply he'd hurt her, or how concerned she was about meeting with Gates.

With each passing mile, she grew more restless. She was desperate to work out a backup plan, in case they couldn't reach Gates. The one time she'd broached the subject of calling the Atlanta police to escort them to the meeting, to provide security for the exchange, Jake flatly turned the idea down.

"The cops will want to know where we got the virus, will have to call in Homeland Security—which Scofield said to avoid—will have a boatload of red tape and questions that will delay us…" He vigorously shook his head. "No. No way. The idea is to keep this as simple and low-key as possible. Go in, hand off the ring and get out. Period. Clean, surgical, fast. Bringing in the cops is the opposite of low-key, Paige."

"Okay! I get it. I just wish we had some kind of contingency, some fallback plan in case—"

"In case I screw up?"

Paige balled her hands, growling her frustration with Jake. "No! Just in case something goes wrong."

He took a deep breath and blew it out slowly. "Look, I know the plan's not perfect, but I can think on my feet. It's what I do, Paige. This kind of assignment is what I'm trained for."

"I know, but…planning and problem solving are who *I* am."

Jake drummed the steering wheel with his thumbs, his mouth pulled in a grim line. "Scofield trusted me to see this through. Why can't you?"

Paige's lungs contracted. She did trust Jake, didn't she? So why was it so hard to let go of the restless need to call in outside help? They'd come this far alone. The transfer of the ring was a simple enough process.

Go in, hand off the ring and get out. They could do that alone. Right?

After a moment, when she still hadn't answered him, Jake turned to meet her gaze. His dark eyes held a penetrating seriousness that matched their grave situation. But something more as well…

A question. A plea. A *need*.

Her answer, her *trust* meant a great deal to him, though he'd never say as much. Seeing this yearning, this…*vulnerability* in her hero warrior rocked her to her core. For all his posturing and protests, despite his emotional distance and barriers, Jake cared. Enough to need her trust. Not just on some strategic level, but on a deeply personal level.

For a man who'd felt betrayed and rejected so many times in his life, trust was not only hard to give, but also as much of a need as oxygen or water. Or love.

She tried to swallow past the lump in her throat, tell him that she did trust him, that he could trust her—with his heart…

But his cell rang.

The moment was lost. The spell broken. The gossamer connection severed.

Jake snatched the phone up from the console between the seats and checked the caller ID. His eyes widened. "It's Gates."

Jake thumbed the answer button and raised the phone to his ear. "Hello?"

"This is Will Gates. I see by my caller ID that you've called here several times today. Is there something I can do for you?"

"Yes, sir. Thank you for calling back. My name is Jake McCall, and I'm a friend of Brent Scofield's."

He paused briefly to see how Gates reacted to the name.

Silence. Then, warily, "Go on."

Pulling in a deep breath, Jake launched into an explanation, starting from the day Scofield had hired him as a bodyguard and finishing with their request to meet him and release the nanotube into the care and keeping of the CDC. "We could meet you at your office if you'd like, but I thought it might be better if we—"

"No! Not my office. That'd be tricky on many levels. Security protocols, the attention you'd attract. I—" Gates hesitated, and Jake heard him sigh, the sound full of the man's indecision and reluctance to get involved. "Are you sure there's no other way? Homeland Security—"

"Is not an option, according to Scofield. He believes there are individuals within relevant agencies with ties to the terrorists. But as soon as you get the virus locked up at CDC, you do whatever you feel you must."

"I don't know. Are you sure the nanotube is safe? I can't expose my family to a deadly virus."

Jake spent the next five minutes convincing Gates to cooperate and getting detailed directions to the man's house. "Remember, this has to stay under the radar, so no police. We give you the ring, and you take it to the CDC labs for safekeeping and further testing. No fuss, no muss."

I just wish we had some kind of contingency, some fallback plan in case—

In case I screw up?

His earlier exchange with Paige resounded in his head like a gong. He'd come dangerously close to showing his hand to her, to letting her see his selfish reason for wanting to finish this mission without outside help.

She might not blame him for his earlier failures in this assignment, but he couldn't let them rest. He needed to redeem himself, he needed to finish this on his own terms. He needed to prove to her, to *himself,* that he wasn't the failure his earlier screwups indicated. How could he even *think* about tackling commitment, a future relationship, if he couldn't even get this simple assignment right? How could he justify asking Paige to depend on him for her future safety and happiness if he couldn't even protect her and the ring through this simple transfer?

Pride goeth before destruction….

The phrase one of his foster mothers used to quote buzzed through his head, incriminating him. Acid pooled in his gut. Now was not the time for vacillation and indecision. It was time for action. Determination. Purpose.

Jake had suggested meeting at a neutral location but Gates insisted his house was safe.

"I'll send my wife and kids to the movies. When can you be here?" Gates's voice brought him out of his turbulent thoughts.

Firming his resolve, Jake answered, "Two hours, max."

* * *

Ninety minutes later, Jake and Paige stopped near the Atlanta city limits for gasoline and to use the restroom. Gates's house was a matter of minutes from the quickie mart where they refueled and refreshed, and the closer they got to their destination, the more Paige's nerves jangled, the more her nervous nausea grew. She still believed they needed a backup plan. The lack of a contingency plan tied her in knots, screamed for attention.

Standing at the sink in the ladies' room, Paige splashed cool water on her face and took deep breaths, fighting the urge to throw up.

Scofield trusted me to see this through. Why can't you? The pain in Jake's voice when he'd asked for her cooperation reverberated in her thoughts, battling with the voice of reason. She did trust Jake, she told herself. Making alternate plans didn't detract from her faith in his skills. It simply made good sense. Right? Or did her desire for extra security, for a fallback plan, undermine the trust she was trying to build with Jake, the trust he needed from her?

Paige braced her arms on the sink and stared at a face she barely recognized. She was a mess. Her hair was loose and tousled. She wore no makeup. The creases and dark circles around her eyes spoke of the lack of sleep she'd had last night.

Her heart gave a painful thump. She couldn't regret last night, despite Jake's change of heart this morning. Giving herself to Jake was a decision she'd made for herself, for her heart, because it was right for *her*.

She'd followed Jake's judgment throughout this nightmare scenario, but she needed to feel she had some control over the outcome of the exchange. She was on the Green Monster again, in the backseat with Ringleader and Beefy Guy. Her gut roiled, and she made up her mind. Jake needed her trust, but she needed security, control. Backup.

With a trembling hand, she pulled the prepaid cell from her purse and dialed.

Chapter 15

Standing beside Jake on William Gates's stoop, Paige pressed a hand to her swirling stomach and waited for Brent's contact to answer the door. The CDC researcher lived in an upscale neighborhood, his house a virtual carbon copy of the other McMansions lining the street. When they got no response to their doorbell summons, Paige wondered briefly if they had the wrong house.

Jake cast her a worried side glance. "You okay?"

She took a calming breath and nodded. "Just ready for this to be over."

"Amen to that."

They waited another few seconds, then Jake tried the doorbell again and added a knock. Finally, after what seemed an awfully long delay for someone who should have been expecting them, Gates opened his front door. He looked just like the picture they'd found of him on the internet when they stopped for lunch at a fast-food joint with Wi-Fi. Except...

His expression was wan, nervous. Terrified.

Warning bells clanged in Paige's head. Beside her, Jake tensed.

"William Gates?" Jake asked, offering his hand. "I'm the one who called—"

"I'm sorry, but I'm terribly busy and expecting company—" Gates said in a rush, closing the door as he spoke.

Jake shot an arm out to brace the door. "*We're* the ones who called. We—"

"Yes," came a voice behind Gates. "Come in."

The door opened, revealing a man with a gun behind the CDC researcher.

Ringleader, aka Steward.

"We've been expecting you." A gloating smile tugged the corner of Steward's mouth.

Before she could blink, Jake yanked her behind him and whipped his gun from his waistband. Under his breath, he growled, "Get out of here, Paige. Run!"

Icy terror washed through Paige, rooting her.

"Not so fast," Steward said smoothly, angling his weapon toward Gates's head. "Put the gun down, or I'll waste him." Flicking a glance over Jake's shoulder, he shouted, "Get them in here, and let's get this over with."

"Go!" Jake shoved her, took the first step down from the stoop. She stumbled with him but came up short as four men rounded the sides of the house and closed in on them. They weren't brash enough to flash their weapons on the residential street, but Paige didn't doubt they were armed.

Jake swung his gun up, but one of Steward's men was already on top of him, tackling him. Jake swung at his captor, struggled to get free. And received a hard blow to the jaw for his efforts.

"Jake!" Greasy fear balled in her gut.

Jake's lip was swollen and bleeding, and he looked dazed as the thug jerked him to his feet. Took Jake's gun.

Paige's gut pitched.

They were trapped. Surrounded. Outnumbered.

With hasty steps, the other men closed in and hustled them back to the stoop. Inside.

The thud of the closing door echoed with a finality that sent chills to Paige's bones.

Gates's throat convulsed as he swallowed. "Please, *no*. I swear I don't have what you want. I don't know anything about—"

"Shut up!" Steward snapped, jabbing harder with his gun. To his men, he said, "Take them all to the back room."

As the goons herded them roughly to the back of the house, Jake shot a lethal glare at Steward. "Let Paige and Gates go. You don't need them."

Steward stuck his face in Jake's. "I'm calling the shots now, hero." He turned his gaze toward Paige, her hand. The ring. "Besides, Ms. Bancroft has what we need."

Paige tucked her hand behind her back. Too little. Too late.

Dear God, she couldn't let these men get the virus. Brent had been clear about the devastation the virus would wreak if terrorists released it on the public. Her gaze flew to Jake's.

He was working on a plan, wasn't he? Mr. I'm-trained-to-think-on-my-feet. His expression revealed nothing.

Paige scrambled. Stalled. Maybe if she bought him time…

As they were led into a windowless back room, she faced Steward, squaring her shoulders and faking a courage she didn't feel. "How did you know we were coming here?"

He turned up a palm dismissively. "Same way we've monitored you for days. We bugged your sister's phone."

Fresh fear writhed in Paige, thinking of these men eavesdropping on Holly's calls. "H-how?"

Steward shrugged, his expression bored. "We followed her to the emergency room when they took Scofield in from the church. Let's just say that during the commotion, she… wasn't especially vigilant over her purse. I planted the bug in seconds, and she was never the wiser."

Paige's stomach seesawed. "Don't you dare hurt my sister!"

Steward scoffed. "I have no interest in harming your sister. She was a tool to find you."

Just as Jake had warned.

Guilt swirled through her. She'd defied Jake more than once to call Holly. If she'd listened to him…

Scofield trusted me to see this through. Why can't you?

"That still doesn't explain how you knew we'd be here," Jake said. "Paige never mentioned Gates's name or where we were headed when she talked to Holly this morning." He sent her a glance, as if to confirm he was right.

A prickle skittered down her spine. She *hadn't* said anything to Holly about their plan for today! So how—?

"I didn't say she did." Steward smirked. "Holly heard it from their father."

Paige jolted. "My dad? But—"

Holly had said their father had talked to Brent.

Call Paige and check on her. I have arrangements to handle.

Her dad knew she was here? What else had Brent confided to her father?

Her heart thundered, anxiety building. What arrangements was her father making?

"Now, are you going to give us the ring with the nanotube—" Steward stepped toward her, his hand extended "—or do we have to cut off your finger to get it?"

She gasped and shrank back, only to bump into the thick chest of one of the other henchmen.

"She doesn't have the virus. I do."

All heads swiveled to face Jake. His face was stony, unflinching. He sounded so sincere, she almost believed him. The staccato beat of her pulse kicked faster.

Steward's expression darkened. "She told us the nanotube was encased in a glass bead that Scofield built into her ring."

Paige swallowed hard, working to steady her voice. "I lied."

Steward swung his glare back toward her. If she could just stall a little longer, maybe...

"I also told you the bead was in my engagement ring, didn't I? I guess by now you've discovered that was a lie. And I told you I'd hocked my wedding ring. Also a lie."

Steward's hands balled at his sides, and a muscle in his cheek twitched. His gaze narrowed on her as if he was trying to decide what to believe.

"Hell, Steward, just off them both, and we'll search 'em when they're dead," the goon behind her grumbled. "You know they have it here somewhere. This is taking too effing long."

A car door slammed outside. Voices drifted in. Young voices. Female voices.

Gates tensed. Gasped. His eyes grew wild and desperate.

"Will? We're home!" a woman called. "The movie was sold out."

In that moment of distraction, Jake launched an elbow into the gut of the ape behind him. Spun. Sliced a stiff hand into the goon's throat. One down. Four left.

Following Jake's lead, Paige stomped hard on the instep of the man behind her. He howled in pain but grabbed her arm, wrenching it behind her. Lashing out with her free hand, she gouged at her captor's eyes. Kneed him in the groin. He sank to the floor, clutching his stomach, but still had the presence of mind to swipe at her legs. With a hard blow to the back of her knees, he brought her to the floor. Paige used the adrenaline coursing through her to fuel her fight. She kicked at the thug, battering him with her feet.

From the corner of her eye, she saw Jake battling two men at once.

A door squeaked. "Will, what—?"

A gun fired.

"Elaine!"

Children screamed. Gates lunged for the door. Another pop of gunfire.

Steward shouted to his men. In the chaos, Piage glanced toward Jake. He was bleeding but still fighting. She had to help him. Swing the odds in their favor...

Her ears ringing, Paige searched the floor. Surely her thug had dropped his weapon. Or she could steal it. Or—

Bingo! She saw a silver gun on the carpet...just a few feet away...

She stretched toward it, reaching—

And a hard shoe came down on her wrist, crushing her arm. Pain shot to her shoulder.

"Nice try, Ms. Bancroft." Steward crouched over her pinned hand.

And wrenched the gaudy wedding ring from her finger.

Horror sliced through her. She couldn't let him take the nanotube!

Brent's desperate plea rasped in her head. *Keep the bead safe...at all costs. National security...*

"Jake!" she screamed. "He has the ring!"

Jake tensed, a sinking sensation settling in his gut.

For a few moments, they'd had Steward and his men off guard, had been gaining ground. But with her panicked cry, Paige had given Steward exactly what he needed. Solid evidence that the nanotube was in the ring.

And with the ring in Steward's possession, he and his men had no reason left to keep any of them alive.

The tumult and confusion he'd capitalized on when Gates's family arrived unexpectedly was already fading to a tense standoff.

Gates lay on the floor, blood seeping from his arm. His wife cowered beside him.

Another of Steward's men shuffled back into the room, dragging two preteen girls, both deathly pale and sobbing, in by the arm. Three more innocents caught up in this hellish situation. More lives at stake, more ways Jake could mess up and get civilians killed.

The man who'd been holding Paige rose slowly from the floor, murder in his eyes as he seized her arm again. The man Jake had incapacitated was still unconscious, but another ape, the one who'd fired on Gates, still held his weapon to Jake's temple.

The advantage they'd gained briefly had swung decidedly back into Steward's favor.

"Please," Gates rasped, "don't hurt my family. They have nothing to do with any of this!"

Jake met Paige's gaze briefly. Her eyes pleaded with him to do something. His chest constricted. He'd rather take a knife in his gut than let Paige down. But what choice did he have now?

Knowing how little he could do with Gates and his family at risk, with a gun at his head, with the ring in Steward's possession, Jake was short on options.

"Finally," Steward crowed, examining the ring. "Hmm, damn ugly thing." He arched an imperious eyebrow at Paige. "You let Scofield give you *this* as a token of his affection? Where's your pride?"

Paige stiffened, and rage roiled in Jake's gut.

"Watch your mouth, Steward," he growled.

With a dismissive sneer toward Jake, Steward turned to the thug holding Gates's daughters. "Thurman, have a look."

Thurman released the girls, who rushed to huddle with their parents, and stepped over to take the ring from Steward. Pulling an elaborate-looking jeweler's loupe from his pocket, Thurman walked to a floor lamp for better light. A hush settled over the room.

Jake's mind spun, thinking in fast forward.

After examining the ring for several seconds, Thurman lowered the loupe and faced Steward. "Without an atomic microscope, I can't be sure what it is, but there's definitely something in there. And that is definitely cut glass, not a diamond. I'd say we've got a hit."

Thurman crossed the floor. Held the ring out to Steward.

And Jake threw his head back as hard as he could, bashing the nose of the goon behind him. The next instant, while the man cradled his broken nose, Jake wrenched free and lunged. Tackled Thurman. Pried the ring from his hand. Rolled toward Paige.

Gasps and startled screams from Gates's girls peppered the air.

Shaken from his smug sense of victory, Steward grabbed for his gun. As Steward and Thurman surged toward him, Jake scrambled mentally. He had to protect the ring, take it out of play, eliminate possession as a factor…

Steward's pistol swung up.

And Jake popped the ring in his mouth. Forced enough spit on his tongue to swallow.

"Jake?" Paige gasped.

Steward's eyes widened in disbelief. "You ass!"

Thurman and Steward exchanged now-what looks.

Jake eased closer to Paige.

"Don't. Move." Steward angled his gun toward Paige. "Or your girlfriend is dead."

"Are you insane?" she hissed.

"Trust me."

She shook her head. "I don't see how—"

The man holding Paige's arm yanked hard, silencing her.

Finally, Steward narrowed a menacing glare on Jake and stepped close. "Don't think you've won. While I'd like to keep Ms. Bancroft alive until we verify the nanotube is in the ring, I'm not above killing some of the other deadweight we've acquired, if it will ensure your cooperation." Twisting to look over his shoulder, Steward looked to the man holding Paige. "Do you have your knife?"

Releasing Paige, the goon stooped to pull a smooth-edged blade from under his pant leg.

Cold dread spun through Jake. Damn. He knew what was coming.

Steward motioned to the other men. "Hold him."

Thurman and the two other thugs moved forward, surrounding Jake. He swung at the first man to reach him, battled the second man's grip when he grabbed his arm, resisted, but within minutes, they had him subdued and spread-eagled on the floor.

To Knife, Steward said, "Cut him. I want that ring back."

"No!" Paige rushed forward, and Steward caught her with an arm around her waist. She struggled, crying. "Please, stop! Don't touch him!"

"Paige, no!" Jake shouted. "Don't give him a reason to hurt you!"

When Knife dropped to one knee beside him, brandishing his blade, Jake shifted his attention to that very real threat, the imminent pain, the likely death awaiting him.

An earthy obscenity filtered through his thoughts. *This is gonna suck.*

Jake gritted his teeth and tensed his stomach muscles.

Knife raised his weapon and plunged it into Jake's gut.

Lightning-hot pain streaked through him. Paige and the female Gateses screamed.

Suddenly, with a blinding flash and deafening boom, all hell broke loose.

Chapter 16

Stunned by the bright light and earsplitting noise, Paige froze. What was happening?

An instant later, men in flak jackets, helmets and gas masks swarmed the room, shouting, "Police! Everyone down! Drop your weapons!"

By the looks of it, the entire Atlanta SWAT department now buzzed through the Gateses' home, armed with assault weapons and riot gear. Steward was knocked to the ground, disarmed. Then Knife. And Thurman.

Relief so sweet it brought tears to her eyes flooded through Paige. Help had arrived. Just in time.

Or almost in time. *Jake!*

Despite the police orders to lie on the floor, hands out, Paige crawled toward Jake in a rush. A large gash on his stomach poured blood on the carpet. Panic surged through her, and she whipped her shirt over her head to stanch the flow. "Help him! Please, he's been stabbed!"

"Get down! Hands out!" She was shoved unceremoniously to the ground beside Jake, and her hands yanked behind her.

With her cheek pressed to the floor, Paige fought the swell of desperation clamoring inside her. Jake angled his head to meet her gaze. Evidence of the pain he suffered radiated from his dark eyes, tightened his mouth and lined his forehead. His skin was growing frighteningly pale. "Paige…"

Brusque hands frisked her. She squirmed, trying to catch the eye of the officer pinning her to the ground. "No! Please, he needs help!"

"Hold still, ma'am."

"But I'm the one who called the police!"

Jake rasped a sharp, strangled sound, drawing Paige's attention.

A new pain and disappointment filled his eyes. "*You…* called them?"

Guilt sliced her to the core. She'd doubted Jake, defied him. Wounded him.

"I'm sorry," she whispered. But he turned his face away.

"Just cooperate, ma'am, and let us get this sorted out," the SWAT officer on her back said. "We actually had more than one call. Earlier today, we had two reports of a biohazard being delivered to this residence."

"Two calls?" Paige's thoughts spun. Around her she heard the grumbles and grunts of Steward's men being subdued and cuffed. The Gates girls crying. More police officers arriving.

The SWAT member finished patting her down and helped her to her feet. "First call came in early today from Louisiana. A man. Said his daughter was in danger."

Her heart tripped. "My dad called you, too?"

The officer gave her an appraising look. "Are you Paige Bancroft?"

"Yes!" Now they were getting somewhere.

The officer nodded. "En route, we received reports of gunfire called in by neighbors, then heard screams as we arrived. We had to consider everyone suspect until we knew we had the situation under our control. Just be patient, and we'll sort this out."

Frustration and fear for Jake gnawed her stomach. "We don't have time for patience! Jake's been stabbed! He's dying!"

The policeman jerked his head toward the floor where Jake lay bleeding. "We're doing all we can. An ambulance is en route."

Paige dropped her gaze to find two men huddled over Jake. One patted him down for weapons while another worked to stop the bleeding from his abdomen. His eyes were closed, and he remained eerily still. Terror climbed her throat. Squeezed her chest. "Jake!"

Jake opened his eyes to slits. The commotion around him was a blur. Except for Paige. He focused on her, even as the edges of his vision dimmed. Pain burned his gut, but the sharpest ache centered near his heart. The only relief he had was in knowing Paige was safe.

It was over. The cops would pick up where he'd dropped the ball.

A dry thickening in his throat made it hard to speak, but as he held Paige's gaze he mumbled, "Failed."

Then darkness swallowed him.

"Paige?"

Paige jerked her head up from her contemplation of the emergency-room floor. When she spotted the tall, silver-haired man striding briskly toward her, tears rushed to her eyes. "Daddy!"

She threw herself into her father's arms and sobbed on his shoulder.

"Thank God you're all right!" Neil Bancroft held Paige in a breath-stealing embrace. "When Brent told me what he'd asked you to do—"

She felt the shudder race through her father that finished his sentence for him. For long, silent minutes, they simply held each other, and Paige fought to regain her composure. Now was not the time to fall apart. She'd already given her full statement to the police and repeated it for the FBI. But the nightmare wasn't over.

Jake was still in surgery, fighting for his life.

As long as the doctors had to stitch up his belly anyway, they had decided, with encouragement from law enforcement, to surgically remove the ring from Jake's stomach.

The last word Paige had from William Gates, whose arm had been treated for a surface gunshot wound, was that the ring was in safekeeping with the Atlanta police. Arrangements were being made to transfer the nanotube to Gates's lab at the Centers for Disease Control once a pile of paperwork and red tape was cleared up.

She should have been ecstatic. The virus was safe. Her responsibility to protect PMB-611 was finished.

But Jake was not out of the woods yet. Even now, surgeons were scrambling to repair the damage done by Knife's blade. The hurt, accusing look he'd sent her before he blacked out haunted her.

You...called them?

Swiping at her runny nose and damp eyes, Paige backed out of her father's arms. "Jake was stabbed, Daddy. He lost a lot of blood, and—" Her voice broke, and her eyes filled with tears again. "I hurt him. He asked me to have faith in him, to trust him, but I...I was scared, and—"

When she broke down in tears again, Neil Bancroft escorted her to a chair at the edge of the waiting room. "Ah, Paige, darling, tell me everything. Start at the beginning."

And she did. From Brent's whispered orders to hide the "bead" after he'd been shot to the SWAT team's storming of the Gates residence, Paige left nothing out.

Except her feelings for Jake and the way they'd passed last night.

Her father listened carefully, interrupting only twice to ask questions. When she was done, her father explained how Brent, consumed with guilt and worry for Paige, had summoned Neil to his hospital room and finally confessed to the senior Bancroft his culpability in the unfolding events. Learning the truth from Brent, Neil had immediately called the authorities in Atlanta to arrange police support for the exchange at Gates's house and the company's private plane to bring him to Georgia to find Paige.

Paige shook her head. "But Brent knew Jake was with me. He'd asked Jake to hide the ring and protect me."

Neil leaned back in the formed-plastic chair and sighed. "True. But Brent wanted to be sure you were okay. Like you, he's big on contingencies." Her father paused and furrowed his brow. "Sounds like I owe Jake a great debt of gratitude for keeping you safe."

Her heart twisted. "And I repaid him by defying the one request he made of me. The one thing I knew mattered most to him. Proving my trust."

"Proving?" Neil frowned. "Honey, why should you have to prove—?"

"Paige Bancroft?" a nurse in green scrubs called to the waiting room, interrupting whatever her father had been prepared to say.

She hurried to meet the petite nurse, eager for news of Jake. "I'm Paige."

"Mr. McCall got out of surgery about an hour ago and is about to be moved to a private room. He's awake and asking to see you."

Relief made her knees tremble. "He's all right? They stopped all the bleeding? Repaired all the damage?"

"He'll have to take it easy for several weeks, but, yes. He'll be just fine."

Paige was so relieved to hear Jake was okay, she let the fact that no one had told her Jake had been out of surgery for an hour slide. A wide smile blossomed on her face. "Where is he?"

The nurse directed her down the corridor, and Paige ran down the hospital hall with her father at her heels. As they reached the recovery room, Jake was being wheeled out on a gurney on his way to a private room.

"Jake!" Paige shoved aside one of the nurses and wrapped her hand around Jake's. His color was vastly better than it had been when they rushed him into surgery, and his eyes had the fire and vital intensity back that she'd grown to love. "The nurse said you were asking for me. I would have come sooner, but I only just now heard you were out of surgery."

"I wanted to be sure you were okay." Jake's gaze traveled past her, over her shoulder. "Your father's here."

She nodded. "After Brent got out of his surgery yesterday— jeez, was it only yesterday?—he told Dad what was going on, where I was and how Bancroft Industries was involved. Dad arranged a corporate plane to fly over here this morning so he could find me."

Jake's gaze shifted back to Paige. "Good." He lowered his eyes and angled his head away from her. "Then my work is done. You can go home with him…get back to your family, your job."

Paige's stomach quickened. A hollow, defeated quality permeated Jake's tone. Squeezing his hand, she bent over him. "Not until you're well enough to come with us."

His dark eyes found hers, and the finality she read in their depths jolted her. Scared her.

"Our business together is finished, Paige. My doctor said he gave the ring to the cops. The bead is safe, and so are you. Go home."

"But…" Paige fumbled, crushed by Jake's rejection. "What if Steward has other operatives who come after me to exact revenge, or—"

"No. I just gave my statement to the FBI." His gaze darkened when he mentioned the police, and compunction kicked her in the chest. "According to the guys I gave my statement to, Ralph Thurman, one of the guys at Gates's, is rolling over to cut a deal. He's given up names and details on the terrorist organization. Including people inside the Department of Defense. Those not in custody now, will be soon."

"Who are these terrorists? Who funds them?" her father asked.

Jake shrugged. "The cop didn't know."

"I'll have my people look into it," her father said. "I'm sure we'll hear more, once they've had time to dig further into the investigation."

Neil extended his hand to Jake, and Jake slipped his fingers from Paige's grasp to shake her father's hand. "Son, thank you. You kept my girl safe, and I can never repay that."

"Forget it." Jake nodded to Neil but turned a penetrating gaze to Paige. "I was just doing the job I was hired to do."

His words hit her like ice. Cold. Hard. Final.

There is no us. Not now, not when this is over. He'd said as much this morning, but she'd dared to hope he'd change his mind once they'd delivered the ring. Once they were safe.

Framing his face with her hands, she leaned close, whispering fiercely, "Don't shut me out, Jake. I love you, and if you let me show you how much, I can—"

"Go home with your father, Paige." He wrenched her hands from his cheeks and met her pleas with a stony stare. "You belong with your family. Not here."

"But—"

"Goodbye, Paige."

The nurse she'd shoved aside earlier now pushed Paige back from Jake's side. "Excuse me. We need to take him upstairs now."

As the nurses rolled Jake's gurney toward the elevator, he wouldn't even look at her.

And Paige felt her heart shatter.

Chapter 17

"Want to talk about it?"

When her father spoke, Paige turned from the view of billowing clouds out the small jet window. She didn't pretend not to know what he meant. Her dad wasn't deaf or blind. He'd heard what she told Jake before Jake dismissed her so abruptly, and he'd seen the leak of tears she couldn't contain as they'd left for the airport in a taxi.

She squared her shoulders and struggled to present a brave face. "I really don't know what to say. So much has happened to me, so much has changed in a matter of days. I'm kind of... shell-shocked."

Neil laid a warm hand on her knee. "I take it your feelings for Brent have changed. He told me you'd ended it with him."

Paige sucked in a deep breath for courage. "Actually, my feelings for Brent are the same." She paused, and her father arched an eyebrow in query. "The truth of the matter is, I never loved him."

Now Neil frowned and shifted in his seat to face her more

fully. "My goodness, Paige, what are you saying? You were about to marry him. I thought the two of you were ideal for each other."

She nibbled her bottom lip and scrunched her nose, feeling like a little girl again under her father's heavy stare. "That's… why I accepted his proposal. I saw how happy you were, and logically, we should have been perfect for each other. We have a lot in common. But…"

Same equals boring. Her heart fluttered restlessly when Jake's assessment flitted through her thoughts.

"I tried to love him, Dad, but he just didn't…" *make me burn the way Jake did.*

Her face grew hot, and she turned back to the window briefly to gather her composure and hide the telltale flush in her cheeks.

"He didn't make you happy."

She swallowed hard and screwed up the nerve to face her father's disappointment. "No. I'm sorry, Dad. I know you liked him, and—"

Neil snorted. "Why should my opinion matter?"

She turned her palm up. "Because you're my dad. I've always wanted to make you proud and have your approval."

His scowl deepened. "And you thought I'd approve of your tying yourself to a man you didn't love?"

"I…well, I thought I'd learn to love him. When I analyzed our relationship, I didn't see any reason why we shouldn't have a successful marriage. On paper, we were perfectly matched. And Brent was your choice to take over the company, so logically—"

"Paige Michelle, you have a gift for logic and analysis, but logic and analysis have no place in deciding matters of the heart."

"But—"

He raised a hand to cut her off. "Let's get one thing straight," he said in the deep timbre that had commanded boardrooms for forty years. "*I* am happy about your choice of spouse only if *you* are happy. Where did you get the idea that I would want you to settle for a husband you didn't love?"

She gaped like a fish, but she was speechless.

Zoey had said almost the same thing to her months ago, before she stormed out of the house the last time. Paige scrunched her nose.

"If you believe that, then explain to me why you were so angry with Zoey about her relationship with Derek."

Neil stiffened. "Angry? I was never angry with Zoey. I want Zoey to be happy, to be safe, same as I do you. She's the one who lost her temper when I tried to reason with her."

Paige rolled her eyes. She didn't want to argue semantics with her dad. Considering she shared her father's opinion of Derek, playing devil's advocate on Zoey's behalf felt odd enough. But her father's answer meant a great deal to Paige. "Zoey says she loves Derek. She says he makes her happy. So why can't you accept her choice of husband and be happy for her?"

Her father's expression darkened, his brow creasing with worry lines. "I believe she does love Derek, and that's what bothers me. Because he doesn't love her. I'd stake my life on that." He poked the armrest for emphasis. "He hasn't married her. Instead, he's dragged her around the country, spending her money to play poker wherever he can find a game." Neil's jaw tightened. "The guy's a con. He's using her for her money, and when he tires of her or once he's emptied her accounts, he'll dump her and break her heart. How can I support her in something I know is going to bring her trouble and heartache down the road?"

"I hope you're wrong about Derek, but...I'm afraid you're right." Paige's belly rolled with concern for her sister's well-being. She missed Zoey, missed her sister's bright smiles and exuberance. Her zest for life. Her friendship.

"Now..." Her father readjusted his suit coat, tugging at the sleeves, his nonverbal cue that he considered the matter closed and was moving on. "About this Jake McCall. You told him you love him. But does he make you truly happy, or are your feelings for him something you engineered through critical analysis and statistics based on your shared traits?"

Neil cut a side glance and lifted the corner of his mouth.

Paige blinked, startled to realize her father was teasing her. They hadn't teased each other in years. Not since she graduated college and joined the family business. She hadn't wanted anyone to think she had an inside track at the company because of her personal relationship with her dad. She had kept their relationship at Bancroft strictly professional, all business.

Looking back, she now saw how that formality had spilled over into their private relationship. The spontaneous jokes and hugs had dwindled, replaced with shop talk and professional politeness. Had that lack of familial warmth in recent years contributed to her feeling that she had to earn his approval by marrying Brent?

Setting that issue aside for the moment, she focused on his question. Did she love Jake?

She curled her fingers into the plush leather armrest. "My feelings for Jake are a moot point at best, considering he wants no part of a relationship with me."

"Are you sure about that?"

Paige jerked her gaze up to meet her father's. "He said as much. More than once." Leaning her head back, she angled her head toward the puffy clouds out her window. "The thing is…he grew up in foster homes and never felt he had a stable home or real love. Then he lost the family he adopted when he became a SEAL because he was forced off the team after an injury. And because several close SEAL friends died, both in the line of duty and once back home. He's been burned too often, had his trust betrayed—" Her heart throbbed painfully with guilt. "—and so he won't give his heart to a relationship again." She sighed and glanced back at her father. "I tried to show him how much I love him. Tried to prove to him that my love was real and wouldn't change, but—"

"Hold it right there, young lady." Her father aimed a finger at her, his tone stern.

Her heart pounded the way it did when she'd been scolded as a child.

"At the hospital, you said something about proving your trust as well, and I didn't get a chance to address it then. But I can't let it pass again." He took her hand in hers and squeezed, his green gaze softening. "Paige, love and trust and loyalty, all the building blocks of a solid relationship, aren't something you should have to prove or earn or work for. Either they are there, or they aren't. Love you have to earn isn't real love. Trust you have to prove isn't authentic. Love isn't meant to be analyzed or fit into a schedule. How do you explain the fact that in a matter of days you've lost your heart to a man so different from you?"

Her pulse slowed, and she held her breath. "I can't explain it. It's crazy. It just…happened."

"Love defies the odds. Love doesn't follow criteria." His eyes brightened with an intensity that speared to her core. "Paige, honey, real love is *unconditional*."

She blinked, stared at him as she processed what he was saying. Intellectually, she already knew everything he was saying, but a small voice inside her whispered that somewhere along the line, her brain and her heart had gotten their wires crossed.

"You didn't need to marry Brent to make me happy or earn my approval or my love, sweetie. You have it. Always. Forever. No matter what. No strings attached."

She gripped her father's hand with both of hers. "And you have mine, Daddy."

He squeezed her hands tighter, underlining his next point. "If you love Jake, you shouldn't have to prove it to him, either. He may have a hard time accepting it, letting it past his protective shields, but if your love is real, he'll know it, deep down. He'll feel it. Real love shines through every word, every action, every look and touch."

Paige chewed her bottom lip, mulling over her father's admonition.

"Sweetie, I know control is important to you, but you can't

make someone love you. Just like you have no control over who you fall in love with."

Paige's pulse scampered. *No control...*

Was that why her feelings for Jake scared her so much?

"Real love is deep, abiding...and has no qualifiers. Can you say that about your feelings for Jake?"

A sob rose in her chest, tears puddling in her eyes. "Yes. Absolutely."

Her father sat back and drew a deep, thoughtful breath. "And yet...you are here with me, instead of at his bedside."

The air whooshed from her lungs. "But..." She rasped and had to stop to find the breath to speak. "You heard him! He sent me away. He didn't want me there!"

"I also saw the look in his eyes when you turned and walked away. Paige, that man loves you. I'm betting he pushed you away because he didn't want to risk rejection. Or he believed he was sparing you some kind of pain or disappointment."

Her heart was a rock beneath her ribs. Cold, hard, heavy.

"And I played right into his fears of loss by leaving." Her gut pitched. What had she done?

"We're almost home now, and your mother and Holly are frantic to see you and assure themselves that you are safe. But whenever you're ready to return to Atlanta, I'll make sure you get priority on the flight schedule."

Tears spilled from her eyelashes as she threw her arms around her father's neck. "Thank you, Dad. I love you."

Jake tossed down his fork and shoved the plate of mystery meat aside. He wasn't hungry.

Throwing back the blanket on the hospital bed, he slid his legs to the floor. He wasn't tired, either. He was restless, sick of being cooped up in this hospital room.

Three days post-op, his pain was well under control, and he could walk without feeling his gut was going to split open. He should have been released yesterday, but because his blood pressure had been slightly elevated since his surgery, he'd been kept an extra night. For observation.

But Jake didn't need medical professionals to tell him why his blood pressure was up. He knew the reason.

He'd screwed up with Paige. Let her walk away. Lost the best thing that ever happened to him.

He'd had nothing but time to think as he lay in his bed and stared at the acoustic tile ceiling. Time to realize what he'd lost. Time to look at why he'd pushed her away. Time to recall his SEAL team CO grating, "Fear is inevitable in this job. You can either make fear your friend, use it to sharpen your senses and push you to achieve more. Or you can allow fear to be your enemy, let it lead you to failure.

He'd failed with Paige because his fear still stood sentinel over his heart. He knew why.

He squeezed the bedsheets in his fists and gritted his teeth. At first he'd been hurt that she hadn't believed in him, hadn't trusted him to handle the situation at Gates's and had called the authorities. Then he'd been disgusted with himself, ashamed that his arrogant pride and determination to finish the assignment without outside help had nearly gotten Paige and other innocent civilians killed. He admitted, belatedly, that she'd made the right call. The number of unexpected variables that cropped up, from Steward learning of the transfer at Gates's to Gates's wife and daughters returning early, had quickly spiraled the situation out of control. He'd needed a contingency plan after all. Thank God Paige had arranged one.

Finally, this morning, after a sleepless night of self-recrimination, he'd moved past his pointless should-haves and if-onlys and realized an important truth. It didn't matter who did what or how the crisis had ended.

It was over.

The virus sample was safe. Paige was safe. And according to the FBI agents who'd questioned him multiple times over the past several days, the men behind the raid on Paige's wedding and the attempts to steal the virus had been rounded up in a nationwide sweep. The homegrown terrorist cell had been on the Homeland Security radar for years. The men inside the

Department of Defense whom Brent had believed to be traitors were, in fact, investigating Brent's communications with the cell. All Jake had to do now was be available to testify at the terrorists' trial.

And figure out what to do about Paige, how to move past his debilitating fear of loss.

His doctor had promised he could be released today, but so far, no one had been by to sign the papers that would spring him. Pressing a hand to the stitches just below his ribs, Jake hobbled restlessly toward the small window to look out. The hazy Atlanta skyline sprawled across the horizon. He stared without really seeing until a knock at his door brought him around.

"Jake?"

He recognized Holly immediately, though her resemblance to Paige had his pulse thumping and his blood pressure, no doubt, spiking again. He hoped the nurse didn't come by now to check his vitals or he'd be stuck here another night.

"Holly, what are you doing here?" He glanced past her to the hall, hoping maybe she hadn't come alone.

"Paige isn't with me," she said, obviously reading the hope in his expression. "Matt, the kids and I were driving through Atlanta on our way back to our home in North Carolina, and I thought I should stop to see you."

"Oh." Jake mentally kicked himself for the idiotic monosyllabic reply and the disappointment he couldn't keep from his tone. He shuffled stiffly back to the bed and sat down. "Going home, huh?"

"We'd already stayed in Lagniappe longer than we intended, but I couldn't leave until I knew Paige was home and safe."

Jake nodded awkwardly, staring at the floor. "Then she's okay?"

Holly moved farther into the room. "She's home and safe. But she's anything but okay."

Jake jerked his head up. "Wh-what's wrong with her?"

Crossing her arms over her chest, Holly stepped closer and

scowled. "She's heartbroken, dummy. She told you she loves you, and you sent her packing!"

Guilt sluiced through him, congealing in his gut as a cold lump of regret. "I never wanted to hurt her."

Holly's expression softened. "I know that. And I know how confusing and complicated relationships can be. Matt and I had our share of issues to work out before we married. What matters is that you don't give up. If you love my sister…and my dad thinks you do—"

Jake stiffened. "Your dad?"

"He was here, remember? He saw the little exchange between you two and read between the lines."

Feeling a bit queasy, he leaned back against the stacked pillows at the head of the bed and groaned.

"Yeah, kinda overwhelming sometimes, isn't it? The whole family knowing your business and adding their two cents?" Holly rested her hip on a corner of the bed and chuckled. "Well get used to it, Jake, because Paige comes with the whole Bancroft brood. Sisters, parents, brother-in-law and kids…"

Holly placed a hand on her belly in a protective gesture, and Jake lifted a corner of his mouth. "Congratulations, by the way. Paige told me you were expecting."

Holly beamed. "Thanks." Then her face sobered. "So this is why I'm here… From the minute Paige got back to Lagniappe with Dad, she's been chomping at the bit to fly back here to be with you. She says she loves you, and she belongs at your side."

Warmth seeped through the cold knot in his gut, buoying his hope.

"She told me about your hang-ups regarding commitment and family, too. Which is why I've spent the last three days finding ways to detain her."

Jake frowned. "Detain her?"

"Yeah. I've done everything I could think of to keep her in Lagniappe. Well, the police helped. They've had lots of questions for her. But I even faked premature labor, the lowest kind of deception, so that she wouldn't jet off to be with you."

Jake stared at Holly, stunned.

"Don't you want to know why?" she asked, flipping up a palm in query.

"Because I hurt her. Because you don't think I deserve her." Statements, not questions.

"Wrong! Because she deserves to know how you really feel. You pushed her away, so it is *your* obligation to be the one to fix this. *You* have to go to *her*."

Jake sat taller, squared his shoulders. "And say what?"

Holly rolled her eyes. "*I love you* would be a good place to start." She paused, angled her head. "Assuming you do."

His nostrils flared as he filled his lungs. "More than anything."

Holly flicked a hand. "Well, there you go. I took the liberty of arranging the Bancroft Industries jet for your convenience. It's waiting at an airstrip in Marietta for you." Holly hiked her purse strap on her shoulder and turned toward the door.

"Wait! I—"

She turned and gave him a patient look. "What?"

"Just because I love her doesn't mean I'm cut out for marriage and family and…and—"

Holly stepped to the edge of the bed and met Jake's gaze with eyes the same shade of jade as Paige's. "No one knows the future, Jake. Giving someone your heart is risky, yes. Scary, sure. It takes a blind leap of faith. But you're not going into this alone. That's the beauty of a marriage. You work at it together. You both give your best, and forgive each other's faults. You're a team. A team cemented by love." She paused and furrowed her brow. "Okay, that sounded corny, but you get the point, right? If you love Paige and can deal with the idea of me—" she struck a pose "—as your sister-in-law, then I suggest you get your ex-SEAL butt to Louisiana and tell my sister how you feel."

She finger waved as she sauntered out of the room. "Gotta run. Matt and the kids are waiting downstairs."

Jake stared at the empty door for long seconds after Holly left. Then laughed.

Paige loved him. Despite all the ways he'd messed up, let her down.

You're not going into this alone. You're a team.

He just hoped Paige would see it that way.

Paige hurriedly tossed the last of the clothes she'd laid out into her suitcase and zipped her luggage shut. If she rushed, she could catch the commercial flight from Lagniappe to Atlanta that left in just over an hour. After innumerable delays, from the FBI questioning her to Holly's false-alarm miscarriage, she was determined to get back to Atlanta, to *Jake,* today. *Now!* Enough delays!

But when she'd called the Bancroft hangar to arrange the company jet her father had promised, she'd learned the jet was out on some mysterious errand, not due to return until later today. Thus the commercial ticket. She was tired of waiting.

When her doorbell rang, she considered ignoring it. She didn't have even a few spare minutes to get rid of a salesman, another reporter or a busybody neighbor. But the ring was followed by an insistent pounding. The urgency of the loud knock gave her pause.

Lugging her suitcase with her, she trooped down to the front door, answered the increasingly insistent summons.

And caught her breath.

Jake's gaze drifted from her face to her suitcase and back. "Going somewhere?"

When she still couldn't find her voice amid her shock and the rush of emotion, she shook her head slowly.

He lifted a corner of his mouth. "Can I come in?"

Holding the edge of the door for support, she nodded and stumbled back to let him in. "A-are you all right? Your injury—"

"Is healing well. It's my heart that's hurting. That's why I'm here." He held her gaze but wiped his hands on his jeans, his jaw tight and tense.

"Wh-why *are* you here?" she finally managed to rasp.

"Because you are."

A desperate hope swelled painfully in her chest, and the sting of tears pricked her sinuses. "I—I was just on my way to Atlanta. To be with you."

"I know. I talked to Holly earlier today."

She blinked her surprise. "You did?"

"She stopped by to see me at the hospital on her way home."

Paige's breath backed up again. "And?"

"She helped me see a lot of things from a different perspective." He rubbed the generous stubble on his jaw, stubble that made him look ruggedly dangerous. An image completely contradicted by the wistful, vulnerable expression in his eyes. "I thought that we were too different to find any common ground for a future. But Holly helped me think in terms of what we could be as a *team*."

A tremble started in her chest and spread through her limbs. Moisture blurred her vision, and she swiped at her eyes. "A team?"

"With the SEALs, I learned that the best teams use the strengths of all the members to build a stronger whole…like at Gates's."

Her body tensed. Guilt for second-guessing Jake flowed through her like tar in her veins.

He shuffled his feet as if he was nervous. "When the situation started getting out of control, when my bag of in-the-moment tricks was running low, your contingency plan saved the day."

She frowned. "What? But I betrayed you. You asked me to trust you and I—"

"Did what I was too thickheaded and stubborn to do. You've been a valuable part of this team," he said, waving a hand between them, "all through this ordeal. Our differences balance each other. You made the right call at Gates's, Paige. I'm the one who failed *you*."

She stiffened her spine and narrowed a sharp look on him.

"Jake McCall, I'm about sick of hearing you talk about how you've failed me, failed Brent, failed…your aunt Petunia!" She stepped forward and poked him in the chest with her finger. "You saved my life on my wedding day. You were up against hugely lopsided odds, and you did what you had to do to protect the most lives. You gave one-hundred-and-ten percent to stop the people bent on weaponizing a deadly virus, and you kept your word to Brent by keeping me alive throughout this ordeal. You are a hero, not a failure. You're…" She paused to swallow hard when a lump clogged her throat. "You're *my* hero."

Jake stared at her, his eyes suspiciously damp. "I'd rather be…your husband."

Paige drew a sharp breath.

"If you can forgive me, for pushing you away. For letting my fear get in the way of telling you how much I love you when I had the chance. Because I do love you, Paige."

Tears flooded her eyes, joy filling her chest until she could barely speak. But her father's wisdom whispered to her. She squared her shoulders, lifted her chin. "Unconditionally?"

Jake wrinkled his brow in question and stepped back, staring at her with a puzzled frown.

Paige's heart cramped. If he didn't give his heart freely, without strings, than was it really love?

Finally, after what felt like a lifetime, but was in reality just a few nerve-racking seconds, Jake's confusion seemed to melt away. A knowing grin spread across his face, and he caught her hand to pull her close. "Completely. Deeply. And unconditionally. I want our marriage to be a partnership where we both are heard, both compromise, both share the best of ourselves…and the worst. Your opinion matters to me, Paige. In fact, I didn't bring you a ring today because I want you to pick the one you like."

She tugged a grin. "Any ring without a secret nanotube in it works for me…as long as it's from you."

Jake drew a deep breath, his eye brightening with expectation. "Does that mean yes? That you'll marry me?"

"Yes, yes, yes!" With a laugh that bubbled from an overflowing heart, Paige launched herself into his arms.

"Ah, ow!" he rasped, bending at the waist and clutching his stomach. "I think you busted my stitches."

Paige jerked back with a gasp, horrified. "Oh no! Oh, Jake, I'm sorry! Do you need a doctor?"

He reached for her, flashing a bright smile, and drew her close again with a satisfied sigh. "No, sweetheart, I have all I need right here in my arms."

As Paige angled her head to accept Jake's kiss, her heart whispered its assurance that she was finally where she belonged.

* * * * *

COMING NEXT MONTH

Available October 26, 2010

#1631 DEADLIER THAN THE MALE
"The Fiercest Heart" by Sharon Sala
"Lethal Lessons" by Colleen Thompson

#1632 P.I. DADDY'S PERSONAL MISSION
The Coltons of Montana
Beth Cornelison

#1633 MEDUSA'S SHEIK
The Medusa Project
Cindy Dees

#1634 HER PRIVATE AVENGER
Elle Kennedy

ROMANTIC SUSPENSE

SRSCNM101C

REQUEST YOUR FREE BOOKS!

2 FREE NOVELS PLUS 2 FREE GIFTS!

Silhouette®

ROMANTIC SUSPENSE

Sparked by Danger, Fueled by Passion.

YES! Please send me 2 FREE Silhouette® Romantic Suspense novels and my 2 FREE gifts (gifts are worth about $10). After receiving them, if I don't wish to receive any more books, I can return the shipping statement marked "cancel." If I don't cancel, I will receive 4 brand-new novels every month and be billed just $4.24 per book in the U.S. or $4.99 per book in Canada. That's a saving of 15% off the cover price! It's quite a bargain! Shipping and handling is just 50¢ per book.* I understand that accepting the 2 free books and gifts places me under no obligation to buy anything. I can always return a shipment and cancel at any time. Even if I never buy another book from Silhouette, the two free books and gifts are mine to keep forever.

240/340 SDN E5Q4

Name	(PLEASE PRINT)
Address	Apt. #
City	State/Prov.	Zip/Postal Code

Signature (if under 18, a parent or guardian must sign)

Mail to the Silhouette Reader Service:

IN U.S.A.: P.O. Box 1867, Buffalo, NY 14240-1867
IN CANADA: P.O. Box 609, Fort Erie, Ontario L2A 5X3

Not valid for current subscribers to Silhouette Romantic Suspense books.

Want to try two free books from another line?
Call 1-800-873-8635 or visit www.morefreebooks.com.

* Terms and prices subject to change without notice. Prices do not include applicable taxes. N.Y. residents add applicable sales tax. Canadian residents will be charged applicable provincial taxes and GST. Offer not valid in Quebec. This offer is limited to one order per household. All orders subject to approval. Credit or debit balances in a customer's account(s) may be offset by any other outstanding balance owed by or to the customer. Please allow 4 to 6 weeks for delivery. Offer available while quantities last.

Your Privacy: Silhouette is committed to protecting your privacy. Our Privacy Policy is available online at www.eHarlequin.com or upon request from the Reader Service. From time to time we make our lists of customers available to reputable third parties who may have a product or service of interest to you. If you would prefer we not share your name and address, please check here. ☐

Help us get it right—We strive for accurate, respectful and relevant communications. To clarify or modify your communication preferences, visit us at www.ReaderService.com/consumerschoice.

SRS10R

HARLEQUIN®

A *Romance*

FOR EVERY MOOD™

Spotlight on

Inspirational

Wholesome romances
that touch the heart and soul.

See the next page
to enjoy a sneak peek from
the Love Inspired® Suspense
inspirational series.

*See below for a sneak peek from
our inspirational line, Love Inspired® Suspense*

*Enjoy this heart-stopping excerpt from
RUNNING BLIND
by top author Shirlee McCoy,
available November 2010!*

**The mission trip to Mexico was supposed to be an
adventure. But the thrill turns sour when Jenna Dougherty
and her roommate Magdalena are kidnapped.**

"It's okay. I'm here to help." The voice was as deep as the
darkness, but Jenna Dougherty didn't believe the lie. She
could do nothing but lie still as hands slid down her arms,
felt the rope around her wrists.

"I'm going to use a knife to cut you free, Jenna. Hold
still."

The cold blade of a knife pressed close to her head before
her gag fell away.

"I—" she started, but her mouth was dry, and she could
do nothing but suck in air.

"Shhh. Whatever needs to be said can be said when
we're out of here." Nick spoke quietly, his hand gentle on
her cheek. There and gone as he sliced through the ropes on
her wrists and ankles.

He pulled her upright. "Come on. We may be on
borrowed time."

"I can't leave my friend," Jenna rasped out.

"There's no one here. Just us."

"She has to be here." Jenna took a step away.

"There's no one here. Let's go before that changes."

"It's dark. Maybe if we find a light…"

"What did you say?"

"We need to turn on the light. I can't leave until I know that—"

"What can you see, Jenna?"

"Nothing."

"No shadows? No light?"

"No."

"It's broad daylight. There's light spilling in from the window I climbed in through. You can't see it?"

She went cold at his words.

"I can't see anything."

"You've got a nasty bruise on your forehead. Maybe that has something to do with it." His fingers traced the tender flesh on her forehead.

"It doesn't matter *how* it happened. I'm blind!"

Can Nick help Jenna find her friend or will chasing this trail have Jenna running blindly again into danger?

Find out in RUNNING BLIND, available in November 2010 only from Love Inspired Suspense.